DREARY DAY IN TEXAS

THE SETTLERS
BOOK FOUR

REG QUIST

Dreary Day in Texas
Paperback Edition
Copyright © 2023 Reg Quist

CKN Christian Publishing
An Imprint of Wolfpack Publishing
9850 S. Maryland Parkway, Suite A-5 #323
Las Vegas, Nevada 89183

cknchristianpublishing.com

Paperback ISBN 978-1-63977-456-2
eBook ISBN 978-1-63977-455-5
LCCN 2023937183

ALSO BY REG QUIST

Novels

The Church at Third and Main

Hamilton Robb

Noah Gates

Terry of the Double C

Just John

Just John: The Complete Journey

Just John

Northward to Home

Reluctant Redemption

Reluctant Redemption: The Complete Series

Reluctant Redemption (Book 1)

A Winding Trail to Justice (Book 2)

Rough Road to Redemption (Book 3)

Mac's Way

Mac's Way: The Complete Series

Mac's Way

Mac's Land

Mac's Law

Danny

Danny: The Complete Trilogy

The Truth of The Matter (Book 1)

DREARY DAY IN TEXAS

PROLOGUE

Sheriff Rory Jamison was astride his big gelding, staring at the dust cloud boiling up in the north and blowing toward the fort. Although it was deep into the fall season, easing into winter, the skies had been clear and sunny, if not particularly warm. The single skiff of snow that had dropped weeks ago was gone without a trace. A couple of showers had also soaked in and disappeared. The road was dry but still, that was a lot of dust.

As the cloud neared the stage company's horse barns, with perhaps a half mile to go, Tate drove his stage into town. Coming in from the north, he would drop his passengers at the hotel and then return to the stage corrals to be rigged out for the next run. He pulled to a halt beside the sheriff.

Curious, and sensing that the dust cloud might somehow involve him, Rory hollered over to the stage whip, "What's going on out there, Tate?"

Tate's response reflected his normal approach to the difficulties of life: anger, frustration, and assurance of his own rightness.

1

"What's going on out there?" the man asks. I'll tell you what's going on. Some fool is driving his herd along the road. With all those empty miles off to the east, there for his using. Wouldn't give me the right of way neither. I had to take this rig off into the grassland by more than a mile and hump the whole kit and caboodle over hill and hollow to pass them. There're maybe two thousand head and a cavvy of horses. Longhorns. Mixed stuff. Cows and calves. Steers. Scrubs such as we ain't seen in this area for years. Should all be shot, cattle and drovers alike."

Rory, familiar with his friend's ways, thanked the man and said, "Maybe I'll just ride up there and take a look."

He rode almost to the horse barns, and by then, he could clearly see the truth of what the stage whip had told him. Knowing it was too late for talk and having no choice but to stop the herd from entering the town, he stepped to the ground and lifted his Big Fifty from its scabbard. He untied the leather pouch he had drawn tight around the workings of the big gun to keep the dust out and checked the load. The weapon was ready. Fishing two more loads from his jacket pocket, holding them in the fingers of his left hand, he dropped to one knee. The plodding herd was now almost upon the big barn and corrals.

His left shoulder still wasn't completely healed from the bullet that had taken flesh and bone a few weeks earlier, but he could use it if he was careful. Holding the weight of the rifle in his right hand, he propped his left elbow on his left knee and cradled the forestock of the fifty in his left hand.

A herd that large would normally be wider at the front, but it seemed clear that the riders had slimmed it down to seven or eight beeves, narrow enough to hold to the road and be pushed through town. As sheriff, carrying the burden of the county and town's safety on his shoulders, Rory couldn't let that happen.

Taking careful sight on the big lead steer, Rory squeezed the trigger. In perfect timing with a boom to waken the dead and gain the full attention of the drovers, the steer folded his front legs and dropped in front of the next animal. As quickly as the sheriff could lever and reload the fifty, two more steers dropped to the ground, one of them kicking up a dust cloud of his own making, before taking his final breath. The startled animals directly beside and behind the dead steers turned in fright, a couple to the side, pushing against the point riders, while the remainder turned back into the herd. The repeated boom and roar of the fifty had folks running into the street, slamming store doors open and emptying out of saloons to see what was happening.

The point riders, leaving the herd to itself, kicked their animals into a run, heading directly toward the shooter.

The point rider on Rory's right pulled a rifle of some sort. And even though his horse was moving too fast and too erratically for accurate shooting, took a careless one-handed aim—regardless of the risk to the residents—that fired toward the town. The other point rider was coming on also, but he hadn't yet reached for a weapon. Seeing the risk was from the right, Rory took aim again and dropped the rider's animal. As the horse's front legs folded, its nose went into the dirt of the road, and its hind end rose into the air, resulting in a complete flip. The rider flew over the animal's head and took a solid fall onto the road, rolled and twisted a couple of times and lay flat, unmoving.

Rory swung his reloaded fifty to the other point rider, but that man, perhaps being wiser, left his rifle in the scabbard and took evasive action, turning sharply back toward the herd.

The half-wild cattle, just recently driven from Roaring Creek's hidden valleys and canyons in Wyoming, were completely out of control. When the lead steer went down, the drag riders were too far back to see what was going on. They kept pushing the herd forward, while the front animals were forcing themselves back, creating a melee. Finally, the herd burst into the open grassland to the east with the riders chasing, hoping to turn them into a mill, but that wouldn't be happening for a mile or two. The swing and flank riders from the east side were riding for their lives, hoping to stay ahead of the stampeding herd.

One more man rode forward, and after a few words together, he and the point man came slowly toward Rory, cautious of the fifty and the damage it could do. Both men held their empty hands well away from their holsters.

Rory, somewhat satisfied, mounted again, slid the fifty into its scabbard, and swung the sides of his coat apart to give him easy access to his Colt .44s. Someone from town, Rory didn't know who, was kneeling beside the downed rider.

He sat still, allowing the two cattlemen to approach him. As they closed the distance, he recognized the men. With a burst of shock and anger, he hollered, "Micah? Junior? What has your fool father got you doing now?"

Without waiting for an answer, he said, "You're under arrest. Both of you. And when your father wakes up, he'll be under arrest too. What kind a fool would drive a herd of longhorns right through a town? No one but Boon

Wardle and his equally foolish sons. Ride ahead of me to the jailhouse. I'm sure you know that if you touch a weapon, you'll be dead the next moment."

Micah opened his mouth as if to say something in rebuttal. The sheriff ignored the effort, simply pointing his finger toward town and the small jail.

Under his breath, Rory was muttering, "Haven't learned a single thing from their first visit to Stevensville and the fort. Be better, all around, if they were to stay to their hidden hills and valleys."

1

RORY WAS SOMEWHERE BETWEEN FULL-OUT ANGER AND amazement that anyone would think of driving a herd of longhorns through the center of a town. He would see to the old man when time allowed, but right at the moment, he was dealing with the sons, neither of which seemed to sense the stupidity of their actions.

Saying nothing at all, afraid that if he spoke, he would say something he'd be sorry for later, Rory disarmed the two Wardle brothers, pushed them, a bit roughly, into the cell and slammed the door. A single turn of the key, along with the fact their father would be under care at the doctor's office, would have all the Wardles the sheriff knew about off the street. It would also mean that the herd drovers would be chasing half-wild cattle and a bunch of saddle horses, with no one to direct their work. Rory was so upset that he couldn't find any sympathy for their situation, no matter how deep into his conscience he dug.

Micah, the eldest Wardle son, tried to ask the sheriff what his intentions were, but he received no answer.

Unless a weary and disgusted glance was taken as an answer. In the silence of the little jailhouse, Rory went to the gun rack and picked up the single pair of blacksmith-made handcuffs the county owned. They were a crude affair, but they were sturdy, and he had to admit that. Anyone locked into them was not going to be taking them off without a key or a metal cutting saw.

With the cuffs dangling from his hand, he left the jailhouse, locking the door behind himself.

He was feeling a bit guilty now. Not for what he had already done, but for what he was about to do. It was, actually, more like a guilty pleasure, something that may have been lying in the back of his mind since the Wardles' first visit. It wasn't his normal nature, but the Wardle family had so angered and frustrated him on their first visit, only weeks before, that the thoughts may have lain in his mind, in anticipation for some time, never truly expecting to have an opportunity to act on it.

Now he was going to add fresh misery to the misery the senior Wardle was already encompassed with.

The two blocks to the doctor's house were a longer walk than Rory felt like undertaking, so he swung into the saddle and kicked the gelding into a slow trot. The handcuffs still dangled from the fingers of his right hand.

Rory's anger was dissipating slightly as he opened the door to the medical clinic. There was no one in the waiting room, so he strode across to the surgery office door and knocked. His impatience for a job that needed doing wouldn't allow him to wait for an answer to his knock. Instead, he hollered out, "You got Old Man Wardle in there, Doc?"

"Come in, Sheriff," someone said quietly enough that Rory almost missed it, as it filtered its way through the wooden door. Grasping the knob and twisting, Rory pushed the door open. There, on the gurney, lay Boon Wardle, the head fool of a foolish clan of mountain cattlemen. He looked to be unconscious until Rory saw him open his eyes, look at the ceiling, groan, and then close them again. The doctor was working on Wardle's cheek with a curved needle and a long piece of thread. The doctor's helper was busy with a soft cloth and a pan of warm water, attempting to remove road grit that had literally ground its way into the old man's skin, even where his shirt had been torn off in his fall. She had a big job ahead of her. There seemed to be scrapes and torn skin everywhere Rory looked.

Wardle's torn shirt and pants, along with his already ragged long johns, were stacked on top of his boots in the corner of the room. He was draped with a folded bedsheet from the waist down.

Tammy was a young ranch girl who had come to town seeking a way off her family holdings, whether that meant a job in town or marriage to another rancher. Just so long as it meant a change. She had mentioned settling in the big city, which in her case would mean Denver, but after a long, heated discussion with her parents, she had settled for the fort. She had become a valuable assistant to the doctor, and she was making her own money to be spent any way she wished, so the first half of her plan had been completed.

Given the way the young ranchers and cowboys gathered around on the lawn after church services on a Sunday morning, shyly pointing quick glances her way, her hopes for the second half remained alive.

Rory said, "How goes it, Tammy? When you get the worst of the grime off, do you think you could figure a way to clean the stupid out of his head?"

Tammy decided it was a good time to remain quiet, but the doctor spoke up. "He'll have some scars to remember this day by, Sheriff. And to remind him that he can't fly like the birds. The hurts from the fall will heal. Eventually. The cuts and the bruises too. Can't say about his stupid."

Wardle simply lay there groaning from time to time.

Rory asked Tammy to move aside just a bit as he bent to look at how the gurney was built. Lifting the covering sheet and kneeling, while bending his head to look under the thin mattress, he was pleased to see a metal support railing running the full length. One on each side. He flicked open one of the handcuff links and snapped it closed around the metal railing. With the key, he locked it then stood and took Wardle's right arm and pulled it toward the edge of the gurney. He snapped the other cuff around that wrist and twisted the key. As he let the arm drop, Wardle became aware of what the sheriff had done. His display of anger was immediate.

The chain on the cuffs was longer than it would be on manufactured handcuffs giving ample freedom of movement for simple functions. Wardle snapped his arm up and down, moving from the surface of the gurney to the limit of his movements and then repeating that effort. He growled out the first words Rory had heard from him since entering the surgery.

"What do you think you're doing, kid? Get these things off and right now. I demand it."

Rory had his temper back under control. But not his disgust. That would last a while. He looked his prisoner in the eye, wondering what the real limitations on his authority were. He knew he couldn't up and shoot a man, or hang him, no matter the wanting to, or how much the action would fit the needs of the hour. But up to that point, he had some latitude.

"In case you haven't figured it out by now, Wardle, you're under arrest. The cuffs are to keep you here, so I'll know where you are. When Doc is finished with you, I'll march you across town where you can share our single cell with your two idiot sons. Then I'll stand you in front of the judge. All of you. You're not going to walk out of this one. But it will be up to the judge to make the final decision. In the meantime, you lie quiet and do what Doc says, or Tammy. You do or say anything at all to offend this young lady and you'll answer personally to me. That's different from answering to the sheriff. The sheriff has to play by the rules. I don't."

After leaving the doctor's office, Rory knew he needed some quiet time and a cup of coffee. Or three. Not wanting to get into any discussions at the dining room, he rode a couple of blocks south to the Mexican cantina. There he would be able to sit in private, remaining quiet while he worked through the current situation. The drone of Spanish from the other patrons would only work to help him concentrate.

2

STEPPING BACK INTO THE JAILHOUSE, RORY WENT TO THE peg above the marshal's desk and lifted the cell door key down. He unlocked the door and ushered the two prisoners out. He pointed at two chairs and said, "Sit."

The sheriff lifted one of his .44s out of its holster and laid it on the desk in front of him. As a means of intimidation, and to emphasize his determination, he spun the cylinder, ending with the quiet comment, "Full. And ready."

Very slowly, still fighting back the last of his anger, and trying to carefully pick his first words, Rory turned his eyes first to Micah Wardle and then to the younger brother, Junior.

Rory had worked and lived beside the two youngest Wardles, Key, now Stevensville marshal, and his sister, Tempest. He had grown fond of both of them. That each showed more common sense than the rest of the family was a good start for their life in Stevensville. Tempest was a very attractive young lady who had arrived in Stevensville wearing ranch clothing, although stylish ones. She had since moved on to more town-oriented wear, but her strong, trim figure and her riding ability would always point her in the direction of the ranch life.

Key had proven himself as a lawman, taking firm charge whenever he had been challenged.

Finally, sensing that Junior, although not the youngest of the sons, was familiar with being the younger brother to Micah, with all that normally came in that designation, Rory fixed his eyes firmly on Micah.

"You've had a couple of hours to think if that exercise isn't too far beyond your natural abilities. So, I have a logical question for you.

"Did you really believe you could drive a couple thousand half-wild longhorns and a cavvy of horses through a town without tearing the town to pieces, and endangering everyone on the streets and sidewalks?"

Although Micah chewed his bottom lip while he studied the sheriff, he said nothing. In his place, Junior asked, "Is Pa dead?"

"No, but he might be willing to have someone shoot him. He's banged and scratched up some, and the doc has exercised his stitching skills in a couple of places. And I expect he hurts just about everywhere."

The two young men were silent for a half minute, but finally, Micah spoke.

"We were following Pa's orders."

Rory laughed. Not a happy laugh, but more a laugh of derision, before saying, "Just following orders. One of the stupidest excuses for outlandish behavior ever spoken. And a common one, I'm afraid. Did you not see the trouble your sister averted with that foolish old man the first time he rode up to the marshal's office in Stevensville? He might be the only man still alive that ever held a rifle on me. I've been shot a few times. In fact,

I'm still healing from the last time, just a few weeks ago. Never really took to it, though.

"No, I can't think of another man who ever threatened me with a weapon and can still sit and talk about it. Here's a bit of advice, don't either of you attempt the exercise. I don't like shooting folks, but I've discovered I'd rather be the one doing the shooting, than the other way around."

Rory's voice firmed up, demonstrating the returning anger he was feeling.

"Now, I asked you a question. I need a better answer than 'Pa told me to do it.'"

Micah shuffled his feet, put his elbows on his knees, and bent his head, pulling his eyes away from the sheriff's stern gaze.

"You might not know this, Rory, depending on what kind of a man your father is—or was. Sorry, I just remembered; I was told before about the dry-gulching in the gold camp. Forgot right at the moment.

"I think the other boys would support me when I say Pa is not an easy man. Not easy to live with or work with either one. As kids, it was out of the question to defy an order. And I'll have to say that as far as the ranch and the cattle went, he was seldom wrong, although he refused to see past the longhorn breed.

"Dealing with family like we were just another part of the ranch was what we came to expect.

"Sometimes a fella can lose track of the fact that he's now an adult and a good cattleman in his own right. And I'll have to admit, too, that I never gave a single thought to what would happen when the herd entered the town."

After giving his brother a moment to pick up the talk again, Junior said, "I'll have to agree with what Micah says. And I'll also have to say I never gave the town a thought. I suppose I just thought the cattle would walk through, and we'd be gone. But I've looked at the traffic on the street and how narrow the street is, and I can see we were heading for a disaster. I'm truly sorry I didn't see it before. And I didn't really remember from our other visit. You might remember that we had a discussion with you at that time too."

Micah slowly raised his head, as if it was the most difficult thing he had ever done, before saying, "Pa was wrong. Junior and I, and the cowboys, too, for that matter, were just as wrong. We should have all known. We skirted the hills behind Laramie, hitting the trail to the south of the town, so that wasn't a problem. This is the first real town we've come to. I'll admit that pushing the stage out into the grass bothered me a bit, but not enough, so's I thought to do anything about it."

Rory studied the two men long enough to think through his plan before finally saying, "Alright. Here's what you're going to do. You're going to go right now and gather up that herd. You're still under arrest, but I'm granting you your parole on your promise to come at my calling. You're going to send a couple of men back with strong horses and rope. I want those dead animals off the road by nightfall. Off the road and far away. You pull them to where the stench of their rotting hides won't keep the townsfolk awake at night.

"You're going to find some unused grass. I don't care if you have to drive your bunch twenty miles, but don't you encroach on another rancher. And keep them bunched, especially the bulls. I'll guarantee you that if one of your bulls gets loose, you won't have to go looking for him. There's not a man in this part of Colorado that will leave a longhorn bull on the grass. That's one of the reasons they all carry rifles.

"Your father is under arrest, and he's not getting parole until the judge says so. Of all the foolish things to do, he took a wild, blind shot toward the town. He was shooting at me, but he missed by a long way. Took the front window out of the saddle shop and scared half the life out of the owner. That's not going to be overlooked or forgotten. I'll not have anyone taking wild shots in this town. Marshal Wiley won't either, and I know that for a fact. The marshal is away for a couple of days, but he's going to want to talk to you all when he returns.

"Now get out of here and gather up that herd. I'm going to leave you with a piece of advice. If you're smart at all, you'd best listen.

"No one here wants a herd of longhorns as neighbors. You'll find that everyone has long since gone into at least crossbreds with beefier animals or gone with full-bred stock from the east. So, here's my advice. While your father is laid up, where he can't shout you into obedience, you gather up that bunch and you turn them around. You're only a few day's drive from Cheyenne. You push them up there, and you sell to the first buyer foolish enough to make you an offer. You take the cash and you put it in the bank. Then, with all winter ahead of you, you look for the land you want and the animals you want. When you locate a ranch site, the rails will take you east where you will have a wide choice of animals to purchase. I'll be disappointed if I see you staying with those thousand-pound grasshoppers of yours.

"For once, take the lead on the Mirrored W. Sell, and then tell your father what you've done. Now get out of here."

3

A WEEK AND A BIT LATER, MICAH AND JUNIOR WARDLE rode back into town. They stopped first at the livery, putting up their animals after the long ride.

"Treat them well and check the shoes. They've put on some miles."

The liveryman accepted the reins from the two men and led the tired geldings back into the dim barn. Unlike most liverymen, Kegs wasn't a talker. He saw no need for an answer, but if he had spoken, the Wardle men might have heard him say something like, "Don't you be telling me my business, Sprout."

Late fall afternoon darkness was descending on the old fort, but the lights still shone in the saloon and the hotel dining room. The weary riders may opt for a drink later, but they needed some grub before the cook blew out the light. Walking in, they were surprised to see Sheriff Jamison sitting in the back corner having dinner with their father, still dangling the handcuffs from his one wrist. The news they had to share held the more cautious Micah back some, but Junior, alive with the self-confidence of youth and the correctness of their actions, stepped right up to their table, pulled out a chair, and sat down.

"Even'n, Pa. Good to see you up and around. Even'n to you too, Sheriff."

Boon Wardle lay his fork down on his plate, slid his chair back just a bit, turned his head, first to Junior, and then, as if his neck was stiff and sore, turned his entire body to look at his eldest son, who still stood in the doorway.

"Well. What have you two got to say for yourselves? You ain't been in town or anywhere around. And where is the herd? And the riders?"

As Micah was using the last of his courage to approach the table, Junior offered, "Riders are paid off, Pa. Remuda is on rented land with a rancher, west some miles. We'll gather them back up in the spring, supposing that's what we'll still wish to do. The cattle are in Cheyenne or in boxcars, where they should have been weeks ago, sav'n the long ride down here and back up, over the same miles, wearing off what little beef those scrubs carried."

Watching and listening, and then studying Boon Wardle's face as it colored up and his lips puffed out, Rory waited for the explosion. But it didn't come. Instead, the old man's shoulders slumped, and he closed his eyes as if he was feeling a different pain than what he had been experiencing since parting ways with his running horse. Defeated, he finally dropped his head and said, almost in a whisper, "Should have never left the mountains."

Hoping to smooth over the news, Micah asked, "How are you feeling, Pa? You took a bit of a tumble."

"You think so? 'A bit of a tumble,' he says. This here

so-called sheriff, not old enough to know up from down, goes and shoots the best horse I ever owned. In his dying, he throws me over his head, flying like a bird with no wings, like a Christmas goose headed for the oven, landing on my belly and face, and tossed every which way before I finally stopped moving. And he says I took a bit of a tumble."

"Ya, that all may be so, Pop, except that part about the horse. That animal was a knothead and you know it. Never trusted the thing myself. But none of that tells me how you find yourself right this very minute."

"If you're really wanting to know, I'm hurting. Every part of me hurts. Can't hardly shuffle one foot ahead of the other, can't sit, can't stand, can't hardly tolerate lying on a bed. I hurt. That's how I am. And now, on top of all that, this here sheriff, he up and shot three of our best steers, animals ready for market, on top of the horse. And to make matters worse, he's planning to stand me before the judge. You two also. Stand us before the judge like common criminals.

"There was a day I'd have explained Wardle's law to him. Explained it so he'd never forget. Ain't rightly written in no law book you can read, but it's all in my head, right there for the remembering. He'd have left out of our mountains with his tail between his legs and never come back.

"Stand Boon Wardle before a judge. Why…"

Junior, becoming braver as the conversation moved along, said, "I kind of think he means it, Pa. I'm not too sure what he plans to charge us with, but when you pulled the trigger, aiming nowhere special, and did it right in town, I suspect some folks may have been a little upset. This is no wild cattle-drive town. I'm not say'n it's all fancy dress and pink teas and such, but folks here live peaceable, shopping and going to church on Sunday. If you had read Key's letters carefully, or at all, you might have remembered that."

The only comment from Boon Wardle came out more as a grunt or a growl than actual words before he picked up his fork and resumed eating.

The waitress, half frightened to approach the table with all the loud talk going on, finally eased over that way. Quietly, she said, "If you two plan to take dinner this evening, you'd best order now. Amber is already letting the fire die down in the cookstove. Anyway, the choices are roast beef and potatoes, what's left of them, along with some greens and all the brown gravy you want. That or nothing. What will it be?"

Micah, grinning at the way the choices were laid out, smiled and said, "That beef sounds good. What do you think, little brother?"

With the two orders taken and the girl just about to turn away, Boon Wardle said, "Don't you be getting your hopes up too high on that beef. Pretty stringy. Be a week getting it out of my teeth."

The waitress grinned and said, "Why, sir, that's your beef. Animal wasn't hardly on the ground when Amber ran right down to the butcher's and had one mostly black brute dragged down to the slaughterhouse. He was bled out, butchered, and skinned an hour after the sheriff shot him. He's been hanging in the icehouse up until now."

Rory and the two boys laughed until there were tears running down their faces. Micah finally straightened up and said, "Why, Pa, just imagine, stringy meat like that, you may put the whole city of Chicago off beef. That's where we sold the herd into."

That brought Boon back into the conversation.

"How much did you get for the animals?"

Micah told him the per pound offer, and then said, "We could have tried to graze them over the winter with no land and no hay, and water that is seldom found on the flatlands. Instead, we can put this check in the bank and take the winter to find some land. You could even ride back up to Laramie, Pa. Try again to talk Mother into seeing your good points."

"Don't have to ride anywhere. Couldn't anyway. Not sure I could even climb onto a wagon. Your Ma rode into town yesterday in a fringe-top buggy. Riding beside her was My Way. Him and another Indian. Came along to keep her safe. As soon as she was in the hotel, the Indians turned right around and headed north again."

4

JUDGE ANDERS P. YOKAM WAS THE LAST TO ENTER THE small, temporary courtroom. Distaining the use of a judge's robe, which he found to be foolish and totally out of place on the frontier, he was wearing the same suit and necktie he wore to church and everywhere else. It was, in fact, the only suit he owned, and he desired no other.

Before he took his seat, he cast his eyes over the court gathering. The chairs set out for the occasion were all full, with men and women both standing shoulder to shoulder and a few more leaning in the windows and single doorways. The only ones in attendance that he recognized were the sheriff, the town marshal, and the owner of the saddlery whose window had been shot out. He assumed the three men sitting front and center were the ones charged with some kind of offense. Startled by the blue bruises and the black thread still hanging from the stitched-up cut on the big man's cheek, the judge decided rightly, that this was the man who took the dreadful fall from his horse, in sight of the entire town.

He couldn't see the two other stitched-up cuts on the rancher's shoulder, covered by a newly bought shirt.

He did not yet know what offenses the sheriff intended to name off, but he was certainly aware of the threat to the town from the longhorn herd and the subsequent shooting. He trusted the sheriff to bring a reasonable argument to his court.

The judge took special note of a mature, very attractive, and well-dressed lady sitting in the second row of chairs. With no idea who she was, he couldn't help wondering what her connection might be to these wilderness ranchers sitting before him. Most of the rest of the people jammed into the small room were curiosity seekers, who came to see the only show in town.

He sat, banged his gavel once on the desk, indicating in the absence of a court clerk who would, in a bigger court, shout out the information that court was in session. He shuffled some blank papers lying before him, adjusted his pen until it was carefully aligned with the papers, cleared his throat, and said, "Sheriff Jamison, I believe you have business to bring before the court this day."

Rory stood, never enjoying this part of his law work, and answered, "Yes, sir. This has to do with the Wardle family who were intent on driving their Mirrored W herd through town with no regard for the life and property of the townsfolk.

"Sitting before you is Mr. Boon Wardle, the owner of the Mirrored W, and the father to Micah and Junior Wardle, two of his sons. After considerable discussion with these three men, I have become convinced that the sons were following their father's orders and were, in spite of the fact that they are clearly adults, unable to argue with their father or dissuade him from his

23

intended travel route. I would, therefore, recommend that Micah and Junior be released with a stern warning from the court and a modest fine for the costs and inconvenience they have brought upon the town.

"Boon Wardle was the instigator of the tragedy that was sure to occur if two thousand longhorns and a herd of horses had been loosed into the town. And I am not convinced that he even yet understands what peril he came close to inflicting. He has offered no apology or explanation. I'm not at all sure that he wouldn't do the exact same thing again.

"In addition, Mr. Wardle carelessly and thoughtlessly fired his rifle into the town. He admits that he was shooting at me, but he was riding a running horse at the time. He had little, if any, control of his weapon, with the result that the shot took out the front window of the saddlery and missed, striking Mr. Sales by only inches.

"We take these two matters seriously, sir, and ask that the court deal with Mr. Wardle in an appropriate manner. As a side matter, I may mention that I don't take kindly to being shot at, as sheriff or as a citizen."

The judge had been scribbling notes as fast as he could dip ink from the small bottle sitting on the edge of the desk and scratch the sheriff's words onto the paper.

Except for some shuffling of feet and one man coughing, the room fell to silence as Judge Yokam reviewed his notes. As the minutes passed, there was more shuffling and a few whispers. The sheriff, knowing the judge was about to call for order if the noise didn't stop, turned and looked over the crowd, showing his displeasure. That was enough to bring silence again.

As Rory turned, he couldn't miss the almost humorous look on Mrs. Wardle's face. He was left wondering what the look signified but had no more time to contemplate, as the judge cleared his throat and began to speak.

"Micah and Junior Wardle, please stand."

When the two men were standing with their hats in their hands, the judge said, "I sit here looking at two fools. That you have lived all your lives on a remote mountain ranch, and are unfamiliar with towns, impresses me not one bit. I suspect that if your herd was loose and headed for your ranch yard, you would take action to turn them. Yet you failed to say no to your father when he pointed the animals for the town. Do either of you have anything to say for yourselves?"

When neither man spoke, the judge glanced again at his notes before saying, "Hearing nothing from you, this court directs that you will each pay a fine of one hundred dollars, payable immediately to this court. In the event that you cannot or choose not to pay the fine, you will spend the next thirty days in our jail. In addition, you will each write a sincere letter of apology, seeking forgiveness for your thoughtlessness. Those letters will be published, along with your names, in the local paper."

With that, Micah and Junior took their seats again, and the judge directed a stern look at Boon Wardle. Clearing his throat again, he said to the rancher who was still struggling to stand, "I am looking at another fool and the father of fools. Do you have anything to say for yourself, sir?"

Boon Wardle had much to say, but he wisely held his silence.

"Mr. Wardle, this court finds you guilty of endangering the town and its citizens, in addition to the damage to property your foolish rifle shot caused. The fact that the sheriff prevented this disaster removes no guilt at all from your shoulders.

"You will, therefore, reimburse the sheriff, who I understand bought and paid for the replacement glass. You will cover the full cost of the replacement of this window, plus apologize verbally in front of this court. You will also pay to this court a fine of five hundred dollars, and you will be the guest of the sheriff in the town jail for one week. During that week, you will have no visitors other than the person selected to carry your food plates to you. That will give you enough time to write a letter of apology to the town and have it published along with the letters your sons are going to write. And now, sir, you will please turn and direct a sincere apology to Mr. Sales, who is sitting near the back of the room."

Standing in front of a room full of strangers and carefully wording a short apology, while every eye in the place could see the handcuffs draped from one wrist to the other, might have been the most difficult and demeaning thing the old cattleman had ever done. He would have preferred to have a gunfight. But apologize, he did, with Mrs. Wardle now smiling openly.

With the crowd watching, Rory led Boon Wardle across the road to the jail. The clanking of the steel door was the loudest noise the mountain rancher had ever heard. But finally, giving in to the pain that still throbbed through his body, he sat on the edge of the hard bunk, and then, one by one, he raised his feet and then one whole leg onto the cot. When he managed to raise the other leg into a prone position, he stretched out fully and groaned. Rory almost felt sorry for him. Almost, but not quite.

5

IVAN, SHERIFF RORY'S DEPUTY, NERVOUSLY APPROACHED Tempest, leading two saddled horses. There had been many changes in his life since leaving the ranch and the suspect teachings of his friend, Kiril, behind. No longer did he believe that the proper place for a woman was to remain in the shadow of her man, doing his bidding. Kiril had made it sound so attractive, so controlled— everyone knowing their place in life and understanding that someone had to make and carry out the rules, and *that* someone was the man.

But to ride out on a cool fall evening with a pretty girl was a far jump even from his new enlightenment. He had spoken without thinking, voicing the thought that an evening ride might be pleasant, his reactions to this girl's attractiveness making decisions for him rather than the cool, controlled thoughts he always imagined he possessed. But he had, in fact, spoken, and now he had it to do.

He had stepped into the saddle, taken up the reins of the second horse, and trotted to the corner and then, in a

27

slow walk, taken the two blocks to the rooming house where most of the single girls in town had found comfort and companionship. When he came in sight of his destination and found the porch to be housing every available girl, including his own sister, and every one of them with a worrisome grin on her face, he came near to dropping the reins to the led horse and retreating in shame. Perhaps it was humiliation.

Tempest turned the incident around by standing. As she took the steps to ground level, she said, "Why thank you, Ivan. I had been thinking of an evening ride. But when I mentioned it to you, I didn't expect you to go to the trouble of fetching my horse. But now that you're here, why don't you come along with me? You can show me the sights as we ride along."

There was not a girl there that believed Tempest's twisting of the matter, but though the grins remained, not a word was spoken. When the two riders were mounted and lined out toward the main road, Tempest flashed a big smile at Ivan.

"You're a brave man, Ivan. You might have known what the girls would think when you showed up with a spare horse. And, I'm willing to guess, the next time will be worse than the first."

She hesitated, as if thinking through something that had already been thought through thoroughly by the young ranch girl from the Wyoming hills. Being raised in a family of boys had conditioned her to deal with the foolishness of men where affairs of the heart were concerned. Even if those affairs were one-sided at the time. With a smile and a lightness of heart she would have had trouble explaining, she said, "Of course, Ivan, I'm assuming there's enough to see in the Stevensville area that you'll require more than just the one evening to cover it all."

Ivan choked out an answer that may have been agreement or total denial. It would be difficult to know for sure, but it seemed to satisfy Tempest for the time being.

6

Cap Graham had been thinking seriously of giving it all up. His search and chase for Sly Loughty had been long and hard. And fruitless. Oh, he had been close several times, but Loughty was as slippery as an eel. Just when Cap thought he had figured out a trick or a trap that would put Sly in his control, the man would do something totally unexpected, and the chase would begin again, with more hours or days lost. Wasted.

Desperate, nearly broke, and tired of sleeping wherever nightfall found him—all the time recognizing that his body was too old for long, tedious nights on the hard earth, curled up under a groundsheet, praying the rain would hold off—he had decided he could spare a couple of coins for a decent, woman-cooked meal.

That decision had been taken an hour before, and now, staring out the window of the hotel dining room in Stevensville, with a final cup of coffee and a hunger put behind him with a plate of roast beef and brown gravy smothered potatoes, he contemplated his next step.

His thoughts were interrupted when a man settled a

mug of coffee on the table across from him. Without a word, the unexpected guest pulled a chair out and sat down. Their eyes met but no words were spoken until Cap said, with a bit of a grin, although lightness of heart was the furthest thing from his mind, "Why don't you join me, Sheriff?"

"I'll do that, stranger, if for no other reason than to find out how you knew about the badge that I never wear."

"I can always tell. See it from a mile away, badge or no badge. Man carries the badge, and he starts taking on a look. Suspicious. Careful. Wondering. He wonders about every stranger that enters town. Can't no way mistake it once you figure out what to look for. So now it's your turn. Why join me? I'm just about to take my leave, and you'll see me no more."

THE BODIES of his murdered family were long in their graves. His cattle were sold off; the money spent. The ranch was being grazed by neighbors who had not bothered with the nicety of offering rent on the grass, and the lonely graves of his family were growing weeds. His resignation as sheriff of the small village of Slough Hollow had become a dim memory only.

Although all of that was true, and the fact that he could no longer deny his weariness, the other fact was that Sly Loughty was still out there. Out there and free. Or at least as free as a man can be with someone haunting his every move. Someone that would know exactly what to do if he slipped up just once. There could be no doubt of the outcome if he should fall into the hands of the ex-sheriff.

Cap Graham had thought it all through. Many times. He knew the preacher who warned him of a wasted life was correct. Had known it at the time. He also knew that the Word promises, "I will repay." But Cap had no patience for waiting for eternity to set things right. He would handle the case now. Or that's what he told himself anyway all those months ago.

And now he was sitting in the dining room in this pleasant little town with the sheriff sitting across from him, while he waited for an explanation for the visit.

Ivan studied the man, thinking before he spoke. He wasn't sure himself why he had picked out this man. Strangers and travelers were plentiful enough on the Denver Road. There had been a lot of others he might have more appropriately chosen.

"I'm probably not aware of the look you describe in myself. Most likely wishing to be the same man that left the ranch just a bit more than a year ago. But I could be wrong on that. I don't study the image reflected back at me as I stand before the mirror shaving. I'll have to admit there's been more action than I ever thought possible in a small town and the area around. It could be the wild rides and the powder smoke have taken a toll.

"Now, to be honest and fair, you hold that same look. I'm guessing that's what moved my steps this way. So, I'm left with a couple of questions. Are you retired, or do you still carry the badge? And that leads me to wonder what you're doing in my town."

"You're sharp for a young man, Sheriff. Are you town or county?"

"Town has a marshal. I'm county deputy. County sheriff lays himself down for a night up at the fort. Just a short day's ride north. Or sometimes at his ranch, the Double J, just a couple of miles north from here. You'll pass it on your way. But I'm still wondering if I'm looking at an active sheriff and wondering why he would be here. Of course, if you've retired and are on some personal law business, I might want to know about that too."

The back-and-forth statements resulted in a long pause while Sonia refilled their coffee mugs. Cap took a sip, and deeming it to be too hot to drink, leaned back in his chair. Ivan could easily see the weariness in the man. Twisting the coffee mug by the handle, first clockwise and then in reverse, Cap said, "No, no story today. I believe I'll just ride on, my friend. I suspect the trail is growing cold as we sit here. I'll catch up, though. I've only got the one horse and no possibility of buying another. The fugitive has been running his animal too hard. I've seen him in the distance yesterday afternoon and first thing this morning. He'll kill the poor animal if he doesn't steal another first. I believe I'll just ride on. He may stop to eat at this fort you're talking about. Anyway, I've been on the trail a good long time. Another day or two won't make hardly any difference. To him or to me.

"I wish you well, Sheriff. And now, if you'll excuse me?"

Ivan said nothing as the weary man eased to his feet, adjusted his holster, placed his hat carefully on his head, and reached into his pocket for the cost of the meal.

"Lunch is my treat today, Sheriff. Ride careful, and don't you go to upsetting Sheriff Rory when you reach the fort. He's a good man and a good friend, but he don't take no nonsense."

Ivan watched as the man made his way a few feet to his horse, where he tightened the cinch and slowly mounted. With a slight touch of the rein and a gentle nudge with his right spur, the rider moved into the center of the trail, heading north. Watching from his seat in the diner, Ivan thought, *Rides like he was born in the saddle.*

"There's a weary man."

The comment came from Ivan's sister, Sonia, who had been waiting tables in the small dining room ever since she pulled away from the uphill ranch her family had established.

"You're right, little sister, a weary man. And a dangerous man."

7

FOR MOST OF THE RESIDENTS OF THE FORT, THE FIRST
indication of trouble was the echoing sound of the
gunshot. But Kegs, the Fort liveryman, sitting in the
shade of his big barn, saw it all. He was too far away to
do anything to stop it, and he never carried a weapon.
But he was a terror with a rope. Like many liverymen, he
had earned his stripes as a cattleman, staying with the
trade until too many cold mornings and too many rank
horses put him on his feet for good, never again to sit a
saddle without pain.

Sly Loughty—a womanizer, thief, murderer, and
worse—had needed a horse. And he needed it quickly.
Cap Graham, that half-mad ex-sheriff who had made a
misery of his life for too long, was close by. He had seen
him just that morning, somewhere a bit south of that last
little town he galloped around, hoping to not be seen. It
looked as if Cap was just breaking camp. He was sure he,
himself, had not been spotted by his nemesis. Since that
early morning sighting, a fast twenty miles had brought
his latest stolen horse, staggering and wheezing, almost

to the breaking point. Escape was all that mattered now. It was time to make his last desperate attempt at disappearing so no one would know who he was or where he went. A change of name, clean up his act, and put enough miles between here and there, and he would be free. He had a few dollars in his pocket, stolen from a rancher who had just drawn his payroll from the bank. He had tried disappearing in times past and failed. This time there would be no failure. He could feel freedom in his bones. He just needed a good riding animal. And the kid who was tying down a canvas sack of supplies had that animal.

Sly leaped off his horse, quickly untied his bedroll and saddlebags, and turned to the fourteen-year-old boy.

"I'll be needing your animal, kid. Just step aside and don't do anything stupid."

Dennis Coulson, tall, thin, but mostly fully grown and feeling the strength of youth and loving the gelding he had raised since its birthing, answered, "Don't you lay a hand on my animal. You do and I'll…"

A single shot ended the sentence. There was no compassion or thought for the youth in the feverish mind of Sly Loughty. There was but a single person in the entire world the man cared for and that was Sly Loughty. As the boy crumpled to the ground and a woman screamed, Kegs jumped from his chair and stood on wobbly legs for a bare second of time, hardly believing what his eyes told him was reality. The other reality his eyes told him was that the shooter was going to escape. There was no one on the street that could stop him. No one already in the saddle or who might hold a weapon on the murderer. No one but Kegs himself. And Kegs hadn't held a gun in his hand for years, and had none handy, in any case. But he had a rope. It was not quite within arm's length but was close by, just a few quick steps away, hanging on a wooden peg inside the livery door. His rheumatism would make him pay a price for jumping from the chair and taking those quick steps, but he soon had the rope in his hand. As he ran toward the road, the fugitive was aboard the stolen gelding and was whipping the beast with his hat and spurring the animal cruelly, even though he was still searching for the second stirrup.

Somehow, without even thinking of it, as if it was the most natural thing in his life, Kegs formed a loop as he ran. If he even saw the liveryman in his frantic attempt at escape, Sly Loughty ignored him. But Kegs had paced his running and his loop swing just as he had thousands of times before. But instead of roping a running long-horn off a horse, he was intent on roping a murderer, while on foot.

With a scream of despair, and more digging of the spurs, Loughty rode exactly where Kegs had figured he would ride. A perfectly timed swing and an accurate throw, and the rope dropped over the fleeing man's head and then over his arms. Even knowing he would be in pain for days following this day, Kegs dug his heels in. The roadbed was firm beneath, but the top inch or so was loosened by the constant turning of wagon wheels and the churning of shod hooves. Bracing himself against being pulled off his feet, Kegs waited for the horse to run out the length of the rope. He had done something no cowboy would do, but in his desperation, he had wrapped the rope twice around his right arm, taking a firm grip with hands that still held some strength. It was an action that could cost the arm when working cattle.

When the rope tightened, Sly Loughty stuck to the

saddle for two long strides of the gelding, pulling Kegs off his feet and into the dust in a mean drag. And then the fugitive and the old cowboy became one, joined together by a fifty-foot hemp rope, as Sly Loughty was jerked mercilessly from the saddle, hung in the air, as if by magic for only a split second, and then dropped to the road. Kegs gripped the rope as if life depended on it. He had landed on his stomach and, although near enough in a daze, still grasped the rope with his every muscle and intent.

The horse ran on as Loughty lay for only a short moment before he began struggling to his feet. The action was stopped when Wiley Hamstead, town marshal at the fort, running full out from the marshal's office, slowed enough to take careful aim and then kicked the murderer firmly beneath the chin. The boot leather was solid, the swing on the marshal's leg accurate, and the chin inviting. Loughty was down and out and would stay that way for some time.

Several men gathered to help Kegs to his feet, but he waved them off, not altogether sure he wanted to get up. The roadway felt unusually comfortable. He might prefer to just lie there for a while. Smiley, another old hand who had chosen the fort as the perfect spot to ease into his remaining years, knelt beside the liveryman, and seeing that he was alive and breathing, turned his head— not quite far enough—and spewed a brown mass onto the roadway.

"Why, I do believe you might be on to someth'n there, ol' son. Don't know why we never thought of 'er before. Work'n the brand'n fire on foot. Now there's someth'n worth the thought. Sav'n the horses fer Sunday afternoon picnics 'n sech. Yes, sir, Kegs, you got you a new idea."

Kegs opened his eyes, took a quick study of his old friend, groaned, and closed his eyes again.

While Marshal Wiley was clamping handcuffs onto Sly Loughty's wrists, with several men waiting to help escort the unconscious man to the jail cell, a new shadow fell across the gathering. Glancing up, Wiley locked eyes with a grieving Samuel Coulson, the father of the murdered boy. As Wiley watched, Coulson slowly and deliberately lifted his Colt from its holster and began to swing it toward the murderer. Wiley leaped to his feet, putting himself between the father and the unconscious murderer. He didn't know who the man was, but he knew the law he had sworn to uphold.

"Hold on now. We'll have no vigilante action here. Put the gun up or I'll put the irons on you too."

One of the men standing there said, "Could be you don't know this man, Marshal. This is Samuel Coulson, father to that boy lying on the road over there, shot down for no reason at all. Way I see it, he has the right."

Wiley had never taken his eyes off the gunman, but it could be that his steady stare softened just a bit.

"I'm terribly saddened by this whole thing Mr. Coulson, but there's still a right way and a wrong way to do things in a civilized society. While I can't possibly understand your loss, I'll not have you adding a crime to a crime. I'd like it if you would give me that Colt and then go back and comfort your wife, if she's here in town with you, and I'll take care of this end of things."

Coulson and the marshal locked eyes for a quarter minute before the grieving father turned and walked away. He carried his Colt dangling from his unfeeling hand. Wiley didn't challenge him on it.

The town had fallen to silence and stayed that way for the remainder of the afternoon, after everyone had done what they could do to help the Coulson family. The doctor came to confirm that young Coulson was dead, before his father gently picked up the young man in his arms and laid him in the back of the family wagon. He would be taken back to their small ranch situated on a picturesque plateau just a bit higher than the town, and lovingly, but sadly, buried in the grove behind the house where willows and aspens thrived in that stream-watered corner of their holdings.

SHERIFF JAMISON HAD RIDDEN to the Double J Ranch for a day of rest, leaving Marshal Wiley in care of the fort. Boon Wardle was still taking up space in the single cell in the small marshal's office. His wife, Belle, given freedoms beyond what the judge had specified, had visited for hours, as well as helping the still hurting man as he shuffled across the road to the dining room for his meals. Not wishing to intrude on a family discussion which he could easily see was close to boiling over at times, Wiley took the cell key off the wall peg and left the two to themselves.

Cap Graham, fresh from his lunch in Stevensville and his discussion with Ivan, was trotting his horse casually north with the larger town Ivan had referred to as the fort, his target for the night. He was well aware that his prey had ridden horses to death in his mad attempt at escape, but so far, over the many months, as sly as he sometimes was, he had gained little, and sometimes nothing at all. Cap was more shrewd and wise on the trail than Sly Loughty was in his wild escape attempts. It was true that Cap had been left behind several times and had totally lost the trail once, the year before, but his reasoning of the geography and the history of the fugitive allowed him to zero in on the trail again. Once, he had missed Sly by less than an hour, judging by the still warm body of his dead horse and the scrambled hoof prints where he had roped a grazing animal. He would catch him yet. He was sure of it. And he had no intention of killing his faithful gelding in the process.

As the ex-sheriff approached the roadway into the Double J, there was a rider waiting, watching his every move. His first instinct was to ignore the man and ride on past, but when the rider stepped his horse into the center of the road and sat there watching Cap's approach, there wasn't much he could do but pull up and wait to hear what the fellow had to say.

Rory tilted his hat just a bit. "Morning, sir. Couldn't help seeing you approaching. Thought we might make our way north together."

The truth was that Rory had no intention of having an unfamiliar rider so close behind him, and to fall back and follow would look strange and untrusting.

"Not as much on visiting as some, but I'll ride along a ways. Heard about a settlement referred to as the fort. Along this way, a slow day's ride. I'm taking a late start, though. Could be darkness will catch up. If you wanted to hurry along, I won't be insulted none."

Rory smiled at the obvious attempt to be rid of him. Speaking casually, he answered, "I've ridden this trail many a time. I expect we can hold the night off long enough. That's a good-looking animal you're riding. Could probably step out and make some time."

"He can and he will if I prod him a little."

"Well then, let's see if we can make the fort in time for dinner."

The fall day was chilly with the threat of rain that

could easily turn to snow at this time of year. Both men pulled their collars up and snugged their hats down tightly against the constant wind.

～

EACH MAN suspicious of the other, they talked little but still held to a companionable pace and entered the town in fewer hours than Cap had expected. As they neared the center of town, Rory said, "I'll be leaving you here, Cap. Hotel has the best food. Cantina we just passed is alright if you prefer spice and aloneness."

Cap had been sizing up the town as they rode and talked. He glanced at Rory and then to the almost empty boardwalks and said, "Pretty little place, what with the mountains and all. Quiet, though. What should I make of that, Sheriff?"

The question and pointed identification caught Rory by surprise, as had the same statement caught Ivan, over lunch some hours before. With a slight tug on the rein, the gelding stopped walking. Rory eased himself in the saddle, placing more weight on his right leg and lifting the left to ease a building cramp, giving him time to put some words together.

"I was all set to point the same title at you, Cap. I noticed when you didn't offer your last name. I expect there's a chance I may have heard it before. The names of lawmen get around and are remembered in the West, same as they do for outlaws. But you're correct; the town is usually much more alive than this. Ride to the office with me. We'll see what Wiley has to say."

Cap didn't bother asking who Wiley was. He simply lifted his stretched-out legs, placed his feet back into the stirrups, and jigged his animal after Rory's gelding.

Rory dismounted and flipped the reins over the hitch rail. Cap did the same. Almost in lockstep, they moved toward the office door. Rory saw Kegs limping toward the two horses, as if to take them under his care, as he most normally did for the sheriff. Rory noticed the limp, and not sure what the next few minutes would demand of him or the horse, waved the liveryman back.

Cap was much the elder and several inches taller than Rory. Although he was a big man, holding to the build and breadth of shoulder from his riding days, he carried little meat on his bones and no fat at all. His eyes were sun damaged, showing squint lines, but still holding a questioning and curious look. He wore his gun as if it didn't exist, seeming to completely ignore the tool of death.

Rory pushed the door open and looked first to the cell, expecting to see Boon Wardle still angry and miserably in pain from his fall. His week wouldn't be up for two more days. But the man he saw lying on the cot was not the Wyoming cattleman. Wiley partially answered his unasked question with, "Been a couple of changes, Sheriff."

"I can see that, Wiley. Want to tell me about it? And where's Boon?"

"I booted his lazy butt out of here. Told him we needed his bed. Warned him not to leave town or cause any more trouble. I do believe that wife of his has a stranglehold on him that's firmer than anything you or I could conjure up.

"Got a new customer, though."

"I can see that. Who is he and what's he in for? Looks a little worse for wear."

Cap answered the questions, one of them at least.

"That's my man, Sheriff. That's Sly Loughty, and a

worse prisoner you couldn't hope to house. I don't know what he's done here to bring him to this, but his back trail would expose about every crime known to mankind. I've been chasing this man nigh on two and a half years. Although I wanted to take him myself, I'll be satisfied just to see him taken."

Rory turned his attention back to Wiley, leaving the other half of his earlier question still to be answered.

Wiley spoke clearly but quietly, almost reverently.

"I don't know if you're familiar with the Coulson family from out west a few miles, Rory. Samuel Coulson and his son, Dennis. The family came to town for a bit of shopping. That man in the cell needed a horse after nearly killing his own. When the boy objected to having his animal taken, this man shot and killed him."

Rory heard Cap suck in a deep breath before something like a heaving, grieving gasp escaped from his lips. As he looked at the old sheriff, he saw the man's hand sneaking toward his Colt. But remembering the oath taken years before, Cap dropped his hand and his chin at about the same time. He then turned and headed for the door.

44

8

time to

CAP WASN'T SEEN AGAIN UNTIL TWO DAYS LATER.

A quick study of the crowd gathered at the Coulson place on that cold, late fall morning would indicate that the entire town, and many from the surrounding ranch country, had wound their way up the switchback trail and now stood in reverent silence in the Coulson yard. Pastor Miller read from the Word and then offered a mercifully short encouragement about God's mercy and promises from the 23rd Psalm. Weeping was heard among the gathering, and a low rumbling of anger and frustration when the mention of Dennis Coulson's short life was spoken.

Rory, as broken inside by the events as any other townsman, was nevertheless vigilant. He had purposely chosen a spot toward the rear of the gathering, where he could cast his eye in every direction without gathering foul looks. When he heard a rustling in the brush off to his left, he turned that way in time to see Cap Graham step from his horse, lift his hat off, holding it in front of his chest, and bow his head. That the old sheriff was hurting and harboring thoughts Rory could only guess at, was plain to see.

It was as if Cap was present in two places at once. His heart was fully with the Coulson family while his mind drifted back over the months and miles to a little ranch out west where a similar event had played itself out. During those brief moments, it was as if his life was totally empty—and pointless. He had failed in protecting his family, and he had failed in catching the murderer that had destroyed them and—now—the Coulson family. He would live with the guilt on top of his heavy losses. There was no one close enough to see the tears streaming down his cheeks.

When the final amen signaled the men that it was time to pick up their shovels and fill the grave, Cap replaced his hat, gathered his reins, and stepped easily into the saddle. He hesitated when he saw Rory walking his way. While he waited, he turned his head and wiped his eyes with the sleeve of his shirt, hoping Rory would not notice. Rory spotted the action but said nothing.

Cap looked down from the height of the saddle as Rory gently took hold of the bridle strap and stroked the animal's neck. The two men, the old sheriff and the younger lawman, studied each other for a mere ten seconds before Rory lifted his hand off the bridle and quietly said, "Come and see me. We should talk."

With no comment of affirmation or otherwise, Cap turned his animal into the light forest and disappeared after just a few steps.

~

THE TOWN WAS quiet while everyone waited for the judge to call a trial date. Sly Loughty remained in jail, manacled, and with a two-man guard around the clock. Rory had asked if he wanted a lawyer. His sneering answer was, "Ain't no book-learned lawman going to come to Sly Loughty's aid now, kid. And don't be making no bets on my life. Or yours either. I ain't finished yet. Not by a long way."

Preferring to avoid any discussion with the murderer, or even talk to him, Rory ignored the foolish statement and turned away.

JUDGE ANDERS P. YOKAM was a determined man. He well knew that to keep the lid on the feelings around the fort, there would soon have to be a court date set for Sly Loughty. But the fact was that Judge Yokam had given Rory time to write letters to several law officers across the West, seeking information on the prisoner. He had included Block Handly on that list, hoping he could pull together whatever information the Federals had gathered over the years. With the murder of Dennis Coulson, he already had all he needed for a conviction, but he hoped the trial and sentence would bring some satisfaction to others who had been unfortunate enough to be confronted by the man in times past.

To speed up the letter movements, Rory had offered to cover for Marshal Wiley if the marshal would make the ride to Cheyenne and work with the telegrapher as he turned the short queries into wires that would cover the miles in seconds instead of the weeks or months the mail would take. He was to wait for the answers, giving him time to renew some acquaintances from when he worked as deputy in the cattle and railway town.

When Wiley rode back into the fort a week later, his

pockets were bulging with wires. Answers from all over the West. Most were simple acknowledgments of crimes committed in the writer's area, along with a few details. In every case, there was satisfaction shown that the man's criminal life would now be in the hands of the court and a no-nonsense judge. But the surprise, which on deeper thought should not have been a surprise at all, was that there were rewards on the man's life from numerous places: banks, towns, counties, and one, larger reward, from the federal government. Clearly, the past life of Sly Loughty had been lived in a dark and miserable place.

Rory made a list of the rewards before passing the wires over to the judge.

What no one knew or suspected was that a couple of sharp news reporters and one writer of penny dreadfuls had picked up the news and were heading toward the fort.

The day of the court hearing was snowy, cold, and miserable. As miserable as the task that lay before Rory and the judge. The prisoner was led across the street in cuffs, both on his wrists and his ankles. The two men who held his elbows were unarmed, assuring that Loughty would have no possibility of twisting toward one of the men and somehow reaching a gun. Ten men formed a box around the prisoner, each with belted handguns, and each with a carbine loaded and at the ready. In addition, Rory had stationed armed men at several high points in the town, roofs mostly, to watch for riders coming to Loughty's aid. His call for volunteers had brought so many men forward that he couldn't begin to use all of them.

The saloon had been cleared of tables, and the chairs set in curved rows focusing on the single table and chair, backed nearly to the rear wall and held for the judge. The bar was closed for the day, as was the cantina at the edge of town. Rory's armed men stood ready throughout the room. The judge was escorted from his already guarded home to the makeshift court-room by Rory himself, along with Ivan, who had ridden up from Stevensville, as well as several trusted ranchers and townsmen. Rory had determined that nothing at all would go wrong if it was within his power to prevent it.

The two newsmen from the East sat side by side, pencils and paper at the ready. The news of the trial would be broadcast far and wide as soon as the writers could push their horses through the snow and cold to the Cheyenne telegraph station.

The trial itself was short and quickly put to the judge's decision. At the mention of a jury, Rory had said, "Judge Yokam, I believe it would be best if you and I handle this ourselves. We've signed on for the jobs before us. The townsmen have not, and I fear this trial will be receiving considerable notice around the coun-try. I don't wish to endanger any potential jurymen with friends of the prisoner seeking revenge."

Reluctantly, the judge allowed that he had the authority to hold court to himself and agreed to do so.

With a simple stating of the facts of the shooting of young Dennis Coulson, as repeated to the court by Kegs, and with Sly Loughty offering no defense except a sneer and a comment about "loser townsmen," the essence of the trial was over in less than five minutes. The final decision was delayed only while Rory read out the numerous crimes committed in other jurisdictions by the prisoner.

Already knowing what his responsibility would be in

the lack of a credible defense, Judge Anders P. Yokam said, "Would the accused please rise?"

Sly Loughty, defiant to the end, pushed his legs forward on the stained floor and slumped as far down on his chair as possible. His final words to the court were, "I ain't doi'n noth'n you say. Never have, never will."

With a disgusted look on his face, the judge said, "As you will, sir. Now, having heard the evidence available and having heard no denial or defense, I am prepared to issue judgment. This is your final opportunity to speak, Mr. Loughty. Have you anything to say that may influence this court?"

The prisoner spat in the direction of the judge's table, but the wad landed harmlessly on the floor.

The judge said, "Mr. Loughty, without the acknowledgment of the existence of pure evil in this world, and a spiritual personage who represents that evil, there is no explanation for a man such as yourself. It grieves me to know that you will enter eternity having turned back any opportunity to repent of that evil, but enter eternity you will, as I now sentence you to death by hanging for the murder of Dennis Coulson. You will be taken by the sheriff and imprisoned until such time as it is possible for this sentence to be carried out. Court is dismissed."

The shouts and joyful expressions from the makeshift courthouse could be heard at the far end of the street.

RORY HAD GIVEN much thought to the problems he knew he would be facing after the trial. There could have been no possible sentence but death for Sly Loughty. He considered transporting the prisoner to the state facility at Denver, but he could sense that the town would be deeply unhappy about that. And who could judge the possible actions of emotion-filled men and women? He knew other communities had built scaffolds in their towns and held a public hanging, almost like a gruesome festival. But the very idea was repugnant to him. Death was not a festival, no matter the prisoner's past wrong-doings. He hated the very idea of taking on and carrying out the sentence, but it was that or resign from his position, and that didn't seem to be the answer either.

Using the guise of needing to be alone, he had saddled up and ridden out, scouting in several directions, seeking a location for what he had in mind. The winter weather was cold and miserable, and his riding held no enjoyment at all. But the goal was accomplished. Seeing what he thought might be the perfect situation, he sat on his saddle, picturing everything as he believed it should be done. He pulled his gloves off and blew on his hands until the blood flowed again, if reluctantly. Then he held the somewhat warm hands over his ears and, in his mind, worked his way through the entire process, from the start at the jailhouse to this spot of forest and then the necessaries from there on.

He would need several men. A good, steady horse, probably the tallest mount that Kegs had at the livery, an eighteen-hand Clyde—gray with feet as big as platters, but calm and easy to work with. He would have to discuss the idea with Kegs. Add rope to his list. And steady nerves. A man can purchase rope at several places in town, but nerves? You can't buy those.

The day before, he had set two men to digging a grave in the farthest, most remote corner of the grave-yard. A coffin would be set beside the open grave, waiting for its dreadful burden.

There were several military graves in the yard. The couple of acres set aside for the purpose of housing the dead had originally been for the military. The executed criminal would be held well away from the honorable military and civilian graves.

He would tell no one of his plans.

When the prisoner was spirited out the back door of the jailhouse in the dark of night, the normal contingent of guards would be left in place, as if the prisoner was still in the cell and needing guarding.

The few potential troublemakers talking it up in the saloon were calmed down with the promise that he would act soon and with final dispatch. They didn't like it, but the respect Rory had gained over his time as sheriff won the day for him.

When the chosen date came, if there had been a courthouse clock, it might have bonged out five times, indicating that there was yet about one hour before first light and two hours before full morning. But there was no courthouse and no clock, except the one Rory had inherited from his father, a large, almost cumbersome railway pocket watch. He had looked at it a discouraging number of times during the night, as the minutes seemed to crawl along. But finally, he was able to quietly say, "Let's move out."

For this unpleasant night's task, he had invited only the steadiest men he knew. Ivan, of course. And to the surprise of all involved, Micah and Junior Wardle. Kegs was there only because he would lead his big Clydesdale gelding, and the fact that he wouldn't hear of being left behind. He also claimed to have the necessary knowledge of ropes.

"Had to deal with a rustling problem down in Arizona, a few years back. Ugly business, but final.

Learned some things. Come in handy again, I'm suspecting."

Samuel Coulson had been invited, but answered, "No, Sheriff. I have no wish to add more grim pictures to my overloaded mind than I am already burdened with."

Sheriff Cap Graham simply informed Rory that he would be there. It didn't sound as if there was any room for discussion.

Marshal Wiley was staying back to complete the ruse of carefully guarding the prisoner. He stepped into the overly hot jailhouse after taking a careful look around outside.

"As clear as it's ever going to be, Sheriff."

"Let's do it, men."

9

EXCEPT FOR A BIT OF VAGRANT LIGHT THAT SOMEHOW leaked through the solid gray overcast, reflecting off the snow, the night was as black as any of the men could remember. Rory led the way, following the tracks of his earlier scouting ride.

Leading the procession, Rory thought of the darkness of the night, comparing it to the darkness of his own thoughts and the dismal gloominess of Sly Loughty's entire life. He finally forced his mind back to a neutral, almost thoughtless position, simply riding forward up the slight grade west of the fort. The trail would be approximately three miles, ending in a grove of huge cottonwoods, a couple of them conveniently bent and broken by previous storms, leaving behind a couple of branches needed this night. He had taken the trouble to assure himself that the land was, yet, unclaimed by any potential settler.

He pulled to a halt a short walk from the chosen location, a slight downward grade ending in a flat area a few feet lower. The trees he had chosen were at the top of the grade. The grade would act as an inducement for the heavy Clyde to take a few quick steps. Those few would be all that was required.

The men dismounted, and in silence, tied their animals to convenient branches. The animal carrying Sly Loughty was led forward by Ivan. The prisoner had been gagged before leaving his cell. Rory wanted no shouting to arouse the sleeping town.

Kegs brought the Clyde up, passing the halter lead to Ivan, before he stepped away to do his job with the rope. Ivan tried to turn the horses so Loughty wouldn't have to watch the preparation of the rope, but the man sneered and refused to be turned away.

A convenient stump gave Kegs a raised platform on which to stand while he slipped the rope around the prisoner's neck. He then stepped back down while he threw the other end of the rope over a high, horizontal branch. While that was being done, several men lifted Sly Loughty out of the saddle and onto the back of the Clyde. They held him there while Kegs completed his ropework.

Unseen by any of the men, Sketch Brisco, sketch artist and writer of penny dreadful stories, was hunched down behind some close-by shrubbery. He had a paper pad on his knee. His pencil was literally flying across the page, creating a permanent remembrance of the event. The fact that he was there with no one knowing about his presence confirmed his claim to be the best sleuth in the writing business.

Sheriff Cap Graham stood back a few feet, holding his hat in front of his chest. Rory glanced his way just once. The slowly brightening day revealed a look on his face of unimaginable grief.

Turning the Clyde to where he was facing down the

grade, Micah Wardle held a firm grip on the halter cheek strap, all the while looking back, watching for Rory's signal. Rory stood behind the animal with a poplar switch in his hand. The prisoner's gag had been removed. When Kegs signaled his readiness, Rory said, "Final time to say your piece, Sly." When no words came, he stepped back a bit and slashed the poplar switch across the animal's rump.

10

THE MEN WHO HAD PARTICIPATED IN THE NIGHT'S activities shook hands all around, vowing silence on their parts in the sad affair. With Rory's thanks, the men separated to go to their homes. Ivan, without a word to anyone, stepped into the saddle and headed south to Stevensville. Rory reported to the judge and then rode out, saying nothing to anyone other than Wiley, who agreed to keep a watch over the town and county affairs, both.

There was some feeling of letdown among a certain cohort in the small town, the ones who felt that violence should begat violence. But for the most part, the reaction was relief.

Wiley completed the matter of the trial and execution of Sly Loughty. The coffin lid was left off for several hours, allowing anyone who wished to view the remains of the murderer. Few made the walk through the snow to the farthest corner of the graveyard. By noon the crude wooden box holding its grim burden was lowered down, and the frozen clumps of dirt and gravel shoveled on top. There was no internment service and only a brief discussion about a headstone naming the resident of the plot. Marshal Wiley said, "Leave the headstone with me, men. You've all done your part. And more."

ONE WEEK LATER, Rory rode onto the Double J Ranch yard and stabled his horse. He feared the family may have a hardened view of him after the news of the events at the fort reached the ranch. Thankful that no one was at the barn, he groomed his gelding and walked toward his own cabin. His thoughts of solitude were interrupted when Nancy ran across the snow-covered yard and threw herself at him, hugging him tightly while saying nothing.

Finally, she eased off and took a half step back. She looked him in the eye and then gripped him in a hug again, this time weeping and saying, "Oh, Rory. Rory. What you've put yourself through."

The words were mixed in with sniffles and pauses while his cousin caught her breath.

"Come to the house. Father just returned from town with donuts. And coffee's ready. Oh, Rory, we've wondered where you were this past week. We've all been praying and wringing our hands. Come to the house. Everyone wants to see you."

"I'll need to heat water and take a bath first. I'm afraid I'm carrying the odor of horse, campfires, and unpleasantness with me."

"You can bathe later. Come."

THE NORMAL JOY of the family gatherings was put aside to make way for seriousness. George stopped any foolish questions with, "Son, the details of your job are private to you until you wish to share them. The concern of the family right now is not about the job or the county. It is about you. Is the burden weighing you down to the point where it's time to step aside? How are you doing? Inside, I mean. In your heart and mind."

Rory had been looking around the table at his family. They were all there, even Hannah and the boys. He said nothing, but he wondered why Hannah wasn't at her teaching job. Perhaps it was Saturday. Had he really lost track of the day? He would let the mystery go for the time being.

"I'm alright, George. I knew this job would hold some unpleasantness. A lawman deals with unpleasant situations and unpleasant people. Otherwise, we wouldn't need lawmen. A few days of staring into a campfire has burned the hurt and hate away. I'll be fine. I need a day of family, a bath, and a change of clothing. Then I'll be fine. I'm fine now, for that matter."

THE FIRST PERSON THAT RORY SAW ON HIS RETURN TO THE fort was Cap Graham. The old sheriff was sitting in the half-barrel chair in front of the jailhouse. Rory stepped off the gelding and grinned at the older man.

"Cold, Cap. Too cold for sitting out."

"Trying not to make a nuisance of myself with the marshal, Rory. Figured to give him some privacy while he sorts some things out."

"What kinds of things could be demanding privacy in a little town like this?"

"Wires. Wires and letters delivered by stage whips. Don't know where they all come from or what they're about. They're not for me; that's all I really know. Anyway, breathing air with a bit of a bite to it is refreshing. Gives a man time to think. Work some things through."

"Well, Cap, I would agree with all of that. Which leaves just the question of what you're thinking about."

"I guess it will come as no surprise to you that I'm thinking of my future. Not that I can see much of a future. But even the bit I see has to be spent somewhere. Of course, I still own the ranch out west, but that opens questions I may not wish answers for."

"I am surprised at you, Cap. The answer is right in front of you, plain as day. Do you remember at the funeral I asked you to come see me? This is your future. I knew it then. I know it now. I thought you would have figured it out by now. I'm going to deputize you as a county deputy sheriff. You're going to stay right here and help me. Teach me the things I don't know yet. Things you learned long ago.

"I have to travel some. It's a big county. You'll be needed right here taking care of county matters while Wiley handles the town. So there. That's settled. Let's walk over and get a cup of coffee and see if Amber might have enough leftovers to put a chicken sandwich together for me."

"Settled, is it?"

"As settled as the date on the calendar."

Entering the dining room, a feminine voice immediately called the two men over to a table containing Boon and Belle Wardle.

"Afternoon, Boon. Mrs. Wardle."

Boon's greeting was to slide a chair away from the table with his foot, and say, "Sit."

Mrs. Wardle said, "Boon, try to remember some of the things we've been talking about."

The growl emanating from the big man's throat caused Rory to laugh, and ask, "May I ask what you've been talking about that brought such a reaction?"

"We've been talking about manners. And the absence of them."

Rory took a long look, first at Mrs. Wardle and then at Boon. The old man looked as if he had just had a plate of cold mutton, its grease congealing around the edges of the gray meat, placed before him for his lunch.

Rory burst into laughter. An exercise he didn't often enter into. Then, deciding he had stumbled upon a private matter, he ignored it and settled himself, asking, "Can I assume, since you invited us over to your table, that there's something on your mind that involves me or Deputy Graham?"

Belle Wardle waited for a discretionary moment, giving her husband the opportunity to speak. When he remained silent, she said, sounding like a schoolteacher trying to mend a recess dispute, "Boon has something he wishes to say to you, Sheriff."

Rory waited while Boon worked his jaw and glanced again at his wife. Seeing no relief from that direction, he cleared his throat, shuffled a bit on his chair, and said, "The thing is, I've lived in the mountains all my life. Folks raised me and the others of us in the far outback of Kentucky. No schooling for the young'uns nor no law for the older folks. Church was all there was for higher learning, and the old pastor I grew up under had never went to school himself, and could only read poorly and slowly. But full of opinions, and most of those leaning toward standing on our own two feet and keeping our women under control.

"Came west well before the war. Pa, he figured when his sons could no longer push their feet down into his leftover wore-out boots, they'd growed to where they could make out on their own. The girls were picked off one by one by neighbor boys. Boys set out on their own. Ain't never seen nor heard hide nor hair of any of the bunch again. Headed west is all. Came out on a Missouri River boat. Never did learn me no gentle ways.

"Met Belle here in Benton, up in Montana. Had me

enough money to buy two horses and a little besides, and we set out. Got married all fit and proper first, else she wouldn't come with me.

"Rode and scouted the land, pushing a half dozen longhorn critters and one bull that must have escaped from some driven herd. Found them along the way up in Wyoming. Settled in the prettiest corner of the mountains we ever did see. Named the area Roaring Creek, and since there was no one to argue about it, the name stuck.

"By the next spring we had us a son and six calves. Bought more beef critters from those who were turning back from the wagon trains. Grew more calves and another son."

Belle stopped her husband with a raised hand.

"You can write your biography someday, Boon. But for right now, tell the Sheriff what we agreed on."

"Dang it, woman, old preacher back in the hills was right. Give a woman too much rope and she'll hang you with it. Anyway, Sheriff, me and Belle are going to try again to see if we can live on the same piece of ground, withouten we go to war. We'd like to do it here in town, let the boys do the ranching. But Belle, she's big on having a clean slate. That seems to include me offering you an apology, whether it's for what I have done or what I nearly done, which isn't exactly clear to me. But here I am offering you my hand in peace and hoping we can start over clean."

With that, the old mountain man held out his hand, and Rory seized it with a grin. There was no need for further talk between them. Rory figured Boon had suffered enough.

As was typical in all the dining rooms Rory was familiar with, the waitress was keeping their coffee mugs full. Deputy Graham had sat in silence through the entire conversation, but Rory could see he had missed nothing.

Wishing to build on a new and fragile friendship, Rory asked, "So what's next? Have you found a place you like here, or will you look down in Stevensville?"

Belle quickly answered, "We're taking the buggy to Stevensville in the morning. Boon figures he's up to taking the ride now. He's still hurting, but it's getting better. We need to see Tempest and Key. I haven't been down there yet, and I know the stories from up here will have reached them long ago. I'm kind of surprised they haven't come up here to see their father, but we'll sort that out down there. I'm sure we'll be back, looking for a place here. A little bigger town will suit us better."

The meeting ended with that. The Wardles left, and the two lawmen settled in to talk about the county and the need for law and order.

12

Knowing his commitment to ride with Block Handly and the other federal deputy marshals was only a couple of weeks away, Rory left the town in Cap's care the next morning, after a leisurely breakfast and further discussions with both Cap and Wiley about the policing of the town and county, and rode east. By early afternoon he was tying off at the Gridley ranch. Horace was in the big corral, busy with some calves. He hollered a welcome, and when he had completed filling the feed trough with fresh hay, he pushed the fork into the stack and walked to the gate. Rory was holding the gate open, watching for any animal that might sense an opportunity for freedom. The two men shook hands, with Horace saying, "What brings you out here on a cold day, Rory? I'm hoping there's no more trouble. Not for a while anyway."

"No law trouble I know of, Horace. But I'm committed to going south for a few weeks along with the federal deputy marshal from Denver. They're hoping to clean up that stolen gold coin matter from last year. You may have heard of it, although the trouble didn't come north of Stevensville, so far as I know. I thought since I was going to be gone for a time, I'd come out now and have a visit. Talk some."

Horace gave the sheriff a wondering look, and then said, "I'm all finished up here, and it's cold. We'll put your animal in the barn. Warmer there. Then we'll go have us a visit. The womenfolk will be happy to see you."

Rory pushed his private thoughts and his nervousness down, thinking *I hope so*, and moved his animal into the barn.

The men kicked the snow off their boots on the back porch. Horace was about to reach for the knob when the door opened, and there stood the smiling Julia.

"Well, well, we have a visitor. A stranger, yet. Who is that with you, Father?"

"Just some saddle tramp riding the grub line. I'm hoping if we give him a cup of coffee, we can be rid of him."

Ignoring her father, Julia grabbed both of Rory's hands in her own and pulled him inside.

"It's a cold day for riding, but welcome. I'm hoping you're not on the trail on a miserable day like this."

"No trail. Not in that sense anyway."

The men hung up their coats, and Rory unbuckled his gun belt, slinging the double holster rig over an unused peg. He then lifted a smaller holster from the big coat pocket and slipped it behind his belt on the left side. He had found he liked the right-hand cross-draw, and with his new determination to rid himself of the big rig, out of courtesy when he was in a home, the much smaller .32-caliber revolver was discrete and didn't leave him defenseless.

Dinah Gridley, Julia's mother, had immediately refilled the big coffeepot from the small hand pump that had recently been installed on the countertop. As she pumped, she asked, "How are things in town, Rory? Has it all about quieted down?"

"Mostly quiet. And I've found a well-experienced and qualified older man to act as a deputy for me. I've left him in charge, and he'll be in charge until I get back from Texas."

Julia looked a bit stricken as she said, "We've known you were going to go, but we had no idea when. Is it soon then?"

"Just a couple of days, now. I don't want to go, and I don't really think it's my job but Block Handly, a deputy US marshal, and a man I respect, asked me to join him. I couldn't find a decent way to say no. We've gotten to the bottom of the case in our county, and I'm for letting the rest go. There was rustled cattle sold to a rancher who paid with stolen money; federal money. For some reason or so, Block's higher-ups have told him, the people in Washington want to pursue it. It seems like a small amount of money compared to how the government spends, but the order came from on high, so Block can either go or quit his job. That's a poor choice when all a man knows is the law work he's been doing all those years.

"There's supposed to be some other federals riding along and some Texas Rangers meeting us down there. Apparently, the Rangers are having a problem paying their men, so their presence isn't guaranteed. Hopefully, it will get settled quickly and painlessly. We already have names and locations, so that's a good start. Block has been studying the weather records, such as they are. He says that by the time we get there, a windy spring should be in the air. Again, we can only hope."

Julia, sitting beside him, reached for his hand, folding it into both of hers. She looked directly into his eyes, knocking him off his internal balance for just a moment, as if her look was drawing him in, begging for a kiss, like that same look had, months ago when they were riding together doing the census.

"You'll be, won't you, Rory?"

Dragging up enough willpower from somewhere, he pulled his eyes away and mumbled, "Always."

Dinah broke the momentary spell, saying, "Coffee's ready. Will you have a piece of cake, Rory?"

It was a wasted question with an obvious answer. Without waiting for the answer, Dinah was pulling cake plates from the cabinet and lifting the cake from the cold pantry.

Wanting to get home before full dark and knowing no other way, Rory brought the conversation around to the reason for his visit.

"Horace. Dinah. I'm not quite sure what the proper thing to do is, so I'll just barge right in. The reason for my visit today is to ask you for your permission to visit when I return from Texas, with the purpose of courting your daughter."

Horace burst out laughing, while Dinah broke into a big smile. Julia pointed a strange, wondering look at Rory. Rory was totally befuddled, not having any idea what to do or say next. The reactions were not at all what he had expected.

Horace settled down after a few seconds, looked across the table at Rory, and said, "Oh, I think that would be alright. Probably a waste of time, but still alright. You come whenever you wish."

Julia was still staring at him, almost as befuddled as Rory was. Dinah, still smiling, said, "What my undiplomatic husband is trying to say, Rory, is that you're really asking permission for something you've been doing for some time now. You seem to be the only one that didn't realize that."

More gently than either of the parents had, Julia addressed her suitor.

"Rory, I would love to have you visit. And to be courted. But what you don't seem to understand is that you began the courting the first time we climbed into a buggy together, that time the two men were terrorizing our home. I had made up my mind before we got to the rise of land off toward the barn. The only thing was, that you dropped off the buggy and left me in the dark up by the barn. That kind of put a temporary stop to the courting. But I've forgiven you for that. And I have been talking about spending some time in town. Like most ranch girls, I'm not really needed here, and I may be able to find a job in one of the stores. That way, we could see each other more easily. But whatever happens, I'll wait for you to call. And whenever you have a question to ask, I'll be ready with an answer."

Rory took another bite of cake, washing it down with coffee, trying not to choke, while he tried to gain his mental feet again.

He finally said, "I have a piece of news and then another question. The news is that I have offered to sell my half of the Double J to the family, and they've accepted my offer. It will be a few weeks before it's all done, but the decision is made. I don't see myself having time for ranching while I hold this job, and it's only fair that my cousins get an opportunity to work the ranch as they wish, and gain from their work. The thing that goes along with that news is that I have purchased a small block of land on a rise off to the west of town a few miles. The owners wanted to follow their adult kids to their new lives farther west, so they offered it through a newspaper ad. There's a smaller house and some outbuildings. They have an orchard well begun, and the land includes an uphill plateau that holds maybe three hundred acres of good grass and a trail between the two. I've let the new deputy move into the house with me. I can live there until a new house is ready. I've hired the contractor from town to build a new house as soon as the ground can be prepared. The house should be completed by the end of summer."

There was a flurry of questions about the new house and the orchard, but finally, Rory was able to address the other matter on his mind.

"Folks, I have to hurry along. I need to be in town first thing in the morning, and I'd like to make the most of the ride back in daylight. I have a question that you may not have thought about.

"You know about the murder of the Coulson boy and the trial. Although it hasn't been published in our local paper, I'm sure you know that the carrying out of the sentence fell on me. I expect the whole story is in the bigger papers. I'll not talk details, but I'll say it was the most difficult thing I've ever done, as just and fair as the sentence was, and as deserving as the murderer was. There is no denying that my job and my life can leave scars. I've hoped to keep them under control, and I believe I have, for the most part.

"The question now, relating back to my wish to court Julia, is, does my job and the things I have had to do, bother you, and is it going to put a barrier between your family and me, Horace, or between you and me if we're together, Julia?"

There was silence long enough for the question to sink in, and an answer dragged out. Horace said, "Rory, I've never talked about my past with you, and I don't wish to now. Not in any detail, anyway. Just know that I have not always been a rancher. Some years before the war, a buddy and I decided to see the West at government expense. The army was looking for men to join their Indian fighting and wagon train protection details. We joined together. It wasn't long before I found myself disagreeing with the army's approach to the Indians, but there was no way out until my two years enlistment was up. As it turned out, I saw more blood and more horror in that two years than I ever again want to see. And in our last big fight, just one month before my release, my friend was killed. I held him in my arms as he bled to death, with not a single one of us knowing what to do."

He stopped talking then and held his eyes firmly on the tabletop.

Julia again took up Rory's hand in hers and said, "And you might remember, Rory, that mother beat a man near to death with a block of firewood. And I turned my shotgun on another man. It's not all exactly the same, Rory, but it's close enough to let you know that we're not made from crystal glass."

Rory stood, overwhelmed by the acceptance from the family, and with no more words to share, dropped the .32 into his coat pocket, slung his gun belt around his waist, and pulled his coat on. When he had his hat in place he turned back to the table and said, "Julia, if you're in town, you might want to look up that builder and go over his plans. Give him suggestions.

"And thanks for the coffee and cake."

As he reached for the doorknob, Horace wisely said quietly, "I'm guessing you can get your horse by yourself."

Rory simply nodded, thankful that Horace wouldn't be following him to the barn where the parting would be even more awkward.

13

IN DENVER, HE PUT HIS HORSE UP AND BOOKED A HOTEL room before making his way to the federal marshal's office. He was expecting to find Block Handly and at least two other marshals ready to move. What he found instead was that the marshal's Denver branch chief, and Block Handly's boss, had been shunted aside.

After greeting Rory himself, Block said, "Rory, you need to meet Mr. Glover Harrison. Mr. Harrison, this is Sheriff Rory Jamison. Rory has agreed to join us on the Texas matter."

Rory stepped toward the man with his hand out, saying, "Pleased to meet you, Mr. Harrison."

Harrison looked at the outstretched hand and then cast his eyes over Rory, from head to foot. Making no effort to complete the handshake, he said, "I doubt that you will need any outside help, Mr. Handly. If you figure you need a cowboy to handle horses for you, I'm sure you can find one along the way."

Rory pulled his hand back and looked at Block, then at the two men who were standing a few feet away, looking as if they were embarrassed by what was going on. Donavan Gaines was hunched down over his desk, his forehead settled into the upturned palm of his hand, with the office door closed.

"What's happening Block? Is your bunch ready to go?"

Block sounded apologetic when he said, "There's been some changes, Rory. Mr. Harrison has come out from Washington to oversee the operation." He didn't seem to know what to say after that.

Harrison said, "What Deputy Handly is trying to say is that we will be delaying for at least one week to give us a chance to go over the evidence and form a comprehensive plan. If that doesn't suit you, Sheriff, you are free to ride back home. You shouldn't be a part of this in any case, but since Handly has invited you, I won't forbid it."

Rory had been long enough in the job to have considerable confidence. Further, his father had often enough warned him against getting involved with fools. He had no intention of waiting or rethinking anything. The time to move had been set and, in his mind, was still set, and not open for reconsideration for any but the firmest of reasons.

Already full of frustration and disgusted at the arrogance of the Washington man, Rory said, "Mr. Harrison, I've left an active growing county with spring just around the corner. A county that voted me into office and is depending on my being there and available. Spring will be an invitation for the settlers, but especially the gold seekers, to arrive in large numbers in our towns. Not all of them will be there with benevolent purposes in mind. I should be there. But I promised my friend I'd ride to Texas to wrap up the matter that has apparently so bothered the folks in Washington. Now you have to understand that I don't care one whit about the folks in Washington or what they want. This whole matter should be considered closed. It's a mighty long ride to where it's been reported the thieves' hangout is. Many days of riding with little, if anything, to be gained. Lives have been lost in getting the matter this far, and the little bit of stolen money is insufficient to justify further lost lives. But I made a commitment, and I will see it through. So, here's what's going to happen. I'm going to go to my hotel, enjoy a fine dinner this evening and a night's sleep. At seven tomorrow morning, my horse will be saddled and ready, tied to the hitch rail in front of the hotel. Block knows which hotel that is. I will be having breakfast. At half past the hour, I will be in the saddle. If the federal marshals are there and ready to move, I will join them. I'm guessing you won't be among them, Mr. Harrison. You appear to be more of an easy-chair type of lawman.

"There is this one opportunity only, Mr. Harrison, if you want my help. Tomorrow morning, I will either be riding to Texas beside the marshals, or I will be riding north, back to where my first responsibilities lie. And I won't be coming back if you should request my presence later."

With that, he glanced at Block and the two officers who were staring at him with their mouths hanging open, then back at Harrison, who was bursting with anger and insult. He then turned his back and left the office. Donavan Gaines had glanced up at the sound of Rory's raised voice. With troubled eyes, he watched the young man leave the office.

14

AT THE APPOINTED TIME, AS PROMISED, RORY'S GELDING was saddled and ready, tethered in front of the hotel. A few minutes later, his breakfast was laid before him. At half past the hour, he paid his bill and stepped outside. He was just in time to welcome Block Handly as he rode up to the hitch rail. Rory looked farther down the road expecting to see more marshals. There were riders enough in the busy city, but none of them were marshals, loaded and ready for a long ride.

Rory and Block studied each other, each waiting for the other to speak first. Rory outwaited his friend.

"We're on our own, Rory. Harrison called the others off, and he won't budge. He's angry enough to chew nails. I put my offer before him, saying I'd either be joining you, or I'd be presenting my resignation, and would be leaving the service. That moved him to shout, 'Go then and be hanged with you. You and your hillbilly sheriff.'

"Unfortunately, he forbade the others to join me.

Two of them quit on the spot, but that doesn't help us. I'm going. Against my better judgment, but I'm going. What say you, Rory?"

Rory threw the reins over the gelding's neck, lifted his foot to the stirrup, and was soon seated.

"Texas is south."

"I do believe that is correct, Sheriff."

With their thoughts running every which way in their minds, the two friends trotted out of town. There was really nothing to talk about that hadn't already been discussed.

They rode in silence until they cleared the outer limits of the city before Rory said, "I expect there's small settlements all along the way, but how far do you figure to the first larger stop?"

"That would be Pueblo. I've only been there once and never south of there. I can't tell you in miles, but we can figure on three days at a walk. A bit shorter if we step it up some."

"Our animals are fresh. Let's try."

"That will be our last chance for supplies, so far as I know. We'd best take advantage of it."

Three days later, after a night in a Pueblo hotel and graining of their horses, they were camped in a bleak curve of a small rocky hillside. As Rory tended the fire and the camp meal he had put together, Block said, "As far as I could find on the couple of military maps back at the office, when we crossed the Arkansas back there, we put the last sizable water behind us until we reach the Purgatoire. There're apparently a few streams in between. We should be alright, but we'll fill our canteens at every opportunity.

"I've heard tell there's a small settlement of some sort

down on the Purgatoire. Calling itself Trinidad or something like that. Two, maybe three days from here. Somewhat out of our way. West further than we figure to want to be. Could ride more to the east if you think it better. Our supplies are still in good shape."

Rory had thought of little besides the problems facing them since leaving Denver with only Block riding beside him. He had hesitated to say anything. But the fact that they were two men going against an unknowable situation, while one of them was essentially a desk marshal—a detective, he had been told was the new term —was causing him concern. Deepening that concern was the truth that Block was depending on him. By his previous admission, it had been some years since Block had mounted a chase before the Lance Newley affair. And he had been riding a desk since that time.

Rory had struggled with the idea of others depending on his inexperienced leadership, whether it was Ivan or My Way or Sheriff Anthony Clare. But they had started, and he had every intention of completing their mission, successfully, he hoped.

Firm in his own opinion that the entire thing was a fiasco, from the stealing of the original shipment of gold coins and printed bills to the clumsy cattle rustling that had taken place; he saw further efforts to be foolish if not altogether futile. There was no information at all on what else might have been done by the thieves. Certainly, the few cattle rustled on the three ranches Rory had been able to identify and sold to the Texas bunch, didn't account for all the money stolen.

THE SITUATION WAS unknowable until they arrived on the scene. And that presumed that they could find the scene, the location of the herd, and the rustler boss. That boss had been named as Webster Cunningham, Big C Ranch. The location was the Texas Panhandle, a place totally unfamiliar to either of the riders. Further, there was no real endgame outlined for the matter. There was no clear direction from the marshal's upper managers except to bring Webster Cunningham's enterprise to an end. Whether that end was accomplished by arrest, or by death, didn't seem to matter.

To say Rory was troubled would only be the truth. When the sun was directly overhead, they stopped to rest their horses and boil up a cup of coffee. He finally figured out what he wanted to say.

"Block, I'd like it if you would take a good look around us. In every direction. You tell me what you see."

Block hesitated, studying his riding partner, but finally said, "I don't have to look. Been looking all morning. Came near to twisting my neck permanent, studying on our back trail. Discounting rocky hills to the west and grass in every direction, all I see is the horizon. I expect what you're getting at is that this is a mighty big country. Something will come of it someday, but for now, she's a lonely place for two men to be riding."

"Right you are, Block. Now, could you with any confidence, point your finger to where we hope to find our fugitive?"

"No, I couldn't, but you knew that answer before you asked the question. Are you wanting to quit? Give it up? Is that where this conversation is going?"

"It's the same question but pointed back at you, my friend, more than at me. I've ridden some blind trails since stuffing a badge into my pocket, but none so long or blind as this one. Now if you could apply your detecting work, that would be a great help."

Smiling over the smoke of the fire, Block asked, "What did you have in mind for my detecting, as you call it?"

"Oh, I thought perhaps you could close your eyes and turn in a circle three times and then point out our direction with your eyes still closed. That would give us as much confidence as we have now and might prove to be a benefit."

Block answered, "And with that bit of wisdom salted away in our overstretched minds, put that fire out while I stow this gear. We'll head south and a bit east."

Rory grinned as he poured the last of the coffee on the coals.

"The detective has spoken. It is my duty to follow unquestioningly."

Spring might be on the southern horizon, holding a promise of mild days to come, but the news hadn't reached the southern Colorado plains yet. The men had been riding with their warm coats on, but now Block suggested they could hold the wind back better if they used their rain slickers, which were more or less impervious to the wind as they were to water. With the rain gear in place and their hats tied down, they turned up their collars and started their horses at an easy trot. Southeast was the chosen direction. Southeast it would be.

Hours later, as the men were searching for a place to camp, somewhere out of the wind, Rory pointed to a dim outline of low hills a couple of miles into the setting sun. Without a word, they turned their horses in that direction.

As THEY WERE READYING their animals the next morning, Rory pulled his cinch tight and then rested his arms on the saddle. He looked wistfully in the direction of their travel, shook his head, and reached to check the bindings on his saddlebags, his bedroll, and the light canvas panniers he had snugged up behind the saddlebags. The panniers carried most of their food and camp supplies.

"She's a long trail, Block. I'm thinking you'll have something to tell your grandchildren about as you sit by the woodstove enjoying that big government pension. When you're old, is what I mean to say."

"I haven't heard of this pension you talk about. But as to what we're facing now, I'm figuring, again from the military maps back in the office—and you understand those were done by amateurs out on Indian patrol —that the trail from Trinidad to the area where that big Indian fight took place, Adobe Walls they call it, is about a six or seven days' ride. Fewer if we push the horses, but I'm in favor of treating the animals as if we hope to ride them home after this little get-together is behind us."

"That's all true, but we won't get to the end if we don't make a start."

"Very profound. Is that one of those truisms you tell me your father was regularly teaching you?"

Rory grinned at his partner, responding, "The very same."

Block laughed and said, "I wonder what he would have said about you becoming the star of your very own penny dreadful series? Another showed up in the office just the other day. The headline, in bold print, was '**The Truth about the Murder of the Coulson Boy and the**

Hanging of the Villian. Sheriff Rory Does It His Way Again.'"

Rory swallowed his comment with, "Let's get 'er done," and spurred his gelding southeast.

15

WEARY BEYOND MEASURE, RORY AND BLOCK STEPPED from their saddles and loosened the cinches. It might be a toss-up between who was the most weary, the men or the horses. It had been a long ride, with only one break along the way.

Rory privately admitted his own fatigue, but his days in the saddle over the past few years had hardened him to the endurance needed to keep going. Block, on the other hand, was slow to rise to the leather after each stop. Except for the chase and capture of the Lance Newley Gang, Block normally rode a desk in the Denver office. He was showing his strength and determination on the ride south, but the effort was showing on him. Yet a longer stop to recuperate didn't fit into their plans either. Rory decided they would just keep going until Block begged off, needing more rest.

The men had given up on estimating the miles ridden but thinking it through, he instead settled for the number of days in the saddle. That decision led him to recall the incident, three days' ride back, when they had spotted a small cloud of smoke rising. As they had ridden along, a small cabin—more like a shack—backed by a rocky outpost and a nice gathering of trees and lower shrubbery, came in sight not too far off their trail. Their surprise was complete. They expected to see no settlement on the wide prairie over which they had been riding. Rory looked over at Block, and asked, "Who do you suppose would settle out here?"

"Good question, Rory. One thing for sure, whoever it is, he wouldn't have to fuss over gossipy neighbors. Let's slope over that way."

As they topped a small rise that had shaded their view to the south, they saw cattle. The animals were bunched around a water hole that might be natural, fed by a small stream, or it might be a wallow that held the last rain, although neither man could imagine much rain in the land they had been crossing. They swung sharply to the west, narrowing in on the cabin. They were still a half mile away when they saw the cabin door open and a man step out to fill the space. He stood there watching their every move.

As they rode closer, they could see a rifle cradled in his folded arm. A dog came bounding around the shack barking and charging toward the horses. His tail must have been coming close to flying off as he wagged it, indicating loneliness rather than aggression.

As if by agreement, although no words had been spoken, Rory and Block separated, holding their animals a good hundred yards apart. Rory ran his hands over the Sharps Big Fifty in the left side scabbard, lifting it just a bit, and then dropping it to assure himself that it would easily come free. He did the same with the Winchester carbine in the off-side scabbard. Finally, not making a show of it, he unfastened his coat and pushed the flaps to the side, making his two .44s easily available. And visible.

They pulled their mounts to a halt within easy speaking distance. The man in the doorway had made no aggressive move with the rifle but nor had he taken his eyes off his visitors. He seemed to place more emphasis on watching Rory than he did on Block.

The past several days, Block had been more and more deferring to Rory's ideas and suggestions, as if he finally understood that he was into something that he had little training or aptitude for. That realization and knowing the possibilities if they ever found their Webster Cunningham, frightened and sobered him. He held silent now, giving Rory the lead. Rory studied the man for a moment before speaking out. Old for frontier living, but not really old, perhaps forty. Average height for the times but a bit stout, carrying more weight than most bachelors who cook for themselves manage to pile on. Clean-shaven, or at least he had been a short day or two before. Strong and independent. Rory could guess that much from the fact he was there. Only the long gun was in evidence, but a man had to be careful. There was more than one way to conceal a Colt.

"Afternoon, sir. Riding through. Didn't expect to see anyone out here. Or cattle either, comes to that."

"But I see you're rigged out as if you expect to see Napoleon Bonaparte himself, or perhaps Maximilian, come to draft you to the service of the king, fearing you might have to take a stand. Ain't likely, though, see'n as how those two gentlemen were both ushered off this spinning planet by the citizens. Off to a better place. Better for the citizens, that is. Don't know how either man is fair'n.

"But I got noth'n to steal, and there's no reward out

on me that I know of, so you got no gain by doi'n me harm. Small shed out back'l shelter your mounts from the wind. I'll stir up the fire. Expect you could be ready for coffee."

Rory stepped off his horse into the tail-wagging, slobbery, whining welcome from the dog. The animal had a look of a shepherd crossed with a collie, with the aggressive nature of the shepherd, but the people-friendly attitude of the collie. He was a beautiful animal, tall and strong, with intelligent eyes and upright ears, mixed brown-and-gold hair with the typical black streaks of the shepherd. Rory laughed and scratched him behind the ears, talking to him as he would to a child. The dog loved the scratching but couldn't bring himself to stand still long enough to settle into it. He spun in circles, whining and half barking, as if he hadn't seen a human in a year.

"You have a way with animals, partner."

"Dogs and horses mostly, Block. Of course, a cat or two in the barn catching mice is a welcome thing too."

The dog entered the small shack before either of the men, then turned back to the door and started all over with Rory.

"Dog loves visitors. Had a visitor once last year. Same thing as now. You'd think I never pay attention to him. Name's Tex. Me, not the dog. Always wanted to go to Texas, but this is the closest I've been except for one ride down toward the Walls; toward them is what I'm say'n. Didn't come right to where I could see the place, jest aim'n ta find them hold'n a herd down that way. Purposed to tell them boys hiding out down there to leave my cattle alone. Course, I don't rightly know where we are as we set in this here shack. Could be Colorado. Could be. Cain't be sure. But I'd make a small wager this here shack is sett'n on Oklahoma ground. But ya cain't make no name out'a that jumble of letters, so Tex it is. What brings you fellas down this way?"

Rory, the more cautious of the two friends, simply said, "Looking around. Seeing what we could see."

"You could see more from almost anywhere else on this round earth; less'n grass and distance is what fills yer dreams."

"You're correct, Tex. But it isn't so much the grass and distance that attracts our interest. It's more what or who we might find on the grass."

"Lawmen, are ye? Well, that's alright too. Knew a couple a lawmen, back along the years. We weren't friends, though. Fact is, I never felt too drawn to the type. Of course, it's different now. Lot a years have gone past. Served my time. One week in a small-town cell built out'a wood, don't ya know. In fer eat'n another man's chicken. Course it wasn't the eat'n that they objected to. It was how the bird happened to fall inta my cook'n pot."

With that said, Tex roared in laughter as if the remembrance of stealing a chicken had brightened his day.

"No, sir, there's no paper out on me. Oh, they was a little upset that I took a couple a pieces of saw-cut boards out'a that pretty little cell a' their's so's I could step outside for a bit, if ya know's what I mean. But I was a-sett'n right there drinking the sheriff's coffee and sett'n behind his desk when he came back in the morn'n. It's not like I took ta runn'n nor noth'n like thet."

That set the man off in more gales of laughter.

Rory and Block were studying the old man and looking at each other, wondering what they had walked into. Tex saw their looks and said, "Yer think'n I might

87

be a bit teched. Off in my head. I ain't, though. Jest funn'n with ya. Not often I see a visitor out here, and never before a lawman. But none of that tells me what yer doin' out here in the flat of the earth. You goin' after that bunch down by the Walls?"

Rory answered, "Why don't you tell us about that bunch? Right after you tell us how you came to be here, as you say, 'on the flat of the earth.'"

"My tale don't matter none. But that bunch down there now. If'n ya was ta rid the country of them, my herd might have a chance ta grow the way God meant it to. But they make themselves pretty free with my yearling beef. Not that they don't have animals enough for themselves, but these ya see out by the pond 'er eastern. Lost off'n a wagon train, some years ago. Feller told me where they could be found, so I rode out. Sure enough. Down one a them thar coulees over to the west. Was plumb full a the beasts? All black hides and look'n good. I drove them to better graze and waited. Three years now and look at 'em. Time ta go ta market. Put some money in my britches.

"So, dang, now I done went an' told you what brought me here."

Block grinned at the old man and said, "We'll keep your secret if secret it be, but why don't you tell us about the bunch down by the Walls you mentioned? Can't be any harm in that, and it may save you from feeding them any longer."

～

THE OLD MAN told them what he knew. Which wasn't much. Only that they were holding a herd in the small canyons and side ravines along what they had said was

Cottonwood Creek. There was grass everywhere. Water was the thing. And that was found in the Cottonwood Valley and over into the Canadian River rough country.

"She ain't no Rocky Mountains, don't ya know, but hilly and rough, none the less. Shelter fer the windy months and water all the year round. I kep' to m'self, jest tak'n a look around. Expect all told, they may have something over a thousand heads, maybe more. Blotted brands, mostly. Rebrands. Tough look'n riders. One man in charge is how I seen it. Always with two rough look'n fellas sid'n him. Gunmen.

"Squats in a poor-built shelter worked into a small side canyon off the Cottonwood. Riders 'r hunkered down close by in whatever they can find fer shelter. Three, four of 'em in dugouts along the creek. Now, about that creek. The fella I talked to later called it Cottonwood Creek, but I suspect there's a hundred Cottonwood Creeks spread across this fair land, and no one naming one knowing anything about the others. Still, it's as good a name as any.

"Warm, a dugout is. Spent me one long winter in a hole in the ground left by the previous owner. Shar'n it with half the snakes and spiders God put in Montana. Or it coulda been Wyoming."

Rory had taken it all in and was putting it together in his mind, forming a mental picture. Needing everything Tex had to offer, he asked, "How many riders would you say, Tex?"

Tex didn't answer until he had dumped ground coffee into the boiling water in the big, blue enameled pot. Only then did he turn toward his visitors, and say, "Don't need many men. Not many an honest rider would want ta work out a winter down there, nohow. Them they has 'er most likely on the lamb, hid'n out, don't ya know.

89

Cattle got nowhere ta go. Grass 'n water. Thet's all a dumb beast needs. Ain't look'n fer no social life. Jest like me 'n dog. Feed 'n water. And wood fer the stove. But as t' yer question, I'd say there's no more than six, maybe eight riders. Ya have ta understand, I weren't on no sight see'n nor pleasure excursion. I was doin' my best ta not be noticed. Didn't rightly take a study on the riders. Snoop'n mostly."

"Did you talk to anyone?"

"Didn't intend to less'n it was the head man. But he was keep'n pretty much to hisself. Him and his two gunmen.

"Turned out there was a guard rider. Called me to a stop maybe a mile north a the valley. Alright fella, though. Didn't offer no real threat. Jest wanted ta know who I was and what I wanted. Told him I wanted his bunch ta leave my herd alone. Told him they had all the beef they needed fer their dinners. He laughed 'n said he'd talk to the big man. In answer ta my question he said the man's name was Webster Cunningham, er somethin' like that. Rebrand their bunch with a Big C."

The two lawmen had looked at each other and knew it was time to ride on.

When their horses were ready, cinches tightened, and the dog roughed behind the ears again. Rory reached into his pannier and drew out a small sack of ground coffee and two cans of peaches.

"Tex, I expect it takes some effort to bring in new supplies. We appreciate your visiting with us. And your sharing. We're not over well stocked ourselves, but here's some coffee and something to gladden your sweet tooth. Thanks again. Perhaps we'll see you once more, on our way back home."

"Ride car'ful, you two. That there Webster

Cunningham ain't there because he enjoys the climate. Nor the countryside, though I'll grant the canyon the Cottonwood runs through is pretty enough. If ya likes that kind a thing, is what I'm try'n ta say.

"You ride easy. He may not take ta yer snoop'n around."

around.

16

THE TWO LAWMEN HAD RIDDEN A FULL HOUR IN SILENCE.
As they passed Tex's pond, they had taken notice of the
brand on his stock. It looked like a bent single line, like a
broken stick.

"Story behind that brand," was all Block had to say.

"Story behind how one man alone could catch and
brand all those animals too."

"You have a suspicious mind, Sheriff."

Nodding to that truth, Rory turned his gelding just a
bit, setting the direction as more east, and still just a bit
south, pointing to where Tex had said he'd found the
stolen herd. As if the time on horseback and the distance
traveled had taken some of the town and city rush out of
them, it was another full hour before Block said, "You're
quiet partner."

"Just waiting for your thoughts. And no hurry on
that. I don't know if Tex picked up on it or not, but I
could see your gears going around. Thought there might
be smoke coming from your ears before we had a chance
to get on our way."

"I didn't know it showed like that."

"I suspect that's what you called detective work. Detecting truth. Sorting it out from the rest of the nonsense that old man shoveled at us."

"Are you suggesting that every word spoken back there was not the gospel truth?" asked Block, with a big grin on his face.

"Well, I believed that part of Tex having been arrested. Not sure about the chicken story. Good story, though. And I've never heard of a wooden cell, but a fella working the law in a tiny village can get desperate, so I guess it's possible. But none of that matters for our needs. What did you make of his claiming to have ridden down to tell the rustlers to leave his steers alone?"

Block grinned again and said, "Mighty long ride if I understand the geography anywhere correctly. It's doubtful on both ends. Can't imagine anyone riding three or four days to steal a steer when he has hundreds of his own. And how would he know about Tex's herd in the first place? Then, I'm asking myself why a band of rustlers wouldn't simply help themselves to Tex's entire herd. It's not as if one man could fight off that bunch."

A half minute passed as the horses plodded through what must, by that time, be Oklahoma grass. Taking a rough guess at their location, Rory answered, "I'm doubting all the way around on the story, except possibly how Tex came to be there in the first place. Such things have happened. His wouldn't be the only herd that grew from a few lost cattle as wagons plodded across the land. I haven't heard of any wagons coming this way. Seems out of the way. Off any known route to anywhere. But then, there's no reason why I would have heard. Could have been wagons traveling almost anywhere. It raises questions about Indians, though. The Big C bunch could fight a small, meat-gathering bunch off, but a man alone would have no chance."

"Could be the Indians simply prefer buffalo and leave the cattle alone."

"Could be."

"As far as that goes, Rory, we're pretty vulnerable to roaming Indians our own selves."

"There was a half dozen watching us a couple of days ago, but they just watched and then rode off to the west."

"You didn't say anything, and I didn't see them." There was worry and a bit of accusation in the words Block spoke.

"If they had shown aggression, I sure enough would have said something."

"Alright, but how about we agree that if you see others, you let me know."

"Agreed."

～

BRINGING his mind back to where they were before he had thought back to their visiting with Tex, Rory said, "I believe we'll keep our fires small to control the smoke from here on. We must be closing in on where that bunch is gathered up. Keep your eye out for a sheltered spot for tonight."

As afternoon turned toward evening, Block pointed off to the east. Just coming within eyesight was a rough outline of a plateau rising a good distance above the surrounding land. The edges of the plateau had broken and sheared off over time as the winds and storms of history worked on them.

Turning to ride that way, hoping there might be

94

shelter there, they found their desired camp almost immediately. Block turned and led the way into a sheltered space behind a growth of semidesert brush and under a roof of fallen, jumbled rock.

It took no time at all to water the horses and stack the saddles and provisions. Within minutes the fire was lit, and the coffeepot balanced on a flat rock. The two lawmen eased to the ground watching the coffeepot, anxious for a refreshing sip.

Block glanced out the opening to their hideaway, taking in the surrounding area, or as much as he could see through the rock maze and the brush.

"It seems as if we've ridden halfway around the world. Big country."

"It is that, Block. Someday this will all be put to use. The way the grass grows, I'm guessing grain would grow too. Seems dry, but the settlers' ingenuity might find a solution to that. Can't all just be kept as graze. There must be a limit to how many cow critters the country needs. We've crossed enough grass to feed half the cattle in the entire world."

"What do you see us doing next, Rory, now that we must be close to our target?"

"First, we need to ask ourselves what we're doing here, while we ignore all the need for law work in our own jurisdictions. Then, we need to ask ourselves who gets hurt if Webster Cunningham is never found and caught. Who would care? After that, we might want to know who benefits if he is caught. Finally, we might want to ask ourselves how much we have to accomplish before we'll call it a done deal."

After taking a guarded look of his partner, Block said, "You've been studying on this. I can tell that by the questions. Perhaps you should turn your badge in and become a detective."

"You've made that mention before, Block, but it still doesn't sit right in my mind."

They remained quiet while the dinner was put together. They had been taking turns at the fire. From clear evidence, it was decided that Block was the better cook, but the difference was negligible and unimportant. They took turns. This night it was Rory squatted over the small flame, moving from time to time to keep the smoke from his eyes. They were traveling light, by choice. No packhorses. The provisions carried were a bare minimum for the weeks of riding, and the meals were scant and repetitious. But at the end of a long day, their plates were scraped clean, ignoring the fact that they had eaten the same menu the night before.

Block leaned back against a small tree after placing his now empty plate and fork down on the grass. He complimented Rory on the grub, and then said, "Let's jump right to the last question. I've done some thinking too. Not much else to do sitting on the back of a walking animal with miles and miles of open space in every direction.

"As to when we can call it a done deal, my thought is that the cattle are very much secondary. No one is looking for their return, and truth be told, Texas has millions of cattle running loose back east and more millions of buffalo running loose out here. Or, if not millions, enough thousands to make it appear like millions. No, I'd be satisfied if Webster Cunningham was taken out of the picture. If that happened, we could report the fact to Glover Harrison and hope he got back on the train and returned to Washington, and we could get back to our own jobs."

Rory mulled this over in his mind for a short while before asking, "Alright, then we have to ask ourselves why the man matters. The guess is that most of the stolen money has been spent already, and only a small portion of that on rustled cattle. No one seems to have any idea where the rest of the money went or who benefited. The government is not going to get it back.

"The original story was that Cunningham wanted to build a cattle empire out here and do it quickly. But look around here and tell me why that would be so. Where is the market? Where would dependable riders come from? What about the buffalo that still cross this land, going anywhere they want? Any buffalo herd would sweep up a cattle herd and simply carry it along, and the owner would never sort them out. And how long would Cunningham hope to ranch here without having to face Comanche, Apache, or any other belligerent?

"Then, ask why a man with money would choose to live here. Perhaps in ten or twenty years, there may be some settlement, but right now, I can't make sense of it unless he's forward-looking enough to want to grab up a lot of land before anyone else claims it. Even if that were true, though, any claim he had would be weak. Who even owns the land? Is it Texas, the Indians, or does anyone know? You don't own something until that ownership is acknowledged by some authority. The whole thing has my mind going in circles and meeting itself on the corners."

There was another gap filled with silence before Block said, "My suspicious mind, or as you might characterize it, my detecting, wants to know why Glover Harrison is so very adamant that Webster Cunningham be shot and killed. Oh, he didn't say it quite that openly, but he said several times that trying to haul a prisoner all the way back to Denver was hopeless, or at the very least, difficult and unnecessary. Even the day before we left, after you were at the office and he finally ordered me to go, although he pulled back the other marshals, he said a couple of times that it would not be good for the country to have Cunningham running loose."

17

THE TWO TIRED DEPUTY MARSHALS WOKE BEFORE FULL
light, startled upright in their bedrolls by the flash of
lightning, followed quickly by the crashing roll of
thunder that seemed to go on and on, reverberating
from rock to rock and back again. That was followed by
a sudden downpour of rain and a drop in temperature
that brought a chill to their camp. Their rock roof kept
them dry during the initial few minutes of the storm, but
they were unsure of the near future. They had ridden up
a slight rise in entering the folds of rock. It might be
enough to keep the floor of the shelter dry. Their horses
were tethered close by, where they could reach both a bit
of graze as well as shelter.

While Rory put the coffeepot over a small flame,
Block put their camp in order, placing both bedrolls on a
shelf of rock well above any flood line. The saddlebags
and panniers were added to the stash. There was no
room for the saddles. Lying them on the highest part of
the sandy floor was the best Block could do.

The sun never did make any real impact on the morning. Without discussion, the men drank the coffeepot dry, foregoing any thoughts of food.

Block walked to the entrance as far as he could while keeping out of the steady downpour. The lightning and thunder had moved off to the east, although the sounds in the distance were still audible, leaving the black clouds and the steady rain behind. He turned back to the fire, rubbing his hands together against the chill in the air.

"Dull morning. Dreary. After all the sun and wind, we've got a dreary day in Texas. I couldn't see much of the sky, but what I could see was black. Roiling clouds in every direction. Not a hint of sunlight. Makes a fella long for his home fires."

Rory answered, "We've been needing a day of rest, and we couldn't hope for a better camp. I'm for holding right here. In fact, why don't you spread your bed again and close your eyes for the morning? I'll stay dry right here and keep watch."

With, "Wake me if you get sleepy," Block lifted his bedroll down and stretched out.

The hours dragged on, with Rory taking a turn resting after a small lunch and another consumed pot of coffee.

The constant crash of thunder following peals of lightning ended about midmorning, but the miserable, cold rain persisted. On the second day in camp, the lawmen were again looking for a dawn, knowing full well the weather had settled in. Block hesitated before speaking, knowing how Rory was in the habit of charging in, somehow needing to get to the conclusion of the situation so he could get on to the next one. But no one had ever managed to force the weather to change, and he saw no hope of the morning turning into a sunshiny afternoon. He thought through what he wanted to say before turning to his riding partner. Finally, he pointed his coffee cup toward the opening of the rock and brush shelter and said, "Partner, we've already been gone from home too long, but I'm thinking our target will have gone to roost, and we'd almost have to stumble onto them to locate their hideaway. Then we'd have some work to do before we dug them out. Even being careful, there's always the danger of them seeing us before we saw them. That could result in an unhappy ending."

Rory grinned at Block, answering, "What you're trying to say is that our chances of finding another dry shelter tonight is not all that good. And another day away from home isn't likely to change much up there. I agree. Fill that coffeepot again, and we'll sit tight."

The mention of home caused the two men's minds to focus on their own situations. Block wondered how his wife and kids were faring and if, by any chance, Glover Harrison might have given it up and gone back to Washington. He thought little about the marshal's office and the work left unattended. There were other agents there to fill in for him.

Rory was concerned about his deputies. Buck, especially, concerned him. He had been left alone up at MacNair's Hill. And now spring would soon be drawing hundreds of miners and hanger-ons into the district. Buck would be needing help, but Rory couldn't help him much sitting in a rock cavern in Texas with the rain pouring down.

He thought of Ivan, not yet knowing about the

budding romance between the deputy and the lovely Tempest Wardle. Nor did he know about the developments at the fort, nor how the building of his new home was progressing. He had thoughts of Julia, whom he wished to make his wife when they returned home.

18

RORY HAD NO WAY OF KNOWING IT, BUT CAP GRAHAM, who Rory had left in charge at the fort, was having his own problems. Just a couple of days after Rory had ridden south, Rad Harbinger walked his horse up to the front of the marshal's office with two horses on leads. Slung over the backs of the led animals were the bodies of Bat Kelly and Reef Malkin.

Rather than tying off and walking to the door of the small office, he simply hollered, "Marshal! Marshal, if you're there, you need to come out. We got to talk."

The marshal wasn't there, but Cap Graham was. He stepped outside, cautious until he knew who was calling and what the situation was. Finally, he stepped onto the boardwalk with his eyes flashing between the mounted rider and the two tied-down bodies.

Rad Harbinger was the first to speak.

"Don't know you, sir. Where's the marshal? Or the sheriff?"

"Sheriff is away for a while. I'm deputy to him. Cap Graham. Not hard to see you've got a story. What is it?"

By this time, men and women both were gathering around, curious and always looking for news in a small town where weeks could go by with nothing to talk about.

"Rad Harbinger. The farm just west a way. Fruit trees and milk cows mostly. Deliver milk around town. These fellas rode up to the house this morning telling us we had to get off our farm, that they were taking over. Threatened my wife and son. Held guns on them. I asked them how they figured to move us off our land. Said they needed the upper range that I wasn't using. Didn't show no backup, either one of them."

"Do you know who these men are?"

"No, sir, I don't. Never seen either before."

One of the bystanders pointed at a body and said, "That's Bat Kelly. Rancher out east. The other is Reef Malkin. Gunman. Worked for Kelly on his B/K Ranch. Hard cases, the both of them. Won't be missed, but that still leaves Ida as a widow and in a hard way."

Cap looked at the man, and asked, "Who's this Ida?"

"Ida Kelly. Wife to the dead man, here. Good woman. Far too good for the likes of Bat."

Cap addressed the man again.

"Can you tell me where the Kelly ranch is?"

With those instructions in his mind, Cap untied his horse and mounted.

"Let's go," he said, to no one in particular, although he could surmise that it would be Harbinger that would be the one following.

An hour of silent riding had them standing in the yard of the B/K Ranch. Alarmed, Ida Kelly rushed from the small frame house.

Cap hated this part of the job, although he had carried out more than just the one assignment before

arriving in Colorado. There were few things more difficult than carrying a body home, laid over a horse or
stretched out on the flat of a door. Never before had he
brought bodies home with the shooter leading them. He
stumbled a bit but finally managed to ask, "Mrs. Kelly?"

"I'm Ida Kelly," the woman said, without moving any
closer to the bodies. "That's my husband and our hired
man. What happened?"

She sounded more composed than was normal in
Cap's mind, raising questions. He managed to say, "This
is Mr. Rad Harbinger. Farmer out west of town. He'll tell
you the story."

Rad lifted his hat and hooked it on the saddle horn,
then wiped his face with a work-worn hand, his fingers
permanently curved from the milking of cows.

"Mrs. Kelly, I'm terribly sorry, but I was left with no
choice. These two were holding my wife under their
guns when me and my boy came from the barn. Threatening they were. Telling her we'd have to get off our
land. That they were taking over. Offered a small bit of
money.

"My wife, she was holding the double-twelve gauge
she uses to keep the rabbits out of her kitchen garden
and away from our fruit trees. My son had picked up his
Henry as he left the barn, and I had my belt gun on, as I
always do. You got to understand, Mrs. Kelly, my wife,
she has no backup in her. We worked long and hard to
get us that little spread, lost two babies over the time,
and raised just the one boy. Sixteen now and growing
into a good man.

"I called these two out. Told them to stand down
and tell me what they wanted. The one man, he turned
his carbine on me. The other held steady on the wife.
The one holding on me, must be your husband; he was

doing the talking. He says he needed the uphill graze we weren't using, and we had to leave. Then he turned his weapon on my son. When he says, 'cost you the boy if you make a fuss,' I shot him. As soon as the wife saw me reach for my .45, she blew the other man off his saddle.

"Ma'am, all your husband had to do is ask. I'm not using that range and wouldn't mind taking a bit of rent for it. I'd have cut in a gate, and he could have driven your animals right on through. All he had to do was ask. Instead, there he is, and my wife and son are trying to get over the fact that we had a shooting on our place. Understand, ma'am, I'm not apologizing. Your man would sure enough have killed the three of us if we hadn't moved first. I don't think he expected us to fight back, else we wouldn't have had the chance. Anyway, that's the truth, and now you need to tell me where to drop these bodies off. I've got cows that need milking this afternoon, but I guess I could take the time to dig a grave if you'll show me where to do it."

"I don't doubt your Mr. Harbinger. Kelly was never smart. A good cattleman, but never smart. And Malkin was nothing but a gunman. A killer. I never could understand why we kept him on. Talked endlessly about feuds he's been a part of and the taking of range from lesser men down in Texas. Talked as if land and the life of others was a big game. My fool husband hung on every word until I believe he began seeing himself in those feuds and range wars, even though he was never anywhere close to one. Built up a foolish yearning in his mind."

Pointing to the two bodies, she said, "Now this is the result. If you'll take those bodies back to town, I'd appreciate it. Bury them in the town cemetery. There's no sense leaving them here. I'll have to sell the place now. Me and the kids can't run this spread without a man."

With that, she turned and walked back into the house, closing the door behind her.

Sitting on his horse, looking at the closed door, Rad Harbinger said, "Nary a tear. We bring her dead husband home, and she jest turns and walks away. Nary a tear."

"They'll come," was all Cap Graham had to say as they turned and rode away.

~

TWO DAYS LATER, there was a gathering of townsfolk and a few ranchers in the town cemetery. Two graves had been dug, but not together. Cap had instructed the undertaker, making the arrangements to bury Reef Malkin off to the side to keep company with Sly Loughty. His box was unceremoniously lowered into the ground, and the hole filled before the gathering for Bat Kelly was scheduled to begin.

Ida Kelly arrived in town driving her buckboard. Her two children held down the seat beside her. There was still no evidence of tears, only a staid determination to hold herself together. When the pastor approached, as if to speak to her, she held up her hand, palm out, and said, "No talk. Just get it done."

Although he was troubled about the entire matter, from the shooting right to the moment of the widow's matter-of-fact instructions, he stepped to the gaping grave and opened his Bible.

Deputy Cap watched from the sidelines, his eyes seldom leaving the widow. When the service was put behind her, she climbed onto the wagon seat after lifting her daughter up. The older boy managed to step onto the spoke of a wheel and lift himself into place. Ignoring the well-wishes of several ladies in attendance, she slapped the rumps of her team with the reins and left the cemetery. Watching still, Cap decided the strong woman hadn't made eye contact with anyone during the sad burial.

Seeing that Ida Kelly was determined to return to the ranch immediately, he set aside his hopes of speaking with her. Instead, he stepped into his saddle and rode to the hotel. He figured there was nothing wrong with a lawman making suggestions that could help a grieving widow. If someone made something of that, well, he had faced adversity before and probably would again. He just needed to find the right man to justify his suggestion.

As it was nearing noon, he hoped to find that man taking lunch in the dining room. Walking into the small eating establishment, it took only a moment to scan the patrons. There, in the back corner, seated by himself, was Micah Wardle. Satisfied with his bit of sleuthing, Cap made his way to Micah's table and pulled a chair back. As he sat down, Micah said, "Why don't you join me, Deputy?"

"Thanks. I will."

"And why are you honoring me this way, Deputy?"

"Because I'm seeing a job of work that needs doing, and I want to find out if you're the one to take it on."

"My friend, you know full well that my family— meaning me and my brother right now, since our father is somewhat laid up—are taking the winter months to search out ranching land. Junior is off now to take a look at the southern part of the state. I'm just kind of biding my time, seeing what comes up. But I'm not in the market for a job."

"I know all that, but this is different. If you're half the

man I think you are, in spite of your recent questionable history, you'll hear me out and only decide when you know the facts."

Both men ordered lunch and coffee. When they were finished with their meals, Cap, having spread his idea in a brief few words before Micah, the two men sat looking at each other. They remained silent, as if the next one to speak would be, somehow, committed to the idea laid out before them.

Finally, tiring of the silence and having been satisfied by not hearing an absolute 'no' to the proposal, Cap said, "Get your horse. Let's go for a ride."

An hour later, they were approaching the borders of the B/K Ranch. They moved closer to the pleasant collections of buildings, wondering what the next half hour would hold for the ranch and the sole owner, the widowed Ida Kelly. The buckboard sat in front of the shed. The team was back in the corral. Cap's hopes lifted a bit when Ida Kelly stepped from the big barn door, a pitchfork in her hand. A colorful piece of cloth was cunningly wrapped around her head like a bandana. She shaded her eyes, watching as they drew closer.

"Mrs. Kelly," Cap said in greeting.

"Long ride, Sheriff, when we could have talked in town if you had something to say to me."

"We could have; that's true enough. But you gave the clear message that you wished to be let alone. I respected that wish, but then I got to thinking that what I wanted to say really couldn't wait, what with you needing to run this ranch by yourself now. So, I rode out. Brought Mr. Micah Wardle along.

"Mr. Wardle, I'd like it if you'd say hello to Mrs. Ida Kelly. Mrs. Kelly, Mr. Wardle is recently down from the Roaring Creek country, up in Wyoming. His family has been ranching up there his entire life. He's still a bit uncurried. Rough around the edges, if you can take my meaning. Got to hold a tight rein when among civilized folks. But a good cattleman, for all that, if the reports I've picked up are accurate. Beside that, he has not one thing in this entire world to do until full spring."

The two younger people were taking close scrutiny of each other. Micah was struck by the self-confidence of the recent widow. It was the first thing he noticed and commented on silently when she walked from the barn. This was no weak-kneed widow lady waiting to lean on others for support. He knew she would be troubled and hurting, but she kept it inside, facing her two visitors in a firm, confident manner. Beyond that, she was a well-put-together lady who, if the burdens of life could be somewhat lifted from her shoulders, could be quite attractive. There were no smiles. He couldn't expect that. But they were in her heart. It would just take some time to ease them out.

MRS. KELLY, looking at Micah Wardle, pushed aside the story that had been repeated in jubilant gossip by a neighbor lady. The story was of the attempt to enter the town with a herd of longhorns, and the sheriff's actions that stopped them. Of course, the best part of the story was of how the father of this man, who sat his horse before her, was hurled through the air as his dead horse fell beneath him. At least the neighbor had thought that was the best part. She roared with glee as she told it, while Ida Kelly held her skeptical silence.

Ida Kelly had not laughed at the telling of the story, and she didn't find it amusing as she surveyed the strong, handsome man sitting tall in his saddle before her. She wasn't a gossip. Despised gossip. And she admired anyone who could face an embarrassing mistake and still make a place in the settlement. But none of that helped her understand why the two men were there, although suspicions were growing in her mind.

Cap, for some reason, now removed his hat. He should have done it as soon as the lady came in sight, but it was too late for that. Almost too late for him to remember his manners, too, after the way he had lived for the past long while.

"Mrs. Kelly, if I could speak right out…"

"Go ahead, Sheriff. It's a long ride if it turns out to be for nothing."

"My past life is best left unspoken of, Mrs. Kelly. But it's fair to say that we have much in common. I understand your feelings of loss right at this moment. Let's just leave it at that. But what might be good to talk about is what you will do next. I walked away from a ranch I loved, making that decision too quickly. After a while, it was too late to go back.

"Now I know you plan to sell and move on. But this is a good ranch. Probably good enough to be worth thinking again about. Micah here, he's prepared to discuss working for you. Keep the ranch moving ahead while you think it over and make careful decisions. I believe Micah to be an honorable man. He's from an honorable family, even if they need a bit of currying here and there, as I've already said.

"I'm going to ride back to town now, Mrs. Kelly. Micah could either stop here, and you two could talk about possibilities, or he could ride back with me."

The sheriff sat on his saddle for a long, silent minute as Micah and Mrs. Kelly studied on each other, with neither saying a word. When he figured enough time had gone by for thinking, Cap turned his horse toward town, but still hesitated. When Micah lifted his reins, about to do the same, Mrs. Kelly said, "I have to get dinner on for me and the kids, Mr. Wardle. Wouldn't be much extra to feed one more."

Micah turned his gelding to the corral, intent on tying up and dismounting. Cap smiled and kicked his mount into a slow lope.

19

MORE HUNDREDS OF MILES TO THE SOUTH THAN THEY cared to think about, the two federal marshals were standing at the mouth of their rocky campsite, studying the sky. The close-by graze was eaten off, and to picket the horses farther away was to put them out of their immediate sight. Neither man was content with that prospect. To lose a horse in this country was to face a long walk and possibly death from any number of sources.

The black, roiling clouds had blown over, only to be replaced with a solid sheet of gray and a continual sprinkle, driven sideways by a never-ending wind. It was clear that the major rainfall had ended.

With neither man knowing anything at all about this corner of Texas, it was only the wildest of guesses what might come next. But their supplies were running toward the bottom of the panniers. The impatience and longing for home and their other responsibilities were pushing their concerns about the miseries of the weather well into second place. They had come to do a job, and they'd best get at it.

Without discussion, Block picked up his saddle and walked toward his horse. Rory began to chuckle, saying, "I guess it's time, is it?"

"Past time. Let's get at it."

They rode from their shelter with caution. Anything at all could have happened during the storm. It wasn't unreasonable to fear that they could ride into a trap if the herd and the riders had been active.

Tex, the old man who had filled the air with unlikely stories, had said the herd was being held toward the old Adobe Walls' site, but not quite so far. Exactly how he knew where that site was, had been troubling Rory's suspicious mind. But regardless of all that, the truth was that he had no idea at all where he was, or the old Walls site was, either one. Discussing the possibilities, the two lawmen decided to head south, and follow along the rim of the plateau that hovered above them, as they searched for signs of a camp.

After an hour of riding, Rory decided the rim they were following resembled the multitude of needles on a pinion pine branch. The ins and outs were endless. They couldn't possibly examine them all. The small inlets between the many curves of the plateau ridge and the moraine at its base might be big and deep enough to hide a camp for Webster Cunningham and his two gunmen, but none of them would hold the herd and riders.

They would keep riding, although both men were convinced that they had to be close to where the herd was held.

After two hours of riding, Rory held his hand out to the side, a signal for Block to stop and be still. They sat unmoving while the wind swirled around and through the side gullies they were following, until finally, the smell on the breeze became clear. Smoke. The wind had been blowing it away. Now it was coming toward them. They looked at each other, knowing their chase was moving toward the end. Neither spoke.

Rory motioned for Block to stay where he was while he, himself, dismounted. He walked forward, step by step, leading the gelding, ready for action if his horse called out to other close-by animals, or if one of the guards was alert on this cloudy and still dreary morning. Block also dismounted and backed his horse into a small channel, staying close to the mouth of the inlet himself so he would have a sight line in all directions.

Watching his partner, Block saw him ground hitch the horse and cautiously, and slowly, ease forward and around another point of the rocky moraine. Rory dropped to his knees, easing his carbine into firing position, then squatting back on his haunches as he studied the situation and the possibilities. Light gray smoke filtered from the inlet, rising to mix with the gray sky and get washed by the still-falling rain.

Looking forward, Block was sure Rory was concerned about something. What it was, he had no way of knowing. That Rory only saw one gunman sheltered out of the wind and rain, sitting side by side with a man who had to be Cunningham, told the sheriff that the second gunman was out there somewhere, possibly holding one of them in his sights. He turned his head and eyed Block. He then held up his hand and a single finger, hoping the marshal would figure it out from there. To emphasize his point, he held up the single finger again and pointed up to the rim that hung precariously above. From the rim, he pointed in a circle around them, accompanying that motion with hunched shoulders, hoping to signify that the one missing gunman could be anywhere. Block nodded in understanding. The two men could only hope they were understanding the same message.

Block sized up the situation around him and decided he would do better with a bit of height advantage. The horse seemed satisfied with the bit of graze in the small side gully, so Block dropped the reins and turned to the short hillside. It was, perhaps, twenty feet to the top of the plateau, with every one of those twenty feet fully exposed and covered with loose dirt and rock. To climb silently was out of the question. But he had no intention of climbing to the top, so the question became—could he gain a bit of height without bringing down the sidehill?

Deciding he had it to do and that his first decision was correct, he stepped into the small opening beside the horse, cradled the carbine in the crook of his elbow, and stepped onto the biggest rock he could see. So far, he was silent. But the next step loosened a rock that was jutting from under a sloping gathering of smaller rocks and gravel, topped off with yellowish dirt and a couple of small plants struggling for survival. It was too late to step back. The jutting rock gave way under the weight of his foot, sliding from its place and relieving the couple of rocks it had been supporting. Those rocks slid downward as well, loosening the entire moraine. In a small thunder of dropping and sliding debris, Block was carried to the gully floor. Nothing had fallen far, perhaps five or six feet, but it had created unnatural noise, with rocks clunking one against the others.

Voicing his shock, and the pain of a well-barked shin, was totally unintended. It was a single word of surprise, but it hung in the air like one of those thunderclaps they had suffered through the past couple of days, only less loud. But still loud enough to catch the attention of Cunningham and his one gunman. With a shout of alarm, both ran from their hiding place, right into Rory's gun. The surprise of Block's shout had caught them all by surprise. Having no friends in the area, the gunman would attempt to earn his keep.

The gunman led the way out of their small camp, holding his Colt, ready to shoot. When he spotted Rory, his finger tightened automatically on the trigger, but it was already too late. With Rory's single shot, he crumpled onto the cave floor and didn't move. It was too late for Cunningham to pull to a stop. He tried to jump over the fallen man but ended up tripping over him instead. As he fell to the ground, Rory reversed the carbine and smacked him on the head with the wooded gunstock. He wasn't dead, nor did Rory wish him dead, but he sagged into unconsciousness with his whole body seeming to relax.

Rory rushed from the narrow enclosure in time to see the second gunman drop to his knees on the top of the plateau and point his weapon at Block. "Noooo...!" shouted Rory, as he raised his carbine. As with the first gunman, Rory's shout was too late. The man on the plateau fired at the scrambling Block and levered in another shell. Before he managed to bring the weapon back into line, Rory's .44-40 carbine was speaking its deadly message. The gunman folded sideways and slid from the plateau, landing in a crumbled heap with rock and debris partially covering him.

With rising anxiety over Block, who had collapsed to the ground and not gotten up, Rory still took time to fasten Cunningham into two sets of handcuffs, securing both his hands and his feet. He then ran to Block.

Dropping to his knees beside his friend, Rory began

to ask how badly he was hurt but was cut off by the deputy marshal waving him away, saying, "Leave me. Get those others."

"Already done and down. Where are you hit?"

Gritting his teeth in, Block held his hand over a spot on his right side, high up, just below the rib cage.

"May not be too bad. Hurts like all the fires of hell, though."

With no further words, Rory began opening Block's coat and then the two shirts he was wearing. After their days on the trail, neither rider would pass a good personal hygiene test. Block's shirts were filthy and odorous. Rory knew that his would be about the same, so he made no comment.

Pulling the layers of clothing aside, he found the wound. Block had it right; only he hadn't made provision for the fact that the shooter had been above him, shooting downward. After only half a minute, Rory said, "Been a while since I read that medical book we kept up in our gold camp, partner, but here's how I see it. Shooting down at an angle, the lead touched the bottom of your ribs and then continued downward. It went right through, leaving a nasty opening at the back. I have no idea what's inside a man at that point, but I'm pretty sure it wasn't designed to accommodate an insertion of lead. Best we can do out here is to clean the wound and head back just as fast as possible. We have our man. I have no intention of searching for the cattle. The cattle can do what they want."

With that plan laid out, and a pot of water warmed over Cunningham's fire, Rory went to Block's pannier and removed a roll of clean, white bandage material Block's wife had insisted they take along. "In case you stub your toe or something," the worried and cynical woman had said. "And there's a can of salve in there too. I don't know what it is, but the fella selling it said it was good for man or beast, and since I'm not always sure where you lie in that definition, you take it along."

RORY WASHED the blood from both front and back wounds, although a new flow soon showed his attempt to be futile. But at least the fresh blood was flowing onto clean, or at least cleaner, skin. He then, very carefully, used the point of his camp knife to ease out the pieces of dirty shirt that had been driven into the wound by the bullet. With the blood flow, he wasn't sure he got them all, but he did what he could. He then folded two cut-off pieces of the bandage material into pads, hoping they would soak up the blood, and when he tied them tight, stop the bleeding altogether. Measuring out enough bandage to take a wrap that would reach around Block's slim waist with enough additional to tie into firm knots, Rory said, "You're going to have to help me here, partner. I need to lift you and wrap this cloth under you."

With a partially stifled cry of pain, Block bent his knees, hooking his boot heels into the wet earth. He then lifted his hips and held the position long enough for Rory to reach under with the bandage.

"OK. Hold it there while I place this pad over the wound."

The effort Block put out doing that caused pain to wrinkle the skin of his face, while the falling rain disguised the tears.

"Alright, you can let down now. I'll just tie this around the front, and then we'll figure out our next moves."

When Rory had done what he could do. he managed to get Block onto his feet and shuffled him along the cliff face to Webster Cunningham's camp. At the back of the little draw, the overhang formed a roof of sorts. It would fall in one day, as most of the others along the plateau had. But for this one day, they were sheltered. Rory rinsed out a coffee mug, using hot coffee from Cunningham's fire, and poured a cup for Block. He then took the dead gunman by the back collar of his coat and dragged him away from the cave entrance so they wouldn't have to look at him. Walking back, he bent and grabbed Cunningham's collar and dragged him back under the shelter.

When the partially reviving Cunningham complained about the rough treatment, Rory simply said, "Shut up. You could be like your guard dog out there, and you still might be. Now I'm going to ask you one simple question, and I want a single-word answer. Are you Webster Cunningham?"

"Yes. But wha..."

Rory cut him off with a backhand across his mouth, and a pointed, wagging finger. Cunningham got the message and shut his mouth.

A VOICE SOUNDED from outside the small shelter. Judging by sound, the speaker was close to the camp entrance, but was holding himself off to the side.

"Hello, the camp. Willy here, Mr. Cunningham. I'm seeing dead men out here. Are you alright? What happened? We heard shots."

The man was clearly close. No shouting was required. Rory spoke in his usual voice saying, "Holster your weapon, Willy, and step to where I can see you. Cunningham is alive and well except he's handcuffed and our prisoner. Federal Marshal Jamison here, along with Marshal Handly. Cunningham is under arrest. We're not looking for you or the other cowboys, so don't do anything stupid. Step to where I can see you. Do it now, or I'll come out and get you."

With much hesitation, Willy eased his eyes around the cave entry. Rory saw the move but waited patiently. When Willy made no further move, Rory said, "Trust, Willy. It's all about trust. You trust that my partner and I are who we say we are, and I trust you to show yourself with no gun in your hand. Now would be the time to do that."

Willy stepped away from the entrance rocks and into the clear. When no shots and no threats emerged from the camp, he moved farther into the small space, holding the Colt down by his leg. He stopped when he saw Cunningham stretched out on the rock-strewn floor, trussed in his two sets of handcuffs. The handcuffs spoke of law enforcement. Anyone else was likely to have used ropes or rawhide strips. Making the right decision, Willy said, "I'm going to holster this weapon. Don't you misunderstand when I move."

Rory remained silent as Willy did as he said he would.

Clearly needing an explanation, Rory said, "Willy, I'm assuming you're one of the riders in charge of the herd. Is that correct?"

"I'm foreman for Mr. Cunningham's Big C herd, if that's what you're asking."

"I won't ask if you already know this, Willy, lest you incriminate yourself, and I'm forced to do something I really don't want to do. The Big C herd is a stolen herd. I haven't seen the animals yet, but I believe any brands they carry will be worked over. Rebrands, if you prefer the term. Now, perhaps you and your riders did the branding, and perhaps you didn't. You may be wanted by the law somewhere, or you might not. The thing is, neither I, nor my partner here cares who you are or what you've done. My interest is in what you're going to do. You can probably see that my partner has taken a shot this morning, and we have to be moving to where there's help. You can also see that Mr. Cunningham is my prisoner. We will be pulling out within a half hour."

Willy interrupted to say, "Mighty long way to where any help might be found."

"That's true, Willy, so we can't waste time. Now, as I was going to say, you can clearly see that you and the crew will be receiving no pay from Mr. Cunningham. But there is another opportunity so you can feel you haven't wasted the winter out here on these windy plains. How many men do you have, Willy?"

"Me and six others."

"Understand, Willy, with my partner being wounded, I wasn't going to bother looking for the herd. But with you being here, we now know where the animals are. Or, at least, you do. The other half of my job was to find the herd. With that accomplished, I want the herd moved north. To Pueblo, to be exact. Your pay up until today is probably lost to you, but I can't help that. I'm not paying Cunningham's debts. But you move that herd to Pueblo, and I'll guarantee you a flat hundred fifty dollars each, clean money. That's good pay for maybe ten days of work. Then you're free to go. I won't even ask your names, nor send any other lawdogs after you. Remember what I said? Trust. It's all about trust, Willy."

"Maybe you'd like to tell me why me and the boys shouldn't simply take the herd and have it all."

"I'll tell you and I'll make it simple. That's a rustled herd. I know at least three of the ranches the animals came from. You might have seen what's left of a K Slash or a BL or a Half Anchor under those burned brands. Aw, I see by the look on your face, Willy, that those brands are resting in your memory. So, you understand. You can't sell that herd no matter where you drive it. I've been on this for over a year, Willy, and with the magic of the telegraph, every law man in the West, every bank, every cattle broker, every railway clerk, anyone that has to do with cattle sales knows about the Big C and the blotted brands. Those cattle are useless to you, Willy. Might make my offer attractive. Give you traveling money, if nothing else."

None of what Rory had said was true, but it sounded good coming from his lips, so he held to it.

"Alright. I'll speak for the boys. What do you want to do?"

I want you to find where Cunningham and his pet killers stashed their horses and bring them here. Then you ride back to the herd and get it moving. Round up what you can get in one hour, and leave the rest. Head north and a bit west. I'll find you, and we'll travel together."

With a stern look at the speaker but no further words himself, Willy turned and left the camp. In less than ten minutes, he had five horses standing at the mouth of the cave.

"Found their saddles and tied them on."

"Thanks, Willy. We'll meet you on the trail."

20

RORY LED HIS AND BLOCK'S ANIMALS TO THE CAVE MOUTH and steadied Block as he slowly rose to his feet and shuffled to the horse. The well-trained gelding stood steady while Block fumbled his foot into the stirrup and then, with a solid push from Rory, rose to the saddle. With one hand holding the reins and the other pressing against the wound, Block nodded and, speaking through the pain, said, "Let's get 'er done, partner."

"Right you are, Block. If you feel that wound bleeding again, you let me know. If you get sleepy, you just drop the reins across the gelding's neck and hang on to the horn. He won't leave the bunch."

It was necessary to remove the leg irons from Cunningham for him to mount, but they were replaced immediately after. Rory then went back into the camp and sorted through the bedding, knowing his prisoner would need a blanket or two for the ride north. When he lifted the bedroll from the floor, a large, thick, brown envelope dropped out. He picked it up and opened the top. There were a couple of pages of written notes, mainly a list of names with what Rory guessed were dollar amounts beside them. The second page held a list of properties and bank accounts. Along with the two pages, there was a thick wad of paper money. And in the bottom of the envelope, three tarnished coins. He chuckled and looked out at Cunningham. The prisoner was watching his every move with the most malevolent look Rory had ever seen on his face. As Rory juggled the coins from one hand to the other, he grinned and said, "Just couldn't bring yourself to get rid of all of them, I guess."

At the back of the cave, he found a good supply of food and camp supplies. He stuffed it all into the canvas sacks it had come in and tied it on another saddle.

With what he wanted from the camp tied on one horse or another, and the brown envelope secure in his own saddlebag, he went to the two downed guards. He found their carbines and unbuckled their gun belts. He wasn't in favor of leaving weapons on the ground for a possible enemy to pick up. He went through their pockets, finding a bit of money, some fine turquoise jewelry, and some folded papers. One turquoise necklace he lifted from a guard's neck. He stuffed it all into his saddlebags, tied the guns on the saddle of one of the unridden horses, and mounted himself.

THE RAIN HAD STOPPED FALLING. In his busyness, he hadn't noticed before. Thankful for that break in the weather, he turned his horse north, picked up Cunningham's reins, drove the unridden horses before him, and said, "Let's go home, partner."

Block simply said, "Home. Sounds good." He hadn't

even lifted his head when he spoke. Rory figured the man was doing a fair to middling job of hiding the pain.

Picking up on the frailness of Block's voice, Rory said, "I know you're hurting, old buddy, but you're a deputy marshal. Goes with the territory. You're tough. You can handle it. And don't you even think of quitting on me. We're both going to ride into Denver, look that Washington man in the eye, and say, 'We got your man. Might have been a site easier if you hadn't stood in our way, but here he is.'

"We can't do that if you quit or if you up and die. You die on me, Block, and, so help me, our relationship will be done with. I'll never ride with you again. Can't stand a quitter."

"You drive a hard bargain, Sheriff."

"And don't you forget it."

Then, to brighten the conversation and perhaps take Block's mind off the pain for a moment, Rory said, "Just a bit ago, I realized it's quit raining. I'm glad for that. I've had about enough dreary days."

Block half smiled, saying, "Dreary day in Texas. That's what you predicted a couple of days ago. You can sure call them, partner."

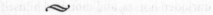

WHEN THEY ROUNDED the end of the plateau after riding a couple of miles, they joined the moving herd. With Rory holding his bunch well to the side, the two groups headed north together. He would never consider himself a good judge of numbers, but trying to count by hundreds, holding his hand in the air to use his fingers to isolate those he had already counted, he figured there was close to eleven hundred animals.

Normally, an unburdened rider would outpace a driven herd by a good bit, but with Block's pain driving deep into him with every step and jerk of the horse holding them back, keeping to the speed of the drive was the best they could do. It was no longer about Webster Cunningham. It was no longer about the Big C herd. It was no longer about officious bureaucrats from Washington. It was now totally about getting Block home safely and alive. It would not be quick, and it would not be easy, but both Block and Rory had done difficult things before. They only had to do it again.

21

HUNDREDS OF MILES TO THE NORTH, BOON AND BELLE Wardle were directing their top buggy toward the livery in Stevensville. Their son Key was the town marshal. Their daughter, Tempest, also lived in the small town, holding down a job at some ranch supply store, or so the last letter had said. But that was some months ago.

Boon had made a much regretted first impression in the town on his previous, and only, visit. He had hesitated when Belle said she was going to visit and insisted he come along. His posterior itched on the buggy seat as he waited for the dreaded but anticipated remarks, some of them unspoken but plain anyway, from the townsfolk.

When Tippet, the long-term and talkative livery man, stepped from the shelter of his big barn, he took a long study of Boon before turning his eyes to the attractive, middle-aged lady sitting beside him. Tippet seemed to know and remember every detail about their town and the country around, going back to Indian days. He certainly remembered the Wardle family's first visit. He had also secured the details of the longhorn herd matter up at the fort. There was no one better or more adept at spreading rumors than the stage whips, and Tippet was friends with all of them. Privately he had chuckled at the thought of the officious Boon Wardle, flying through the air, only to land unceremoniously in the filth of the road. He pushed those memories aside and, guarding his usually mangled English, said, "Afternoon, Mr. and Mrs. Wardle. Welcome to Stevensville."

Stepping closer and moving to the side of the buggy, he held his hand out to Belle.

"Welcome, Mrs. Wardle. It's good to have you visit. I'm sure Key and Tempest will be pleased to see you. May I help you down?"

With Belle safely on the ground, an action she could easily have accomplished herself, Tippet watched Boon stiffly and slowly place one foot onto the little metal step at the side of the buggy and then, very cautiously, lift himself to a hunched over but standing position, fishing with his other foot for the wheel spoke, while holding the back of the seat with a firm grip. Tippet could easily see that the man was still hurting from his fall and that he needed help more than his wife had.

Moving quickly around the buggy, he placed his hand on Boon's foot and guided it to the wheel spoke. All of his literary good intentions forgotten, Tippet said, "Jest hold 'er there, ol' timer. Ease yer weight onta that there spoke and take a deep breath. We'l git ya down in no time at all."

His ire rising at Tippet's words, Boon carelessly dropped one foot to the ground, landing with enough force to jar his entire body, a move that woke up all the sleeping hurts in his legs and back.

"Why, you old fraud!" he shouted. "Who you calling old? And you coming at me with a double-twelve shotgun on my last visit, and now here you are like the town welcoming committee. Buttering up Mrs. Wardle as if you were the mayor. Let go of my arm and step back. Take care of this horse. That's if you think you can handle that simple task without doing injury to the animal."

"I'll let ye go jest as soon as ye git yer balance there, old-timer. With all that shout'n 'n carry'n on ye forgot ta place yer other foot on ta the ground. I'd hate ta see ya ly'n in the road, all in a heap. Heard ya done that up ta the fort. Folks 'er still tak'n about thet. Wished I'd a seen it. Someth'n ta remember on a cold night a-sett'n by the fire reminis'n 'bout the old'n days. But a man'd think once would be enough a that fer ya."

Under his breath, Tippet said, "Hard ta believe this old blister sired these good kids we got here in town. Or that this fine lady somehow put up with him long enough to git 'er done."

Boon finally got his other foot on the ground just as a loud female voice said, "Father, your shouting's about enough to put the hens off their laying. I'm happy to see you and all, but I'd be just as happy if you didn't carry on so."

Turning to the side, she threw out her arms and enveloped the lady who was approaching.

"Mother. Oh, Mother. How good it is to see you. It's been so long. Key and I, we'd heard you were up to the fort, but this visit is a surprise. Come, we'll go have a cup of tea and a visit."

Turning to Tippet, she said, "I don't suppose Father has asked yet, but perhaps you could move this buggy under the shed roof and care for the horse. Thanks."

Tippet didn't bother answering as he wrapped the reins into a tight loop to where he could grip the bridle without dragging the leathers on the ground, and led the horse away.

Boon found himself standing alone in the street. With his hands on his hips, he looked all around, noticing the smallness of the town, but also appreciating the orderliness of the buildings gracing the only business street, and the cleanness of the storefronts. He didn't see Key walking up behind him, but he turned at the voice.

"Standing here by yourself. That's what happens when you wear out your welcome on your first visit, Father. And when all your friends can be counted on one hand, with that hand making a fist, and no fingers showing."

Coming within arm's length, Key smiled and held out his hand. Boon, never before shaking a son's hand, and having always had trouble treating them as adults, almost shyly shook his youngest son's welcoming hand.

"It's good to see you, Father. I heard you and Tippet greeting each other and thought I'd stay back until the two of you sorted it out. Good man, Tippet. I believe you could see that right off, but you're more apt to drive folks away than attract them. You'll want to spend some time with Tippet, and get to know him. You'll enjoy each other. Now, come, I've got coffee on in the marshal's office."

22

THE HERD MADE GOOD TIME ON THE LEVEL GRASSLAND. On the third day, about midmorning, the animals Tex had been laying claim to, came into sight. Rory waved Willy over from the herd.

"When we get to where that herd up yonder is huddled around a small pool of water, push those animals off the water and stop long enough for our bunch to get some refreshment. There won't be enough water in that little basin to do the job, so don't be afraid to keep them moving so the trailing bunch might get at least enough to whet their whistles. Then get them moving again. Take that other bunch along with you. I'll go over and get the owner. Tex, he calls himself. Says he was down your way. Talked to someone with the Big C. Any truth to that?"

"He was there, alright. Strange old duck. Filling the air with stories. Yes, I met him. Never did find out why he was there. Snooped around some and rode off north. Never saw him again."

Rory thought of asking about the claim that the Big C

boys were taking his beef but let it go. He had never taken it as a likely story. As he turned to leave, he said, "Keep an eye on Block and Cunningham for me. I'll not be long."

Tex met Rory about halfway between the herd and the small shack he lived in.

"What y'all doin pushing my critters off'n their water? Ya got no right."

"Go pack up your keeping stuff, and all you don't want, leave behind. We're heading for Pueblo. Going to market our beef. And yours, too, like you said you wanted to do. You'll never get a better chance. You can't drive them alone, but these boys will take them along. You cross their hands with a bit of coin after you make your sale, and all will be fine in your world."

Tex started to sputter as he thought of reasons to object, but Rory cut him off.

"We're not stopping, fella. Go back and pack up. Bring your extra horses and the dog. You can easily catch up later this afternoon."

With that, Rory turned back and rode off.

It was two hours later when Tex rode up to the herd. Willy had stopped them again at a small stream. With the dryness of the country, he couldn't afford to pass up even a small water source.

Considering Block's needs, Rory had decreed that there would be no noon stop. They were going to drive hard and long each day, even if they were rolling pounds off the market animals as they moved.

As the evening sky was beginning to dim, the point rider waved his hat over his head and gestured off to his left. With that instruction, the crew eased the herd to the west, into the setting sun. Within a mile there was water. The animals found it first, with their sensitive nostrils.

133

They began to trot; cattle and loose horses together. The crew pulled back and let them go. The cattle didn't break into an all-out run, but they were close to it when the lead animals stopped and pushed their parched mouths into a running stream. The crew, knowing the thirsty animals were not going to wander off, turned farther upstream to clean water. They watered their saddled mounts first before pulling them back to where one man, the chosen wrangler for that day, could hold them. Only then did the men walk to the water themselves, filling their canteens before they drank.

Someone got a fire going, and soon there was coffee. Cunningham had kept his crew well-supplied. There had been ample provisions to bring along for the drive. Bacon and biscuits until the bacon ran out. From there on, it would be beefsteaks fried up in held-over bacon grease. The daily repeated fare didn't do much more than keep them alive and strong enough to keep going. There was little pleasure in the eating.

Rory was cutting Block's steak into small pieces for him when Tex wandered over. He stood silently for the first time Rory could remember. Block was clearly in rough shape. He had been helped from the saddle and laid on the ground. When the food was ready, Rory stacked up three saddles to make a backrest for the marshal and propped him against it. With every move, tears of pain found their way from Block's closed eyes. When Rory laid him against the stacked saddles, one of them moved enough for Block to drop sideways a bit. A gasp and a groan that was hard for Rory to listen to escaped from the patient.

Tex squatted on his haunches and looked at Block, then opened his shirt and saw the dirty, bloody bandage.

He lifted the bandage enough to see the inflamed edge of the wound beneath.

"You got you a sick man here, Marshal. Most likely sicker than you ever thought. Ain't goin to make Pueblo nor anywhere else that matters if'n we cain't do something. I know a bit about these situations. Saw enough in my war. That's not our own big bit of butchery I'm referring to. I managed to miss that one by being somewhere else when the repeated calls for cannon fodder come along. I made a point of it.

"And I don't want to hear one word from you nor anyone else about duty and such. I done more duty than most folks ever considered doin'. And I ai'n talk'n about that neither. No, I had me a piece of another situation, and that's enough talk of that. Thing is, I need to take a look at what's under this bandage."

Rory said, "I take a look every evening. No reason you can't. Might be a help. If you can help me and Block both, we'll welcome it. A few minutes isn't going to hurt, though. We'll just let him finish eating first."

When Rory set Block's empty plate aside, he and Tex held Block in position while the saddles were removed. He was laid back down with just his head resting on his rolled-up bedroll. Block's two shirts were gently opened, and the knot that held the bandage in place untied. Rory laid the two ends of the bandage aside and lifted the grim-looking pad off the wound. It had adhered to the drying mucus that had never stopped leaking from the wound. Pulling it off dragged a groan from the patient. With the damaged skin open to the evening light, Tex gasped. Rory was startled by the growing inflammation around the wound. The skin was far redder than it had been even that morning, and there were clear signs of yellow puss leaking out, along with some discolored blood.

Tex said, "Son, we got to do something. You heat water. As hot as this fella can tolerate. You clean this up, front and back both. If your knife is sharp enough, you give her a wash and a few seconds in the flame of the fire. Then you cut away all that ragged, infected skin. Keep the flies away while I go on a search. If you don't have a clean bandage, you take these and wash them as best you can. And I mean you wash them. Hot water that you'll think is going to take the skin off your hands. If you care about your friend, you'll do as I say. I'll be back."

With that, he resaddled his horse and rode off to the west, toward a rim of rocky upthrust where a border of trees and other growth were showing. The stream they were camped on appeared to grow out of those same rocks and growth. The day was nearing its end. The rapidly setting sun said it would be fully dark when the strange old man returned.

When Tex rode back into camp, he went first to the makeshift kitchen, and said, "Pass me one of those clean pots. The small one. And keep that fire going. We're going to need it."

With the pot in his hand, he rode to where Rory and Block waited.

Tex knelt on the ground with the pot before him. From a saddlebag, he had removed a large handful of plants and a few roots. He stripped the leaves off the plants and dropped them into the pot. With his knife, he stripped and shredded the bark from the roots. He looked at the pot and said, "Not enough, but we'll have to make do. Do better in the morning. Too dark to go on the hunt again."

Willy showed up with a lit lantern. Answering Rory's

unasked question, he said, "Always like to have some light available. Bring 'er along most places. A man never knows what might come up."

Rory acknowledged with a brief 'thank you.'

Tex stood and went to the stream. Rubbing sand roughly all over his wet hands, he scrubbed them as clean as he could, given the situation. He then dropped a bit of hot water into the pot and began kneading the leaves and bark into a mush. One of the cowboys was looking on from a few feet away. He studied the situation for a minute and then turned to the stream. He was back in about ten minutes, carrying a handful of some kind of plant. He squatted beside Tex and held out the plant.

"Seen my mother make a poultice outta this here root, many a time. Might help."

Tex took the root, and as he began stripping it, said, "Right you are. Should have thought of it my own self."

Tex worked silently for a bit and then, as if thinking it all through, said, "Of course, flaxseed might be the best of all for this need. Ain't none anywhere near to where we are, though. Right at this moment, is what I'm try'n to say."

When the roots and leaves were kneaded into a drying mush, Tex said, "Pass me some of that bandage material, Sheriff."

Rory answered, "One of the cowboys had a clean shirt in his bedroll. I cut enough to make two thick pads. We'll put one in front and one on the back. I've heard of making a poultice, Tex, but wouldn't know how myself. I don't know much about the plants and herbs. Might just know enough to poison the patient."

"Well, we're going to try not to poison this one. He's poisoned enough already. We're still three, four days from Pueblo. These men and the cattle will make it alright, but this man won't, unless we can draw that poison out."

With fingers as clean as he could scrub them, Tex wiped the mush from the pot onto the layers of cloth and then folded the cloth into the two thick pads.

"Now, lift him to where I can plaster this on the underside wound. Then I'll hold both in place while you wrap that strip around."

Block said nothing at all while the men worked. The gasps and groans and the pain-filled expressions on his face spoke for him. With everything done that they knew how to do, they buttoned Block's shirt and laid two blankets over him. Morning was a long way off.

Block appeared to have gone to sleep quickly after the men quit rolling him around, causing him pain. The dog, who had already become a favorite with the saddle crew, returned from scrounging bits of fried beef and cut-off rims of fat and gristle. He entered the little camp that held the two marshals as well as Tex and the prisoner. The dog went from one to the other, looking for praise and a scratch behind the ear. He then sniffed all around Block before turning in a couple of circles, looking for a comfortable sleeping position, lay down and rested his head on Block's chest. Somehow, the sleeping Block pulled his arm from under the blankets and rested it on the dog's shoulder.

Rory and Tex stared, surprised at the dog's actions, while Cunningham spoke for the first time that day.

"That's a smart dog."

WHEN RORY RODE BACK to where Block was laid out after taking the last shift on watch, Tex was gone. The dog was back at the fire begging for food and attention. Cunningham had struggled to his feet and had waddled far enough for some privacy. He had then made his slow way to the stream and had a good sand wash, and drank enough water to put the night's foul breath away, along with his thirst. Entering the camp again, he spoke to Rory.

"He said to tell you to get a couple of clean pads ready."

When Tex returned this time, he had a small pannier balanced across the saddle pommel. The pannier was bulging with dry-land plants, roots, and water plants. He passed the canvas bag down to Rory and stepped to the ground, leaving the horse far enough away to keep him from becoming a nuisance in the camp.

"How's the patient?"

"Why don't you ask him? You can see his eyes are open. I believe his fever is down, is about all I know to say."

Tex looked at the man on the ground, and asked, "Feeling any better, Marshal?"

"Might. A little bit. Hard to tell. Ask me again in a couple of days."

"Son, in a couple of days, we won't have to ask. You'll either be up looking for your dinner, or you'll be dead. Ain't none but those two choices. Now, let's take a look at our doctoring."

Rory and Tex worked together to remove the poultices. Tex picked the first one off with the tip of his knife. He dropped it in the grass and flipped it over. The cloth was yellow with puss and a bit of blood.

"Draw'n good," said Tex. "Let's get the other one."

If anything, the pad from Block's back was more discolored than the one in front. Tex studied it for a moment and said, "We ain't going to do it, but if'n you was to peel this pad open, you'd find puss most of the way through. And look, the inflamed skin is already going back to its natural color. Goin' to leave a mark, Marshal, but show'n those marks and tell'n the story will earn you many a drink in any Western town."

He patted Block on the chest with his open hand and said, "You just might live to be a grandpa yet, son."

The poultice treatment was repeated morning and night on the three-day ride to Pueblo.

BLOCK'S long struggle seemed to open Cunningham's mind to where he was prepared to talk to Rory as they rode along. Block was sitting upright in the saddle again, instead of being hunched over the animal's neck.

Rory and Cunningham dropped back a bit so they could talk in private.

Rory started with, "I looked over the list of names on that sheet of paper you were keeping. I see Glover Harrison's name there. Would you like to explain that?"

It took a long time for Cunningham to answer, but finally, he said, "One answer like that surely leads to another. Some of those names represent powerful people. People who could do me harm."

Pushing the man a bit, wanting to get the story, Rory said, "I've never believed the story from the very first of this. From when I found the first tarnished gold coin and then brought down the phony judge and marshal, and heard their unbelievable tales of ranching in the unsettled parts of Texas. I've never believed that was all there was to it. It just didn't make sense. Two trunks of stolen government money that can't be traced. With all the possibilities that set before the thieves. To choose wilderness ranching, fighting off Indians, buffalo herds, and what have you, all hundreds of miles from a known market? Makes no sense.

"But seeing that list of names opens the possibilities some. Of course, I don't know any of those men, but starting with Glover Harrison, and having met him in Denver and seeing what a high position he holds, opened my eyes to those other possibilities. That's going to be investigated, so whatever you might add to it would go down to your favor."

The horses plodded along, kicking up grasshoppers and the odd rabbit, and scaring some ground birds that Rory didn't recognize off their nests. And all that while, Webster Cunningham held to his silence.

But perhaps the sun on his back and the grand, wide-open land all around him, and the gentle movements of the horse, reminded him that only a free man could truly enjoy it all. Perhaps the idea of years in jail was souring on him as the day moved along. Again, the delay was long, but Rory figured they had hours ahead of them on the trail, so he waited. When the captured man began to speak, he had obviously thought to buy every break he could get.

Whatever it was, he finally said, "There's gotta be something in it for me that would make me give you what answers I can."

"All I can do, as you well know, is tell the marshals and the lawyers that you cooperated and didn't fight the inevitable. The only thing I can promise is that facing the judge, and you are surely going to do that, you need to have a better argument for consideration than if you refuse to tell me the story."

Knowing the truth of Rory's statement and grasping what little hope there was, he started talking.

"I'm thinking you've already figured me for a small part in this whole matter. You'd be correct with that thought. There's none of those others sitting out the winter winds of northern Texas with a bunch of ignorant cattle drovers, holding a herd that would get lost in the millions of wild animals in another part of Texas. No, what I was in charge of is small potatoes to all the rest. And the worrisome thing is, I don't have any idea what the rest of the scheme is. I've been told nothing. I was just paid a more than generous amount to care for the herd and told to keep my mouth shut.

"I'll need you to understand, Marshal, that this isn't my caper. I'm just working for those names on the paper, the same as Ronald Thrasher and Mike Wasson were. None of us knew who all is involved, or where the whole thing is going. Our job was to get some money into circulation, preferably through cattle.

"What's being done with the rest of the money, or other money the bosses might have, I wouldn't know.

"The fact is, I'm not supposed to have that paper or those names. I'm just a small part of this. But I'm not going to risk my life by telling you where that paper came from. I'd rather take my chances with the judge."

"But you really haven't answered my question. I asked about Glover Harrison."

"Every name on that paper is higher up the pole than I am. Exactly how it all fits together, I've never known and can't say. I don't know the man you're asking about, only that he's somehow attached to the federal marshals."

Rory decided to accept that statement as the truth,

but just to push a bit harder, hoping for more, he said, "It might interest you to know that Harrison first tried to stop any law from riding south. Then, when Block and I pushed for completion of what we had started last year, he finally allowed the two of us to go, but he held any others back from joining the ride. He also made it very clear to Block that your death would be the most satisfactory conclusion."

That seemed to take away the desire Cunningham had for any more talk. But there were still miles to go. There would be another time.

23

THE GROUP ENTERED PUEBLO BEFORE LUNCH, FOUR DAYS after Tex had applied the first poultice to Block. The men and animals were all exhausted. Seldom had a cattle herd been pushed harder than the Big C herd had been. Willy rode over to where Rory and Tex were standing guard over Cunningham.

"Well, we're here, boss. I've talked to the boys. They're willing to stand over one more day. This is good grass where we are right now. We'll let them get their breath, a day of good graze, and plenty of water before we push them up to the corrals. In the meantime, you can go make your deal with the buyers and find some pay for us. We can sort out Tex's brand, too, if you want."

Tex immediately agreed with the plan before saying, "While you're dealing with the buyers, I'll go with Block and find the hospital, if such a thing exists here. If not, I'll run down a doc somewhere."

Rory rode to the cattle chutes and flagged down a worker, asking where he could find a buyer. With that information, he rode to the small office building and tied up at the front. There was only one man, and he was sitting on a chair on the small porch.

"I see a herd out on the flat. They yours?"

"Most of them. Big C brand and a bunch of mostly blacks branded with a broken stick. That owner will be along later. The boys are sorting them out now. We'll graze them overnight and run them in tomorrow. But there's something you need to know and pass along to your buyers."

"Then you'd best come up here and sit while I listen to your story."

Rory pulled the sheriff badge from his vest pocket and took a seat. "The broken stick bunch are clean as far as I know. The Big C herd is a collection of rustled stock, overbranded Big C. I'm Sheriff Rory Jamison. I've been on the trail of this bunch for the past year. Found them down south a ways, along with the man who arranged for their theft. I'm also a sworn-in deputy federal marshal, and I'm riding with a regular federal marshal. That provides authority to carry the law over crossed borders, either state or county. The marshal's on his way to find some medical help. Took a bullet some days ago, but I believe he'll be fine. I'm willing to sign an affidavit that guarantees your innocence in handling stolen animals. If there are questions, I'll deal with the legal part when I get back to Denver. Have we got a deal?"

The buyer fingered the badge as he rolled it over and over in his fingers, looking first at the badge and then at Rory.

"Heard of you. You made it to the big time. Your own penny dreadful write-up and all. Last magazine had a song all written out, words, notes, and all. Can't sing myself, but I heard a half-drunk cowboy plucking a guitar and singing about Sheriff Rory down at the saloon a couple of nights ago. Not a half-bad song neither."

This was said with a bit of a grin. But seeing Rory didn't wish to continue that conversation, he said, "I'd say we have a deal, Sheriff. You bring your herd in first thing tomorrow. I'll have cars enough, and they'll be on their way east before noon."

The two men shook hands, and Rory rode back to the herd.

~

By NINE THE NEXT MORNING, all the animals had been sold. Tex stuffed the bank draft in his pocket and shook hands all around. He had given each rider fifty dollars for their few days' work.

"I'm on my way to California, boys. Me and the dog. Gotta sell my horses down to the livery and buy me a ticket. Never rode no rails before. But she's a far distance to where I'm going, so I'm taking the easy way."

Rory pulled the man aside for a moment and said, "Tex, don't you be traveling with a wad of cash in your pocket. You'll never reach that ocean you want to see. You go put most of it in the bank. When you get to where you're going, you can transfer it out there."

Tex just nodded and said, "Never would have thought of that."

Rory put his draft in his pocket and paid the riders out of the funds in Cunningham's brown envelope. He, too, shook hands all around, saying, "Fellas, I promised not to ask your names, so I can't do more than thank you and remember you by the work you've done. If you'll take a sheriff's advice, you'll stay clean from here on. I'm hoping to never see a poster with any of your faces on it. Good luck, and thanks."

They rode off with more money in their pockets than most riders ever saw. Silently, Rory wished them good luck.

RORY FOUND the hospital and walked the corridors until he located Block. The doctor was just finishing up putting on a fresh bandage. To answer Rory's question, the doc said, "I don't know what it looked like before the poultices were applied, but it's looking good now. Mr. Handly will be a while regaining his strength, but he should heal up just fine."

Looking at Block, he said, "I don't believe the bullet did any lasting damage, Marshal Handly, but if you were a cat with nine lives, as they say, you would only have eight left. I advise you to treat yourself with kindness, with that in mind."

The lawmen found a cantina that would feed two men desperately in need of baths and clean clothing, and were soon on their way home, pushing the spare horses and Webster Cunningham before them.

24

As Block and Rory neared home, only a few more riding days away, Boon and Belle Wardle were reacquainting themselves with Key and Tempest, their two youngest. At Key's insistence, his father had gone to the livery in search of Tippet. Neither man knew the first thing about how to make or accept an apology, and neither expected it. Boon opened the conversation with, "My son says you're an alright fella. Myself, I still think you're an old pirate with a story to tell that's best not told. You came out with the king's English when you thought to butter yourself up helping my wife, who needs no help at all. But digging out those words put a strain on you, I could see that.

"But I'm new to town and I'll be needing the livery time to time, so I'm willing to forget all your hidden secrets. Might even buy you a coffee if you thought you could stay civil while we drank it."

Tippet looked the man up and down with a grin on his face before saying, "Why, that's about the most awkward and misworded apology I ever did hear. But don't you worry. I've met many a man over my time. One of about every type, I expect. Of course, you're kind of in a cat-a-gory all on your own. Ain't never met a man who thought he could fly before. And there ain't no need to cross the road and pay Ma Gamble, her that owns the dining room, none of her gett'n rich prices jest ta have a sip a coffee. Got 'er right here in my office. Bettr'n that across the road too."

That was the beginning of a daily ritual where the two old men sat outside the livery, wearing heavy coats as the season demanded, and exchanged tales of the past. Anyone listening in would have to wonder which tales were true and which were make-believe stories.

After a couple of rarely peaceful days holding down one of Tippet's chairs, the first verbal explosion belched from Boon Wardle when Deputy Ivan rode up to the hitch rail outside the marshal's office and stepped down. He had been on a long trail of a lost horse, with the owner hollering theft. Two nights on the hard, cold ground and the miles of riding, leading the wandering animal home, had put him in need of sleep and good food. There had been no sign of a thief. It seemed the animal just took his freedom when the opportunity allowed. Ivan stretched the kinks out of his back and stepped toward the door.

Without considering consequences, Tippet pointed with the stem of his pipe and spoke to Boon.

"That's Deputy Ivan Ivanov. Good fella. From a ranch up in the hills above town. Good man on the trail and tough as nails when he has to be. Spark'n yer Tempest. Seems ta be somth'n to it. Ivan, he takes the borrow of my buggy as often as situations allow. Course they go out riding time to time too."

Boon jumped to his feet and, not considering the

volume of his voice, a volume few men could have matched, said, "My Tempest? That's the man who held a rifle on me the last time I was here. Locked me in that cell. There's no way in this world my daughter will be seeing that man. I'll put a stop to that right now."

Tippet started to say, "Seems a bit late," but Wardle was gone.

"Hey you! Sheriff or whatever you call yourself! I want a word with you!"

Ivan turned from the office doorway to see who was making all the noise. Folks along the walk on the opposite side of the road were standing still, having heard the shouts. Tempest, working in the supply store, where the door stood open, also heard, and knew the voice. Hunching her shoulders against the embarrassment, she stepped onto the boardwalk in time to see her father approaching Ivan. She knew trouble when she saw it. Standing still, she was torn between walking across the road—to do what, she wasn't exactly sure—and going back into the store and closing the door, leaving the men to sort out whatever it was. She did neither. Instead, she stood as if rooted to the boardwalk.

Gritting his teeth as he determined to hold his tongue, Ivan waited for Boon to approach. It didn't take long.

"Kid, I'll not have you spending time with my Tempest. Do you hear me clearly on that? I see you with her, you'll answer to me, and you won't enjoy that, I'll guarantee. There's no way I'll have a man such as you are as a son-in-law. You get that idea right out of your mind."

Ivan somehow knew he had to defend himself or forever look weak in front of this man. In spite of his determination to hold his tongue, he heard himself say,

"I'm not so sure I want you as a father-in-law either, but there it is. On the other hand, Tempest and me, we're nowhere close to making that decision. Right now, we enjoy a ride now and then. Anything else will have to wait while we work it out."

At the beginning of the conversation, Tempest had started walking slowly across the road, knowing that half the town was watching and listening and that the other half would know about the situation before the end of the day. She stepped up to her father and said, "Pa, I thought you were going to look for rangeland. Don't you figure this is a good enough time to get busy at that?"

"The boys are taking care of that search."

His voice could still be heard far away.

"Father, if you shout one more time I'm going to pack up and move to the big city. Maybe Ivan and me, we'll go together. Probably Mother will come too. Now go back and sit with Tippet. I'll go over to the bakery and buy a sweet treat for you two old men to enjoy. It might help your sour disposition."

With a final warning look at Ivan, Boon turned back to the livery. Tippet greeted him with, "I'm sure that should fix the situation."

"Shut up, old man. What do you know about it? If you ever had a daughter, you'd do the same."

"Now there ya go again, mak'n noise outa yer mouth when ya don't know one single thing of what yer tak'n about."

"Are you saying that you have a daughter?"

"What I'm say'n is that you've talked enough fer this here one day."

It was early afternoon on a Friday when Rory and Block ventured into the big city. Wending their way through the outskirts of the growing center, they passed a few hovels and run-down shacks that were somehow housing the poorest of the poor. But the trail soon led them into areas holding more promise of prosperity, including the beginnings of some businesses. Folks gathered on the few walkways fronting the stores and saloons, studying on the strange collection of riders and driven horses. Before long, they entered a small Mexican section, with modest adobe homes built among the few businesses. The streets seemed to be taken over by children shouting and playing games Rory knew nothing about. A promising-looking cantina caught Rory's eye. He had developed a taste for the spicy offering in a good cantina. Studying the cantina but speaking to Block, he said, "What do you think, partner? I'm for taking on some lunch."

Block answered, "I was hoping you'd say something like that."

Without consulting Webster Cunningham, they turned their horses' heads in the direction of the tie rail. A young man stepped out and caught one of the riderless horses, leading him to the rail. Knowing other young men would want to do a favor for the gringo riders and collect a coin for their troubles, the fellow moved quickly, gathering the other two loose horses while he waved off his friends, who were beginning to get the idea.

With all the animals secured and Cunningham released from the saddle, Rory found a silver dollar in his pocket and flipped it to his helper. "Will you keep an eye on them for me, muchacho?"

"Si," answered the young man as he skillfully snapped the coin out of the air. The silver disappeared into his pocket while he grinned at Rory. Shifting his eyes between Rory and Cunningham, who was now hand-cuffed, although his feet were no longer hobbled, it was clear the young fellow had questions pressing to be spoken, but he held his tongue.

The lawmen and their prisoner made their way into the cantina and found a clean table. Taking their seats, each man removed his hat and glanced around. Staring into the dark interior, they were able to see the place was about half full, with teenage girls scurrying among the tables, taking orders and delivering plates of food and brown bottles of beer. When a young girl approached their table, Block surprised both of his companions by asking what was available, asking it in what to Rory sounded like flowing, perfect Spanish. The server answered in her native tongue and waited while Block translated for the other men. In a matter of seconds, he spoke their orders, and the girl hurried off. A half-hour later, they were again climbing on their horses after tightening their cinches and counting the weapons that were tied across the saddles of the unridden animals. Rory was careful not to make a show of the counting, knowing what an insult it would be if he showed mistrust of his young helper. Nodding his thanks at the fellow, they turned to the road again as their helper pulled the slipknots and released the other three animals.

As they moved into the center of the city, the traffic increased. They had to take more care of the three unridden horses in case they got tangled up with the many other horses on the road. Their first target was the hotel, where Rory would check in and leave his bedroll and pannier. Only after that would they take the horses to the livery Rory knew best. From there, it was an easy two blocks' walk to the federal marshal's office.

The three men were filthy and weary from the days on the trail. Block had been near enough staggering when he stepped to the ground outside the cantina. Holding still for a moment, he had rested his head against the saddle, while one hand gripped the horn. Rory, nearly as weary but not fighting a gunshot wound, looked over at him and said, "Nearly home, pard. You'll be in your own bed this night."

As they neared the hotel, a young city policeman stepped off the boardwalk, waving the trio of men to a stop while hollering, "Hold up there, you can't be riding down city streets with loose, out-of-control horses and all those guns showing on you. There's to be no weapons worn in the city. I demand that you dismount and lay all those weapons down where I can gather them up and get rid of them."

When neither Rory nor Block paid any attention, the young man began walking along beside Rory, hollering for him to stop. Choosing not to speak, Rory reached down and grabbed the young fellow by the front of his uniform coat and picked him up just far enough so his feet were clear of the ground. The man sputtered and waved his arms, the tightening of the coat preventing him from getting any words out. Rory didn't bother to even look at him. He simply rode to the edge of the boardwalk and released his hold. The desperate policeman fell to the ground and lay there holding his throat, among the laughter of the onlookers.

When Rory returned to Block's side, the marshal grinned and said, "I've known you to be a strong man, Sheriff, but you lifted that fellow with one hand. I don't think I could ever have done that, even when I was younger."

Cunningham had watched the whole incident with mixed fear and admiration. But when Rory pulled between him and Block, Cunningham moved his mount a bit further away, out of arms reach.

The group made a stop at the hotel. Rory untied his bedroll and pannier and took them in with him. Knowing he was filthy, but not caring, with his exhaustion taking a more demanding position than the much-needed bath, Rory approached the desk and said, "Need a room. Two nights. And someone to take this gear up to the room."

The clerk, who had seen ranchers arriving directly from the range, was no stranger to the vagaries of the times, but Rory's condition was pushing the limits.

"Sir, are you sure this is where you wish to be? There are less costly hotels not many blocks away. Perhaps…"

Rory pushed his hat off his forehead and looked at the man. Before he had a chance to say anything, another voice, this time a woman's quiet tone, said, "It's alright, Sid. Give the sheriff room two-one-five, and I'll mind the counter while you take his gear up. Be sure you lock the door and give me the key when you return."

Lifting his hat in thanks, Rory walked back out to the horses and mounted. Almost directly across the road and down a bit of a side street was the livery. As if they were returning home, the three unridden horses trotted right into the big barn as soon as they were close enough to pick up the odor of feed and water. The hostler leaped to his feet, preventing the animals from going farther. Opening the gate to a large box stall, he ushered the mounts in and then held the gate while the three men dismounted outside, before slapping their horses on their rumps, knowing they would follow the first three.

Without discussing their plans, Block took Cunningham by the elbow and led him across the street, while Rory was telling the livery man, "Can you hold those saddles and weapons somewhere safe? They're important to a rustling investigation."

"Sure enough."

Rory swung his saddlebags across one shoulder and followed Block. The two blocks' walk seemed longer than normal, pushing even further against the men's supply of strength and energy, but within ten minutes, the three men stepped inside the marshal's office. With a gasp of surprise, every man in the room stood to their feet. Donavan Gaines, the branch chief, stood with his mouth open, while Glover Harrison appeared to be backing away, disbelief and concern mingling on his face.

Surprising all the marshals, Rory took charge. He instructed Cunningham to sit. The clanking of the chains caught everyone's attention. Block dropped into a chair, leaving Rory to continue with what he had started. The two marshals that had stayed behind in Denver backed away a couple of feet. Donavan Gaines turned toward his office, leaning against the door frame.

Even Rory himself couldn't have said where the voice of unquestioned authority came from. It could be that he had finally hit his limit dealing with tarnished gold coins, rustled cattle, reluctant federal marshals, and the foolishness of the orders laid on the trip south by Glover Harrison.

From the time Denver had come in sight, Rory's anger had been building. He and Block had lain their lives on the line over what amounted to little or nothing in comparison to other federal spending and waste. Seeing Glover Harrison's name on the list of what was shaping up to be, in truth, a white-collar gang of thieves, had been burdening Rory's peace of mind since the moment he saw it. Every step his gelding took on the return trip seemed to drive the anger and frustration deeper into his very being. Going right back to when he was dealing with the phony judge, the knowledge that he had been trapped into a federal matter where he no longer knew who he could trust and who he should doubt, had soured him on government and politics like nothing else ever had. He now laid his saddlebags on a desk and spoke to one of the younger marshals. "Go flag down a buggy and get back here as soon as ever you can. Then you take Marshal Handly to his home. And you see that he gets there safely, right into the house. Then you stand guard until you're relieved."

Without questioning the order, before the man could even get to the door, Rory stepped up to Glover Harrison and, with all the strength he possessed, backed by anger and righteousness, he backhanded the man across the face. Harrison had no chance at all. With a crushed nose and mouth, he simply folded to the floor.

Looking at the second marshal, who, up until this time, had simply been standing there, he said, "This man is under arrest. Put him in the most secure chains you've got and march him to the city lockup. Take Cunningham with you but separate them so they can't talk. You stay and guard them."

With that order given, the junior deputy moved to obey. He hadn't even glanced at his commanding officer, who had pushed himself away from the doorpost and once again come toward the group.

Rory turned to Donavan Gaines. "Your case is Chief. Harrison is in it up to his eyeballs. But he'll hold until another time. Right now, I'm going to the hotel and bed. I may sleep most of the day tomorrow. Or I may not. But I'll be back. I'll be back with the evidence. Then I'm going home. Deputy Handly has been shot and wounded, but the doctor says he'll be alright. He may sleep all of tomorrow, too, but we'll both be back. You can depend on it."

26

RORY LEFT A SILENT OFFICE BEHIND HIM AS HE WALKED out. To have this young county sheriff so dominate the office and the actions of the marshals, was totally unexpected. That those actions and orders were the obviously correct ones, left the marshals with nothing to say. The few minutes since Rory and Block had entered the office were so out of character for the lawmen that they were all shocked into silence. The events of the past few minutes had been so strange and so sudden, with a strong tinge of violence, that even the branch Chief hadn't spoken.

Rory half staggered back to the livery, concerned about his personal rifles. He could point to no direct cause for concern, but a man can get attached to his own shooting weapons. At the livery, he found the hostler working over the six animals left in his care. Rory asked where the saddles and gear were stored. The livery owner silently pulled a key from his pocket and pointed to a door beside his own office. Rory took only a minute to pick out his carbine and the Big Fifty. He locked the door, thanked the man, and returned the key.

When he stepped up to the hotel counter with the two rifles folded into his bent left arm, with his hand gripping the bottoms of the two stocks, he was passed his key with a quiet, "Sleep well, Sheriff." He then turned to the dining room. As always, it was busy and crowded. But he spotted a table tucked into the back corner. It was a table of last resort, undesirable to most customers, and often left empty. But for Rory, it was perfect. He eased through the other chairs and tables and took a seat. Several dining room guests held their eyes on him as he found his seat. One woman held her lace-trimmed handkerchief over her nose and mouth. He knew he was leaving a waft of trail and campfire odor and horse behind him, but he simply didn't care.

He leaned his guns in the corner behind him and laid his hat on an empty chair. The dining room manager was there in no time at all.

"Sir, I can't let you bring those weapons into the dining room. We have a town ordinance against open weapons. I'll have to insist that you leave and take the rifles with you. And those two on your belt, as well."

A voice that surprised both men came from halfway across the room. "I'll vouch for the sheriff, sir. I'll even sit with him while he eats. Just to make sure he doesn't up and shoot someone, you understand. And by the looks of him, he needs to be eating quickly."

Rory looked up into the smiling face of Gale Strombeck, the rancher with the two lovely daughters that he had met on his first visit to the big city. Gale pulled a chair back and aimed a hard look at the manager. When that man didn't move, Strombeck said, "Sir, this man is an extraordinary servant of the people of Colorado. You can see that he's been through it the past while. Now you get him a plate of beef and potatoes and hot gravy. And coffee. Coffee for me too. Hurry off, man, and get it done."

When they were alone, Strombeck turned to look at what had caught Rory's eyes. His two daughters were making their way through the crowd. Strombeck looked at them and simply said, "Not now." The girls grinned and returned to their seats.

Strombeck looked at Rory for a minute before saying, "I've seen some men worn to the bone before, been that way myself more times than I care to remember, but you might be setting a new bottom limit. When did you eat last?"

"Ate just a couple of hours ago. Down at the edge of town. Mexican cantina. The food was good too. But I could eat again. Drink some coffee."

"Taken care of," responded Strombeck. "And then to sleep, I hope. No more chasing bad guys today. And if you don't mind me mentioning it, you might find a tub of hot water to your liking before you roll into the sheets."

Both men laughed at the statement, but by then, a waiter had arrived with a plate of hot food. Another had come with two mugs and a big coffeepot. Rory fiddled with his knife and fork for a moment and then started to eat. Strombeck slurped his coffee and remained quiet, not wishing to draw Rory's attention away from his food.

Between mouthfuls, Rory said, "My friend, if you wished to do something that I would be very grateful for, you could go purchase some new clothing for me. The hat and boots are still alright, but everything in between needs replacing. I'd give you the money, and

161

you could leave the package outside my hotel room door."

Strombeck stood and waved to his daughters, who were still at their table but had hardly taken their eyes off the two men since Rory had entered the dining room. He waved them over. When they arrived, standing beside the small table, he pushed Rory's money toward them and repeated the sheriff's request. Polly scooped up the coins and responded, "Oh, what a glorious opportunity. This could be a dry run for when I'm able to shop for my husband. Or even imagine I am shopping for my husband. Or future…"

"Let it go, little sister. You're dreaming and wishing is growing into an embarrassment."

As they wound their way through the tables and chairs and then linked arms as they left the dining room, Rory saw them whispering and giggling.

Thinking of where the shopping trip could lead, he thought, *Sometimes I'm a bit unwise in my actions.*

Getting his emotional feet back on the ground and admiring the half-empty plate that had been heaped high when it was set before him, he said to Gale Strombeck, "Didn't take them long to put that plate together. It's almost as if they were thinking if they fed me, I might take leave of the place. A man could come to believe his presence wasn't really welcome."

27

CONTRARY TO WHAT HE HAD PREDICTED THE AFTERNOON before, Rory and Block both showed up at the federal office by midmorning. Rory had taken an early breakfast with Gale Strombeck and the girls, Allie and Polly. Allie started the conversation with, "Sheriff, I hope you appreciate that Polly and I were hoping to lay abed for another hour this morning. We'd been looking forward to it ever since we heard about the trip to town. And shopping for you, in addition to being terribly embarrassing as we sorted through the stacks of pants, shirts, and unmentionables, why, that simply tired us out.

"And now, here we are at the crack of dawn, as if we were on the ranch with cows to milk or eggs to gather, just so you could have the pleasure of our company over breakfast."

Rory, partially rested from his long ordeal, answered, "It's a sacrifice I'll remember and treasure in my heart. And this multicolored shirt you forced on me will forever cement the day into my weary mind."

Both girls laughed, while Allie said, "I wish I could believe that."

Polly added, "That shirt is very becoming on you. It's a lovely shirt."

"If you say so."

As the girls and their father stood to leave, Block came in. He and Rory had another cup of coffee together while they decided how to proceed with the day before they were ready to face Donavan Gaines.

DONAVAN GAINES WAS at the marshal's office and waiting. The two returned men, up and ready for the day in spite of their threat to sleep through it, walked into Gaines's private office and took seats without being invited. It had been midmorning by the time they dealt with personal matters, but even that was earlier than Rory had predicted for their arrival.

Rory laid his saddlebags over his knees. He undid the strap on the side that held the incriminating written list of names. But before he produced any evidence, he asked, "Cunningham and Harrison still on ice?"

"They are. I spent a big part of last evening questioning Cunningham. But before I get into that, I need to say that you men did a great job, and I'm more than happy to have you both home in one piece. Block, I'll be praying that you complete your recovery and return to full health. I'll be wanting to hear all you have to tell me, but then you'll be taking a week off to rest and reacquaint yourself with your family. I'm also taking you off fieldwork permanently. You're too valuable to the service to have you traipsing all over the country chasing bad guys.

"And, Rory, as of now, you are no longer a deputy marshal, although we may call on you again. You are relieved with my, and the nation's thanks.

"You are now a county sheriff, which is no low position, I assure you. I met with Anthony Clare, your state man, for breakfast this morning. I sent a runner to his home last evening to arrange it. Because the unraveling of this matter began at the state level, he is claiming the right to be kept in the know as it winds down. And he was pleased to hear of your safe return. Be sure to stop at his office before you leave town.

"One question before we get to what Cunningham has to say. I'm surprised you were able to locate him and the herd so quickly. That's a vast country down there with little, if any, settlement."

Rory answered, since Block hadn't been brought into the gold coin mystery until later.

"You'll remember from my written report back at the start of the whole matter, that I located the crew that was hired to drive the original stolen herd. They admitted they were often lost in that vast country, as you called it, but they still knew north from south. They were able to steer me in the right direction. After that, it was a matter of looking for logical telling points. They would need, at the least, grass, water, and shelter. That led us off the flatlands toward the rise of land we could see in the distance. From there, it just seemed to come together without much input from us."

Gaines listened carefully, studying the two men, knowing they were downplaying their efforts. But he needed to move on, so he left it at that.

"Alright, now to Cunningham. It's plain why there was pressure to kill this man rather than bring him back for trial. I suspect some folks in Washington believe

Cunningham knows too much, although he denies having such knowledge. I couldn't understand Harrison's animosity toward Cunningham at the time. I never once suspected. Harrison is one of the worst types of criminals we have to deal with. A man with authority. A man with experience and connections. A man who has hidden himself inside the very agency that is trying to solve a mysterious crime. A man with a title to hide behind. A man with what has come to be known as presence. He almost commands obedience from his very presence alone. To find that he's a crook and worse, is very upsetting. The marshal's service will, no doubt, have to take a serious look at this thing when the news reaches the head office. But we'll shut him and a few others down. Provided, men, that you have the written evidence Cunningham says you have."

Rory reached into the saddlebag and removed the two pages of handwritten notes taken from Cunningham's pack. He had so far said nothing about the cash that was in the same pack nor the cattle that were impounded and driven north and sold.

"Cunningham says he wasn't supposed to have these. He somehow managed to wiggle them away from someone else. I don't know who that someone might be. And Cunningham refused to say. He was terrified at the very mention of this other person.

"I wrote out copies of these pages this morning for my own records. Although I don't know who these others on the list are, the whole thing appears to be credible. It clears up most of the questions we have all had for over a year, beginning with the phony marshal and judge up at Stevensville, and the tarnished gold coins that led to the theft of the government strongboxes. With this evidence, I believe you could make a visit to the state lockup and have a talk with Mike Wasson, the phony marshal. He's a very small cog in the wheel. He'll be forever a small cog. Spend his life in that position. It probably wouldn't hurt the cause of justice too much if you were to offer him leniency on his sentence, even an early parole, in exchange for his testimony.

"It shouldn't be any great trick to track down the list of properties purchased and other investments on that list, and there's still the possibility that one of the men on the list of names would be only too happy to tell the whole sordid tale if he's offered some kind of deal.

"I'm no lawyer or well-experienced lawman, but if this was my job to wrap up, I'd hold Cunningham and Glover Harrison on ice until you had what you need to make the case. If you show your cards to Washington too soon, you might find it all buried and pushed aside."

Donavan Gaines said, "How would you like to have it as your task to sort out and complete? Even take it all to Washington and follow it through?"

Rory laughed at the thought, probably the first time he'd laughed since leaving the fort.

"There's not one chance in a thousand that I'd take that on. No, you're the federal people. I'm simply a county sheriff, and I need to get back to it."

"You'll be accused of many things in this life, young man, but simply being a county sheriff will not be one of them. You haven't begun to understand who you really are yet."

Rory chose to leave that alone, fearing further complications in his life if the conversations continued.

Donavan Gaines studied Rory as he tapped his teeth with the end of his pencil. He then glanced over at Block, seeking some insight but received only the deputy's blank face. Thinking of nothing that would hold Rory in

Denver, he said, "There's no real reason for you to remain away from home any longer, Sheriff. Just two more questions. The first is when are you people going to get the telegraph up your way? It's a perfect nuisance having to send letters and wait days for a response."

Rory grinned, answering, "If I hear anything, I'll be sure to let you know. In fact, I'll send you a wire."

"Alright, then the second question. What became of the cattle?"

Again, Rory grinned, saying, "Why, we sold them. Drove them north and sold them in Pueblo on our way home. That's a bit of a story that Block can tell you over lunch someday."

"Where are the proceeds of the sale?"

"In my county bank account. Or they will be just as soon as I can get the draft to the bank."

"Were those not federal government cattle?"

Ignoring the fact that the ranchers had been reimbursed with stolen federal money, and hoping Gaines would let it be, he said, "No. They came from my county originally, and that's where the sale proceeds are going back to. I've learned that federal agents are not allowed to enjoy the proceeds of rewards. For the counties, though, it's largely reward money, or the sale of impounded horses, saddles, and such, that finance the lawmen and the judges and courts. Sparsely settled counties such as the one I represent can't possibly raise enough money to support those services from taxes alone. We need another source of income. Rewards on captured criminals and their possessions has proven to be that source."

After another glance between Block and this sheriff, the man said, "Go home, Sheriff. Go home. Rest. Be well. And thanks for all you've done."

Rory wasn't at all sure the subject of captured cattle was ended but, not wishing to prolong his departure, said, "Thank you, Mr. Gaines."

～

As Rory prepared to leave, he shook hands with Gaines and then turned to Block. With the discussion of rewards now behind them, the two men grinned at each other as they shook. They said nothing. It had all been said on the trail as Block had hovered between life and death.

Block thought of the bank draft in his pocket, the one Rory had slipped to him earlier, whispering, "This is just between you and me," he knew there was no need to mention to Gaines that neither man saw a problem with sharing with a fellow worker. That was different from collecting a reward.

～

Leaving the federal office, Rory walked directly to the bank and asked for Hebert Tremblay, the bank president. Within a few minutes, he was sitting in the president's office explaining the rather large bank draft he had laid on the desk. Tremblay listened with rapt attention, fascinated by the experiences of this young sheriff. When the tale of the returned cattle ended, Tremblay said, "So, what do you wish to do with this draft?"

"I want it to be on deposit somewhere safe where I, or the county I work for, can draw on it when necessary. I'm not sure I can really sign for the county. I'm only the sheriff. Perhaps it could be in my personal account. I could keep track of which portion of the account the money is drawn from. Or can it be in a new account in my name as the sheriff of the county? I'll need your advice on those choices.

"I will be opening an account at Stevensville for smaller purchases and deposits. Or for drawing a bit of cash. There are several deputies, in addition to me and the judge, who will be drawing their pay from the account. Our best source of income is from rewards, impounded horses, weapons, and such. But that income is spotty and not dependable, so this larger fund will be important as a backup."

The banker was silent for a full minute, tapping his pencil on the bank draft that lay before him. Finally, he said, "I think, Sheriff, from what you've described, that you need to have an active account in your local area. But most local banks are small, and their security is not always the best. I'm thinking you might be wise to leave the larger amount here, in a separate account from yours, and keep it secure. You'll want to keep the money separate from your own account to avoid misunderstandings, if nothing else.

"We'll open the account in your name. If the managers of the county wish to have it in some other name, we can easily make the change. You can transfer funds by wire draft as you need them. Or you could deposit more here if you found you had excess from some other source."

Rory explained about the check he had written on his own account and given to Block, before saying, "I like the idea of keeping the account here, and separate. We'll open that now, with my signature, if you have time. As you said, if the county people want a different signing authority, we can change it later. But when Block's check comes in, I'd like if you would transfer enough money over to my account to cover it."

A half-hour later, Tremblay stood in the back hallway beside his assistant manager. They watched as Rory made his way through the bank and out the door, adjusting his hat as he went. The assistant asked, "Who is that? I've seen him in here before."

"That is an amazing young man. I'll tell you a story someday. And if chance allows, the next time he comes in, I'll introduce you."

RORY WALKED into the state office and said, "Good morning, Bertha. I'm happy to see you still at the job, keeping the office workers safe from the riff-raff, such as myself."

Lifting his hand from his jacket pocket, he passed her a string of small, teardrop-shaped turquoise beads, beautifully mounted in silver trim, strung on silver loops, creating a string long enough to slip over a person's head, becoming a fine necklace.

"For you to wear and enjoy anytime you wish."

As the clerk was fondling the jewelry and exclaiming over it, Oscar Cator, the state administrator, came out from his office. He was about to speak to Rory when he noticed what Bertha was holding. Wondering what Rory had been up to and what he had brought the secretary, he held his thoughts and remained quiet.

Rory had started surprising Bertha with gifts several visits ago. His first visit to the office was an unpleasant experience. Bertha, misjudging the young town marshal, had tried to block his entrance, using the busyness of the other employees as her excuse.

171

In an attempt to break down the resistance of the obviously unhappy woman, the still teenaged, beginner lawman brought gifts, like chocolate, which prompted a much-needed mellowing effect in the woman. A bit of news leaked out to other visitors, and before long, small tributes were showing up on Bertha's desk with some regularity.

Oscar could see immediately that what Rory had brought for this visit was an expensive piece of jewelry. That, alone, raised questions in his mind.

Bertha wasn't going to be able to simply add this piece to her small collection of tributes that rested on her desk and the wall beside it. There sat two empty chocolate boxes and a few other items, none of them expensive. Pinned to the wall above them was the eagle feather My Way, which the Blackfoot assistant to Ivan, Rory's deputy, had gifted her with, several months before. But to hang the necklace on the wall would be a waste of a fine piece of jewelry that needed to be worn, as well as a temptation for theft. And that was not to mention the possible questions arising from the receipt of a fine piece of jewelry.

Bertha, who had never held a piece so costly, let alone owned or worn one, sputtered a bit, but finally managed to say, "Sheriff. I don't know what to say, or think. This is absolutely beautiful. Where in the world did you get it? I hope you didn't pay as much as I believe this to be worth. Perhaps, oh I don't know. Where, actually, did you get it?"

"It's quite simple, really. I got it off a man down in Texas a few days ago. He's not going to miss it."

"Are you saying he just gave it to you?"

"Actually, what I'm saying is that he was dead. So, I'm sure he doesn't need it any longer."

Oscar watched as Bertha dropped the piece onto her desktop and sagged back into her chair. He wondered if the poor woman was going to faint. Still, he couldn't hold back a chuckle. Bertha gathered herself after a half minute. She looked at the turquoise again and then up at Rory.

"You're teasing, aren't you, Sheriff."

"No, actually, I'm not. It's my fault for not asking if he would donate the piece to you before he died, but things were moving rather quickly right at that time, and then, before I could get a word out, it was too late. So, it's yours, and don't you let its source bother you one bit. The dead man was a criminal. Not a good man. He won't be missed on this earth. You keep the piece and wear it with pleasure."

When Bertha still appeared to be unsure, Rory said, "Bertha, we are lawmen who spend our days hoping to make the country safe for you and the rest of the population. Every one of us has done things we would rather not have had to do. But that's the job. That's because we're dealing with unsavory men. And the odd unsavory woman. And yes, if you feel you need to know, I shot and killed the man who was wearing that. It's important to know that he was trying to kill me at the time. I like the outcome better this way. He was wearing that, but in his pocket, he had a couple of others. I've kept those. They were clearly stolen, and there is no way to track the original owners. To bury the piece with the man makes no sense. So, it's yours. Put the rest out of your mind and enjoy it."

Turning to Oscar, he said, "I've only just come in to pay my respects, boss. I'm anxious to get home. So, hello. And goodbye."

Oscar laughed and took Rory by the arm, saying,

"Not so fast. Come to the office and give me the story. Shorten it if you wish. You might remember that I was involved with the tarnished coin mystery as well. I need to know the ending. If indeed we are at the ending."

Taking a seat in Oscar's office, he picked up where the administrator's last comment left off.

"We won't know if we are at an end until it gets to Washington. But that's now in the hands of the federal marshals. I'm guessing the trail will lead to a very high office, but that is just speculation. And we'll find that this bit we've been dealing with is by no means the whole matter. We'll have to wait and see. But for me, I'm for getting back to where I should have been the whole time. I had no real business joining the search down to Texas, but as a favor to Block, I went along."

"I hear he was seriously wounded, so it's good you were there."

"Perhaps. But the Federals are not short of men. Any number of marshals could have ridden south."

"But then Bertha wouldn't have that string of turquoise," Oscar said that with a grin.

Rory, somewhat concerned by Bertha's reaction, said, "It was a bit messed up when I lifted it off the fella's neck. I believe I washed all the blood off."

"I won't tell her that part, Rory."

"Good decision."

Over the next half hour, the two men filled each other in with the happenings of the past few weeks. Only then would Oscar agree to allow Rory to leave for home with just one final question, "Where in the world did you find that shirt?"

~

RORY RODE FOR HOME, leaving it to Block to post the brands on the stolen horses in the newspaper with instructions to the livery man to sell the animals if no one came forward with a claim after three weeks. Rory himself toted the impounded rifles to the gun shop and sold them. The gun belts and pistols he kept. He would hang them with his growing collection back at the marshal's office at the fort.

28

THREE DAYS LATER, RORY RODE INTO STEVENSVILLE TO A greeting from Ivan and Key. And then another greeting from the midafternoon coffee crowd in Ma Gamble's dining room. The questions flew one by one from the curious, but Rory offered no information beyond "Done and done." The answer satisfied no one, but he offered nothing more.

He swung into the saddle, intent on spending a night in his own cabin on the Double J Ranch. He was in time to meet Hannah on the trail north. This cousin of his who had so enraptured Wiley Hamstead, the man who had accompanied her on the train from the eastern school she had been attending, and who was now the town marshal at the fort, was teaching school in Stevensville. The school day was ended, and she was riding home to the ranch.

"Welcome home, cousin."

"How goes the school teaching, cousin?"

"Struggling. Spring is in the air and in the minds of all the students, most of all, the older ones. They're staring at their readers, but I know their mind's eyes are looking between the ears of their horses, or they're shooting down bad guys and saving the fair maidens, not having any idea what that life is really like."

"Is it that bad?"

"Worse. And worse still, since those ridiculous penny dreadful magazines started popping up all over the territory. Boys and girls alike, sometimes small groups with their heads almost touching, hover over them before hiding them in their desks, as if I didn't know what was going on. And it's even worse that so many of the stories are of your exploits. You, a man most of the students know, at least a little bit, and all know by sight. Life would have been so much easier if you were back on the Double J raising whiteface beef."

"It's not as if I write the stories or make anything from them."

"I know and I'm mostly just teasing. In a way, I sympathize with the young fellows. I've read a couple of the tales and the writer sure makes your life sound interesting. And to top it off, in the last issue, there was a song all written out, melody notes and all. They didn't get the tune quite right, but that hasn't stopped some of the students from singing about 'Sheriff Rory,' morning, noon and night."

"I don't think I want to hear that song. And what you called an interesting life could have several meanings wrapped into it."

"Yes, indeed."

Rory let the verbal silence and the steady clopping of the horse's hooves on the hard-packed trail put an end to the discussion. When he felt he could move on, he asked, "Is it fair to ask how you and Wiley are getting along?"

"Fair, I suppose, but hopeless if you're depending on

me for information, since everyone seems to have more knowledge of the matter than I have."

RORY'S WELCOME BACK to the Double J was as it always had been. Everyone was glad to see him returned in one piece, not having suffered any disasters in his sheriff's duties. His recent experience with a bullet having taken a chunk of flesh and slivers of bone from his shoulder, was about all the wounding any of the family wanted to see. He stayed one night only before riding the rest of the distance to the fort.

During dinner, the family had worked the visiting around to a discussion about the ranch itself. Rory had previously offered to sell his half to the family, and they had accepted. The only matters to discuss were the arrangements for the final payment and the two Double J horses Rory had fallen in love with.

Blood-red bay horses were bred on the ranch, a practice that went back to the time when Rory's father had purchased the first pregnant mare. Since there were two or three foals born each spring, Rory's Uncle George had settled the discussion with, "We're not short of animals. In fact, we're having trouble finding enough time to properly break and train the young ones. Take the two you ride now, and one of the yearlings. Training a new gelding will give you something to take your mind off other things."

With that settled, the matter of payment for the ranch consisted of nothing more than, "When you get it put together, write a check and give it to Jesse Ambrewster, down at the bank. He'll deposit it, and we'll call it a done deal. I wish you good fortune on the ranch. I'll miss it, but this is the right thing to do. And I hope I can still throw my bedroll out here from time to time."

From the moment Rory had ridden onto the Double J Ranch, the dog had not left his side. There was no explaining why the animal, a beautiful big dog folks were calling shepherds, had so attached himself to the sheriff, but the truth was evident. Rory had rescued the half-starved animal when he found Kiril, the mysterious recluse bachelor, dead on his own porch. It was as if the dog was intent on thanking him for the remainder of his life.

As Rory was saddling his gelding for the ride to the fort, George said, "Be a kindness if you were to take the dog along. We've named him Scout, but I don't imagine he'd mind too much if you changed that."

Rory scratched the animal behind the ears and said, as if the dog could understand, "Is that what you want there, Scout? Do you want to come with me?"

The dog gave a half bark and turned quickly in two circles before licking Rory's hand. George laughed. "Well, you asked."

RORY RODE into the fort midmorning the next day, riding straight to the marshal's office. The dog trotted beside him. The chairs on the boardwalk in front of the office were empty, telling Rory that the marshal and deputy sheriff were busy with something. Or they had let the chill in the air drive them inside, closer to the stove and the coffeepot. He swung down and tied off at the rail, then stepped to the door. At the click of the doorknob turning, the men inside placed their hands on their Colts, waiting to see who would block the weak, cloud-filtered sunlight as they entered. At the sight of the familiar face, they relaxed and, almost together, said, "Welcome home, Sheriff."

Rory stepped inside and went directly to the woodstove, which had a low fire burning and a pot of coffee steaming on the top. A two-hour ride first thing in the morning was sure to wake a person up and replace his bed warmth with a late spring chill. He rubbed his hands together over the top of the stove and then poured himself a cup. Only then did he turn to the men. "Morn'n, fellas. That heat feels good. I'm seeing an empty cell, and nothing particular happening in here. Can I take that to mean that everything is under control?"

The dog had curled into a comfortable position where he would have to move for the door to open.

With a smile, Marshal Wiley said, "Under control could stand some refining as to its meaning. But I'm prepared to say that so far today we are reasonably sure there are no bad guys skulking around and no damsels in distress. Of course, it's a big county, so who knows what's happening out there?"

He said that with a wave of his arm, as if to take in the land in every direction.

It never took Rory long to get to the business of the day. Any talk of small, unimportant matters was soon pushed aside.

"I'm pleased to hear things are well in town, and to support what you said, Wiley, I am concerned about the great 'out there.' I'm especially concerned about the gold country. We have one man alone up there. That country might still be snowed in this time of year but I'm thinking I may still have to give it a go. Try to make it up there. But the thought of those snow-covered hills could almost make me wish I was back in Texas. It's not a pretty country down there; very nearly flat. Windy, but warm."

Cap Graham, who had been alone in the district as deputy sheriff since Rory had ridden south, asked, "And how was Texas? Find your man?"

"Found and dealt with."

Cap asked no more, knowing that if the sheriff had wanted to say more, he would have done so. Having been a sheriff himself for many years, Cap knew that some experiences were best not relived.

Rory turned the last free chair in the little office around so he could lean his elbows, and occasionally his coffee mug, on the back. Looking from one man to the other, he asked, "Any excitement at all since I left?"

Wiley answered before Cap could get a word in. Wiley, more educated and better with words, enjoyed using effective vocabulary when telling—or even amplifying—a story, said, "As town marshal, I've had to put a couple of drunks away for the night to keep the peace, but none of that amounted to anything. The big news might be that we have a couple of new citizens. Young. But I'm still considering them as citizens."

Wondering why Wiley had stopped at that point, Rory waited, but not for long. He studied the grinning marshal while he could have completed a slow count of ten before saying, "You'd best complete the story, or I'll have to get on to something else. There must be something I need to be doing."

Cap rose from his chair, rinsed his coffee mug in the bucket of water placed on the stove to be kept warm for that purpose, swung his heavy coat over his shoulders after pushing his arms into the sleeves, and left the office. Both men silently watched the door close. Rory's question, spoken only from his eyes, could not have been any more clear if he had shouted it from the rooftop. Wiley couldn't miss it. He dropped his grin just enough to allow him to speak clearly.

"It's undoubtedly Cap's story to tell, but you can see he's a little reluctant. So here it is. Cap's got a soft side that he works hard to disguise. The softness is well hidden inside a tough shell, made up of firm opinion and rightness. But you dig down some, and the gentleness shows through.

"The softness saved two kids. And stopped the abuse on a harness team. The hardness cost a stage whip his job and near enough his life."

Rory, without looking, reached behind himself and dropped his now empty coffee mug into the bucket. He would tend to it later. With his arms folded on the back of the chair, he practically pinned Wiley to the wall with the intensity of his look. Wiley dropped his grin again and said, "The thing is. What happened is. Cap was just coming from the dining room when the stage pulled in, hours late from fighting snow and wind. Cold. I'll say it was cold. Cold and dark. Whip probably should have stopped out at the stage barns, but it was Tobacco Pete riding the box on that run. You'll remember Pete. He's not the brightest star in the sky. He's known to be hard on horses, stage rolling stock, and passengers too. His one determination appears to be to do his job well, by his own definition.

"Those days are now over for Pete. At least on this particular stage line. I have no idea where he is, but wherever he's hung his hat, he's looking for a job.

"When Pete rolled in that evening, it was bitter cold. The run was late by a considerable amount. The horses were frothing from being pushed hard on a long run, their breath turning to frosty mist and wrapping itself around their heads. Pete himself was suffering with the cold. The old fool pulled the team to a sliding stop, and without waiting for everything to settle down, he stepped onto the wheel rim and then dropped to the road, then to his knees, as if the cold had taken the strength from his legs. He struggled back to his feet and, never bothering to open the stage door, he went around to the boot and pulled out the mail sack. He dropped it on the boardwalk for someone else to carry in and started to climb back to the box. I'm guessing he was in a hurry to return to the barn and finish his day.

"Cap, he hollers up at Pete, 'No passengers?'

"Pete said nothing, but he pointed his thumb toward the door and picked up the reins. Cap reached out, turned the door handle and looked inside. With a roar, he backed out and stepped onto the front wheel hub. From there, he reached up and grabbed Pete's coat, and pulled him right off the box. Cap was roaring in anger and Pete, terrified, was screaming in fear. Fear of Cap, and fear of the drop to the road. Once over the edge of the rig, Cap released his grip, and let gravity take Pete to the ground. Pete was hurt, and still crying out in anger and surprise, but Cap picked him up by the collar and the seat of his pants, backed away a bit to give him room to swing his arms, and threw him against the stage. It all happened so fast that none of us could have done anything. Cap then opened the door again and stepped inside. That's when he called for help. I moved into the doorway to see what had so upset your deputy. A couple of others gathered close.

"There, inside the stage, lying across two of the seats, were a couple of blanket-wrapped kids. Sleeping through all the turmoil, or unconscious, I couldn't tell which. What Pete's plan for them was we've never been able to sort out. The kids were beyond knowing; they were that cold. Cap picked up the closest one and gently passed, what turned out to be a boy of about fourteen to me. 'Take him inside, and get him warmed up,' he instructed, which I would have done anyway, without being told. He then passed the second child out, which turned out to be the boy's sister, a girl of about twelve.

"Cap climbed out of the rig, picked Pete up again, threw him inside and slammed the door shut. There was a horse tied to the rail right there. I've no idea whose horse it was, but Cap he led him over and tied him to the back of the stage. Then he climbed to the seat and got the rig moving. Turned it around and drove it slowly, to save the horses, out to the barns. He came back riding the strange horse. He retied the animal and came inside the dining room.

"We had the kids coats off by that time and were trying to rub some warmth back into their hands so they could hold a soup spoon. Amber warmed up some beef soup and made tea. It seemed half the town was there hoping to help, or at least find out the story. The kids were so cold they couldn't speak, but eventually, between the blankets Amber had warmed in her big oven and the soup and tea; they started to take on life again.

"Cap never did say what happened out at the barns, and I haven't asked, but we've seen nothing at all of Pete since."

Rory asked, "So how did it end?"

"Now, that's the fun part of the story. Cap adopted those kids. What I mean, of course, is he took them under his wing. Bought them clothes. Got them into school. Bought them a horse and saddle each, so they could ride to school. Paid with his own money. Taking care of them, and they look great. Healthy, smiling and all, but with a sad story behind them that you'll want to hear."

"Where are they living?"

"Did I forget to tell you that?" Wiley's grin kept getting wider. "They're living with Cap in that house of yours. Out where your new house is being built. Got a regular family out there. Dealt with a neighbor for some chickens. Talking about getting a milk cow. Come shopping to the mercantile together. Ride to church together. It's a sight to see."

ANY FURTHER QUESTIONS Rory had were pushed aside when the office door opened against the dog, and Julia Gridley poked her head inside. She could go no further. Scout growled a bit, but he moved at Rory's instruction. After a quick study of the girl, the animal must have felt she was alright. He wouldn't let her into the office until she scratched behind his ears and spoke to him.

Rory leaped from his chair with a smile and said, "Julia. It's good to see you. I just got in an hour ago. I was hoping to find time to ride out in the next few days."

"Well, now you don't have to. I'm living in town. I thought it all through and decided that it made no sense to be living on the ranch when the contractor is building my new home here in town. A girl never can tell when the builder might need some advice."

Rory didn't miss that comment about his new house being her new home. But Julia kept on with the short story, saying, "So I came in. Took a room at the boardinghouse, and a job with Mr. Sales, the gunsmith and saddlemaker. He needed someone to keep the place

185

orderly and deal with customers, so he could stay at his work bench. I'm enjoying it. I've already cleaned the place up, sold three pistols, a saddle gun and an old saddle." Grinning widely, she added, "Mr. Sales, he couldn't do without me."

Rory wasn't sure where to take the conversation from that point. There were two reasons. The first was that Wiley continued to hold down the chair behind his desk, and the sheriff rather felt the conversation should be private. That the marshal was listening was evident from the way he raised his eyebrows at the mention of 'my new home.'

The second reason was that he felt the need to get on top of other matters, sheriff's matters, that had, or were, happening in the county and at the fort itself.

"As fine as it is to see you, Julia, there are a couple of things that are needing my attention now. I wonder if we could meet for dinner at the dining room at around six this evening. That way, we can visit as long as we wish."

Smiling, Julia replied, "We can certainly do that, and if this lovelorn sheriff will go home, we could come here for our private visit."

Wiley ventured into the conversation to say, "But this is my home, as well as my workplace. That lonely bunk in the back room is all that separates me from the cold, cold nights."

Julia dug up her most taunting voice, and returned, "Oh my, you poor boy. I'll bet you'd feel better with a bit of tenderness and a good meal. Why don't you ride down to the Double J for a visit with Hannah? I'm sure you two could find something to talk about, and it's only a short ride. Your loneliness will disappear at the very sight of the girl."

Not to be outdone in the inflections of voice, Wiley

whined, "But it's a full two-hour ride, and it's cold outside. And I'd be all alone on that road. There's no telling what calamity might befall a young innocent fella. And what if we should have an emergency here in town while I was gone? The town would hold me responsible, and I'd run the risk of losing my job."

This was all said in good nature as the two were teasing each other.

Rory, who seldom managed to allow his lighter side to break through, said, "I'm sure I could handle anything that came up, Wiley. And you could probably outrun any surprises that met you on the road. If you left midafternoon, you could get there in time for dinner. If anyone asks for you, I'll make up some kind of excuse. And Hannah said just last evening how much she was longing to see you again."

Wiley broke right out in laughter. "Sheriff, that last part is an outright fabrication. I'm ashamed of you. I may never regain my trust in your stories."

Smiling, Rory took Julia by the elbow and turned her to the door.

"Come, I'll walk you back to the saddle shop."

AFTER RETURNING Julia to her job, he spoke to Mr. Sales for a few minutes, although the saddlemaker showed by his actions that he wasn't fond of being distracted from his work. He took the hint and left the small shop.

Cap showed up at that time with something clearly on his mind. Rory had been intent on taking a walk around town, maybe talking with a few folks, but clearly, Cap had something he wished to discuss.

The two men took their seats, with Cap wiping his

face with his callused and wind-chapped hand. He held his eyes on Rory as he said, "Couple of killings while you were gone."

Having gained the sheriff's full attention, Cap told the story of the Bat Kelly and Reef Malkin killings. With Cap's tendency to limit the telling to a brief outline, the story had soon been laid before the sheriff.

Rory listened carefully before saying, "It sounds as if you did all that could be done. I'll think it over, and we'll talk again."

He had a couple of questions on his mind as he stepped into the saddle and rode the short distance to where the builder was constructing his new home. As he neared the site, he pulled the gelding to a stop to give him time to admire, again, the slight rise of land that lifted his home above most of the surrounding country, except to the west, where the succession of ridges eventually became the Front Range of the Rockies. The slightly raised area gave him an open view to the east, taking in the growing village and the many miles of open country beyond, right to the hazy horizon. To the north were forested hills, rising in staggered lifts until his view faded, melding into the forested horizon and misty, spring sky. He was familiar with the magnificence of the mountains to the west. He had ridden through a good part of them, lost more times than he wished to remember.

To the north, just a bit, the river cut a path through the area, and right up into the rocks of the rugged mountains, forcing its way into hidden curves and crannies of rock, where few had ever ventured. Where the river's foaming, churning flow began before making its way east, Rory had seen only a slight portion. But he remembered how welcoming that portion and its sloping banks had been when he finally found his way out of the forested uplands. There were other water flows making their way toward the semi-parched grasslands to the east, but none so big as the one that guided Rory out of the hills the previous summer.

To the south were more staggered hills, and folds in the gentle slopes that eased into the mountains. There were several homes and small farms sprouting up in the area. Some had experimented with fruit trees of various types, meeting with surprising success.

And right there, just a few feet from where his new home was rising from the ground, sat the wooden shelter that the previous owner of this land had put together, just a few years before. A shelter of no particular design or beauty but adequate to hold back the rains of summer and the periodic miserable days of winter. In keeping with the needs of a young family, the building contained three small bedrooms and a large kitchen with a sitting room, all in one. The kitchen cookstove was the only source of heat.

Rory had expected to make do in the place until the new building was built. But now, if Wiley's story proved to be true, and he had no reason to doubt it, Cap and the two young folks had taken up residence there. He and Cap had agreed, before the Texas trip, that the two of them could make do until the new brick and sandstone-trimmed structure was ready for occupancy. But there had been no discussion of adding two growing young people.

Thinking it through on the information he had, Rory decided that a night or two at the hotel wouldn't make any significant dent in his bank balance. He would do that until he and Cap could figure it out.

Happy with all his eyes could take in, he was more

than satisfied with his choice of location for the house. He nudged the gelding with his heels and was soon riding into the yard. Sticks Willoughby, the contractor, stepped from behind a half-unloaded wagon of bricks, hollering, "Sheriff! Welcome home."

Pointing back to where he had just come from, Willoughby hollered, "What do ya think of 'er? If that's not as pretty as a day-old calf, I'll eat my hat. Walls are all up. Roof is on, all but the shingles. The boys are just fitting out the brick and sandstone window trim. Cupboards are in, and most of the flooring. Got some doors to hang."

"You've made good time, Sticks. I know nothing at all about building, but it looks good to me. Is it too soon to ask about completion?"

"I'd be shocked if you didn't ask. And yes, it is too soon for a definite answer, but it's going well. You can see the boys are unloading a final wagonload of bricks, fresh from the kiln. You can still feel the warmth in them. Another bunch are cutting and shaping the sandstone for the trim. Oh, she'll be a beauty; you just wait and see."

Stepping off the gelding and tying it out of the way, Rory hollered over the noise of the workers. "Can you walk me through? Show me how the plans you and I put together turned out?"

"Sure as you're born, Sheriff. Come on in. Bring your imagination with you."

The only question Rory had for the builder was about a change from the original drawing the two men had made together. The back wall had been pushed out several feet on one side, and a room inserted between two bedrooms. At the question, Sticks Willoughby smiled and answered, "Why, that's the space for the bathtub. Your young lady insisted that be included. We've worked a pipe below the floor to drain the thing. She also mentioned something called a water closet. Since I know nothing at all about it, you'll have to sort that out between the two of you.

AN HOUR LATER, trying to get his mind to cope with the concept of a bathtub and a water closet right inside the house, Rory left the builder to his work. He was content with the plan and the progress and was anxious for the completion. He embarrassed himself by thinking of sharing the place with Julia, but he tamped his imagination down and concentrated on his next task.

29

RORY'S NEW HOME SITE TO THE SMALL DAIRY HOLDING OF Rad Harbinger was less than a half-hour ride. He trusted Cap to have done what he thought was right in the case, but ultimately it was not Cap that would answer to the electors. Rory had no intention of causing more trauma than the families involved had already experienced, but he still had questions. He would try to ask them gently.

As he neared the place, Harbinger, and what he supposed was his teenage son, were standing in the barn doorway watching him. With a simple wave, Rory rode up the side of a fenced field of fruit trees toward the house.

Still a little distance from the yard, but looking through the six-foot-high deer fence, Rory said, "Morn'n, folks. Rory Jamison. County Sheriff. Need to have a few minutes with you all if you can put your work aside for just a bit."

Seemingly resigned to the visit, as if he knew the sheriff would eventually arrive at their door, Harbinger quietly said, "Ride on up to the house and come in."

The three men met and shook hands at the yard gate.

"Rad Harbinger, Sheriff. This is my son, Tappen. Prefers to be called Tap."

"Rory Jamison. Pleased to meet you both. I'll not take much of your time."

Nearing the small porch, Rory saw the door swinging open and an apron-clad lady standing there tall and proud, as if guarding the entrance to her personal castle. He could see no sign of back up on the severe, but otherwise pleasant face.

"My wife, Sheriff. Kimberly. Goes mostly by Kim."

"Good morning, Mrs. Harbinger. Rory Jamison, sheriff."

Kim Harbinger looked troubled by the sheriff's visit but, pushing the upsetting thoughts aside, with confidence in her voice, she took a step back and invited them all to enter. As the two men bent to remove their barn boots, Rory said, "Actually, Rad, if you don't mind, I'd like to talk with your wife alone."

Harbinger expressed his doubts by the look on his face, but he could hardly refuse, considering all that had happened. Two men had recently been shot to death in this very yard. That fact was not likely to disappear without more questions. Turning to the three steps leading down to the garden path, he said, "I'll be at my work when you need me."

Rory wiped his already clean riding boots on the mat and stepped inside. Kim Harbinger was slowly backing away, giving more than adequate room for the sheriff to enter, determined to face whatever came with poise and dignity.

She was a tall lady, perhaps even taller than her husband, but slim from the constant work, and attractive, with long, light red hair pulled together at the back of her head and held in place by a twist of red ribbon. Idly, Rory wondered what impact the killing had dealt to this lady.

"Would you like a cup of coffee, Sheriff?"

Rory had already taken his fill of coffee for one morning, but on the chance that it may ease the conversation, he said, "That sounds welcome on a chilly morning. Thank you."

Kim Harbinger poured the coffee, and the two took seats on opposite sides of the kitchen table. As bad as Rory felt for being the cause of the troubled look in the woman's eyes, he had a job to do, and he intended to do it.

Rory couldn't know it, but the lady was thinking, *This man isn't much older than my son.*

"Mrs. Harbinger, I'm sure you were told that I was away for a while on another matter, when an unfortunate incident was pressed upon you. I have just returned this morning. I had only a few minutes with Deputy Cap Graham and didn't know the whole story of the trouble. I'd appreciate it if you would tell me what happened and what part you played in it."

Haltingly at first, concerned that she would say something that would reflect poorly on her actions, and those of her husband and son, she spoke quietly, but finally told the essence of the matter, leaving out no detail that she thought important.

"If I have this right, Mrs. Harbinger, what you're saying is that you shot the hired man, and your husband shot the rancher himself. This was after the rancher demanded that you get off this land, as he intended to take it for himself. Do I have that correct?"

"You have that absolutely correct."

That statement seemed to say it all, as if no further

questions needed to be asked. And it led to a silence that lasted long enough to allow the statement to settle in Rory's mind. Then, with a fierce determination that had been somewhat hidden before, more words blossomed forth from the farmer's wife.

"Sheriff. I did that shooting. I did indeed. Did it with that double-twelve gauge you see on the pegs above the door. That poor excuse for a man was lifting his carbine to take aim at me. Going to shoot me right here in my own doorway. I had no doubt he would shoot a woman, or my son for that matter. I had no choice. I was protecting my men and myself. And our farm that we have worked powerfully hard to build. If you want to know if I'd do it again, my answer would be yes, absolutely. Only I may not wait so long. I thought since, that I should have shot him just as soon as I understood their intent, before he had a chance to lift the rifle."

Her voice was rising, becoming stronger, as the words came out. As she listened to her own telling, all her doubts were removed. Her family had been threatened, and she did what had to be done. She had told the story just that way. It was as if she had spoken the truth and would now stand with that truth.

A further stiffness straightened her spine, a stiffness that lifted her out of her resigned posture when she first sat down. Where she had held her eyes on the tabletop earlier, she was now holding a firm look on the man facing her. She raised her head as she spoke, showing no hesitation or doubt. Rory was left with no indecision about her story, or her determination.

Rory had previously heard the expression "fire in the eyes." Now he was looking at an example of that. Grinning inwardly, he thought, *This is a woman to stand proudly beside her man. A woman much needed in this new land.* She reminded him a lot of his mother, or what he could remember of her. Proud in a good way. Determined. Right in her actions and backing down from no one. The remembrance of Julia standing off the raider at her ranch home also flitted quickly through Rory's mind.

"Thank you, Mrs. Harbinger. I'll be going now. It's a small town. I'm sure we'll be seeing more of each other from time to time."

He rose and lifted his hat off the chair beside him. He wouldn't put it on until he was outside. Leaving the untouched coffee right where it had sat throughout the interview, he stepped toward the door. Kim Harbinger's voice stopped him.

"I understand we are to be near neighbors, Sheriff. I'm told the new house going up to the north is yours."

"Yes. I have just come from there. The builders are moving along, and it shouldn't be too long until I can move in. Not that I own anything that needs moving. But you know what I mean."

"I do know, Sheriff. And if the young lady who stopped by here one evening last week just to, as she said, meet her future neighbors, is as determined as she appears to be, you won't be moving in alone."

There might have been a bit of a smile on her face as she spoke. Julia had obviously not bothered telling her that the critical question had not really been asked or answered yet. There was yet no proposal or planning, except that which was clearly taking place individually and separately, in the minds of the two young people, with Julia clearly taking the lead.

Rory talked to the farmer and his son separately and could find no variance in their stories. Still, in the next few days, he would have to find time to ride out to the

Kelly ranch for a talk with the widow. And with Micah Wardle, if he was still out there.

~

He ARRIVED BACK at the office in time for a late lunch and decided to visit the cantina at the southern edge of town. Cap Graham was in the office. Rory talked him into riding along. They rode in silence, finding it difficult to talk over a sudden gusting and swirling wind that had just come up. Looking all around, holding his hat firmly with one hand, Rory finally leaned toward his deputy and, speaking more loudly than he usually did, said, "If those clouds don't develop into a storm, I'll be surprised."

Showing no particular concern but still conscious of the building storm heads over the mountains, the deputy answered, "So long as it's rain. I've got short-term patience for snow."

"Any snow falling now will be gone by morning."

~

WITH THEIR PLATES of beans and tortillas in front of them, along with a bit of carved chicken—and a side dish holding three small green chilis, a few yellow samples, and one red and wrinkled—the men dug in.

"I've just come from the Harbinger farm. I was out looking at my new place. It's only a short ride to the Harbingers'. Talked with each of them separately. Since there were no witnesses to the action, we only have their word on it. I have no reason to doubt their story, but I'd like to hear what they told you."

Cap was slowly chewing his way through a bitten-off

half of a green chili, chosen from those on offer. As he thought of an answer for Rory, he held the remaining half of the chili in his fingers, held aloft with his bent elbow on the table, as to have the pepper ready for the next bite. He had found on previous occasions that he enjoyed the challenge of the mild green fruit, and not understanding that not all green chilis are born equal, he had picked one at random, based solely on color. As Rory studied his changing facial expressions, he had to break into a smile.

Cap's eyelids were raised almost in horror at what his mouth and taste buds were experiencing. Further antagonizing his already pained eyes was the sweat sprouting from his forehead, dripping onto his nose, while some slithered into his eyes. His nose was flared, as if he was trying to bring in cool air, while at the same time eliminating the thundering heat from the green monster. Rory thought he heard the deputy gasp once as his lips cracked open, trying for more air.

Rory slid his water glass in front of the suffering man. Cap had already drained his own.

"Take your time, Cap. We've got all afternoon."

Cap missed the humor in Rory's words while he took a frantic two-handed grip on the table's edge. The second half of the chili was dropped, long forgotten. Loosening one hand, he reached for the water glass. He took a long drag of water and looked for more, but the only water glasses in sight were empty. He glanced frantically around the small cantina. There were no spittoons, and to make a sudden dash for the door seemed too out of place and demeaning, too damaging to his remaining dignity for Cap to accept.

He tried to swallow the offending chili along with the liquid but was only partially successful. A gulp of beer from a glass placed there by a man sitting at the next table, put an end to the mass in his mouth, but not to the pain that had now migrated to his throat and stomach. The burning on the roof of his mouth was slowly dissipating. With eyes closed and his nostrils still flaring, his sinuses burning and draining, all at the same time, along with a grim determination to not cry out, the older man laid his elbows on the table and sagged onto them. Finally, with a belch that lifted the deputy's shoulders, Rory was sure the long, drawn-out explosion of air could be heard outside the cantina, as the foulness od the deputy's breath wafted across the table. Rory took one whiff and started waving his hat in front of his face. The four Mexicans at the next table were laughing, and enjoying the spectacle. Finally, Cap took a huge breath to replace what he had lost in the belch, leaned back, and looked at the Mexicans. He could barely speak, but while wiping his eyes and cheeks with the sleeves of his shirt, he managed to say, "I always thought the green ones were not so hot."

"Sí, señor. Sometimes that is so. But also, sometimes, not so. You picked a very bad hombre. I think Carlos, he give you that for to laugh. Carlos, he is a good cook, but sometimes he make the trouble. For next time I tell you. Water not much help. Sugar help."

"I'm hoping there will never be another time."

The men laughed again. This time Cap joined them, winning their respect.

When everyone had settled back down, Rory said, "I believe I was asking you about the Rad Harbinger killings."

Over their food, ignoring the rest of the chilis on the side plate, Cap repeated his talks with each of the Harbinger family members. By practice as well as by nature, he kept to the short version without leaving out important details. He continued wiping his eyes. When he was finished, he asked, "Does that match with what you heard from them?"

"Almost word for word. The only addition was Mrs. Harbinger saying she would do it again if need be. Now tell me about your visit to the Kelly spread."

THE SKIES WERE OPENING JUST as the two lawmen arrived at the office after leaving their mounts at the livery. They quickly huddled under the boardwalk overhang and watched as the rain bounced off the road after making small indentations in the dried-out dirt. The steady wind pushed the rain sideways enough that they were feeling the slight flicker of tiny pellets on the exposed skin of their hands and faces. Turning on his heel, Rory opened the office door, pushed the dog out of the way, and entered.

Rory would spend the afternoon going over posters and mail received while he was away. He also wanted to hear the story of the two kids. He dug into the mail first. There were only four envelopes. The first to come into Rory's hands was an advertisement for "unbreakable handcuffs." Although the federal marshals had provided him with four pairs, he set the advertisement aside, thinking about his deputies. By all logic, they needed the cuffs as much as the sheriff did. He would get back to it after some more important matters were dealt with.

The second envelope proved to be holding a bank draft for five hundred dollars. With raised eyebrows, he turned the document so it would pick up the dim, rain-filtered light streaming into the window. He needed to see what bank from which it was drawn. It looked like what was probably a small bank in a town Rory had never heard of. The enclosed letter was addressed to Sheriff Rory Jamison.

Thank you for your part in ridding the nation of Mr. Sly Loughty. I suspect there are still people in our town who lose sleep over the remembrance of this man and the deprivations he visited upon us. We will rest easier now, knowing he will not be returning. The enclosed is sent with our thanks and our good wishes for you and your work.

It was signed by the sheriff.

Racking his memory again, Rory still couldn't remember hearing of any town by that name. He turned the letter and the bank draft over to Cap.

"You ever heard of this town, Cap?"

The answer from Cap was long in coming. The deputy held the letter in one hand and the draft in the other, casting his eyes between them. As so often happened, Rory could see the man's lips moving slightly as he thought his private thoughts. The long delay in answering caused Rory to think there was something personal happening. Something special. Finally, Cap spoke, although he did not raise his head or make eye contact with the sheriff.

"My town. Where my ranch is. And the graves of my family. This sheriff was my deputy. Good man. I'm happy he got the job."

Rory studied the man and waited. When nothing more was said, Rory reached for the two documents. As he folded the letter back into the envelope, he said, "Might be best to leave closed doors closed."

"Some doors never close."

Rory's mind was suddenly dragged back to the murder of his own father, conscious of how often that remembrance flashed through his mind, mostly unbidden, and he felt some of what Cap must be feeling at the mention of his old home country.

"You've never said anything righter than that, Cap. Sorry. I wasn't thinking."

Rory opened the other two envelopes and found bank drafts in each. One was for a lesser amount and one for considerably more than the five hundred from Cap's old hometown. He set them all aside. He would have to discuss the matter with Wiley, whose appointment as marshal was from the town. Perhaps there should be some negotiated split in the reward money between town and county. He would hold the drafts until later. He still hadn't done the planned banking after his trip to Texas. He would attend to the matter as soon as he could get back down to Stevensville.

By midafternoon the town and all its surroundings were saturated and chilled by the heavy storm. Cap and Rory had been hanging around the marshal's office after lunch, but Cap was restless. Pacing the small space, he paused at the window. Looking across the road, toward the hotel, he saw the two rescued young people riding their horses toward the side street that would take them out to the house. Absently, he remarked, "School must have let out early."

Still reading a newspaper that had been left in the office, Rory said, "Why do you say that?"

"Kids are out and on their way home."

"Are you talking about the kids you've taken under your wing?"

"The very same."

"Are they gone, or can you call them over here?"

Without replying, Cap stepped onto the covered walkway in front of the office.

"Yo! Peter."

When the boy turned his head toward the shout, Cap waved them over. When they eased up to the rail, hands on their hats and their chins stuffed into their coat tops, Cap stepped into the rain and tied their horses.

"Get down and come in. You need to meet someone."

The kids did as they were told after first throwing their rain slickers over their saddles to keep them dry. Emmalou couldn't quite reach the saddle, but her brother completed the task before they both ran for shelter. Entering the warm space, Cap said, "Peter, Emmalou, you need to meet Sheriff Rory Jamison. I've told him just a bit about you, but I'm sure he'd like to hear the story directly from you."

Rory stood. Smiling and holding out his hand to the kids, he said, "I'm pleased to meet you both. Come in and have a seat."

When the kids first entered the small office, Scout, who had been sleeping the afternoon away and enjoying the warmth of the wood heater, immediately came to his feet with a small growl. Rory had settled him down with a wave of his hand and a quiet word.

The kids made a fuss over the dog, much to Scout's approval.

Cap stepped into Wiley's private sleeping space and dragged another chair out. Leaving the conversation to Rory, Cap took his seat and remained silent.

Rory had little experience dealing with kids. Looking from one to the other, he saw a timidity in their eyes, as if they were terrified of being in front of the sheriff. Then it came to him that Peter was about the age he was himself when he had lost his mother and sister, and he and his father had set out for the goldfields of Idaho. *Could I possibly have been that young? Or that scared?*

"It's Peter, is it? And Emmalou? I'll remember those names now. By the sound of things, you two have been through some trouble. I'm sorry about that. You're young to have to face up to things that are normally left to the adults. But, it's good you have Cap to care for you and a roof over your heads. But I would like to hear your story. How did you come to be on that stage? Where are you from? Where are your parents? Those sorts of things."

When neither kid spoke, Cap said, "You can trust the sheriff, kids. Tell him your story. I know he'll help you if he possibly can."

Emmalou offered nothing, but her brother quietly said, "Ain't got no parents. Not no more. Don't know what happened to them. Just all of a sudden, they was gone and we was dragged off to what was being called an orphanage. Run by a woman named Gulch. Her and some man. I don't know what his name was, nor who he was. Not her husband, I don't think. He mostly never spoke. Just did what she told him to do. Walked around with a leather switch stuffed into his back pocket. He loved to pull it out and threaten all the kids with it."

"And did he ever beat you with it?"

"He beat all the kids. Seems like he was watching for reasons."

"How many kids were in this orphanage?"

"Eight, counting us and the other two who were bought by the same man who bought us. We four were the oldest. The rest were quite a bit younger. Mrs. Gulch, she wanted rid of us because there were some more younger kids being wagoned in from somewhere away from town. She said we older ones were a nuisance, and we ate too much."

Rory was taking notes. He had picked up on the word *sold*, underlining it on the paper. Troubled by the thought, he said, "What do you mean she sold you? You and two other boys?"

"A man came with a covered wagon. Him and a woman he said was his wife. He said that, although she didn't act like no wife. He needed help with the team and the loose stock he was driving. 'Heading to Oregon,' he said.

"The only time I ever heard Mrs. Gulch's man speak was when he said, 'Awful late in the year to be starting out.'

"Mrs. Gulch soon shut him up, and he slinked out of the room. I don't know how much she was paid for us, but after her and the wagon man whispered a bit, I saw him reach into his pocket and give her some money. She turned to the four of us and said, 'Go get your things and get out. Go with Mr.

Rory was becoming more and more troubled as he listened to the story.

"Where did this all take place? In what town or city?"

"It was way out east. Pa and us, we were heading west ourselves. We'd wagoned through Missouri, but Pa knew we would have to wait till spring and maybe join up with some other wagons. With the railway running, most folks had given up on wagoning, but Pa, he wanted to scout out the land along the way. He'd planned to stop at the first likely place.

"We stopped in this little town, figuring on wintering over, and Pa, he went looking for work. He was scouting around the local farms and ranches to try to hire on. When he didn't come home that night, Ma was worried.

She went looking for him the next day. She told us to stay with the wagon and watch over the stock. We never saw hide nor hair of either of them after that. About a week later, this man rode out to the wagon. Him and another two fellas. Saying nothing at all to Emmalou nor me, they hitched the team and gathered up our other stock. I tried to stop them, but one of the men back-handed me across the face and knocked me to the ground. Took my rifle away. We had no choice but to go with them. They took us into town and around to a house. The man said to get off the wagon, and we done so, afraid of what else he might do. A woman stuck her head out of the door of the little house and said to come in. We never saw the wagon nor our stock again neither.

"Pretty soon, the woman took us by wagon to St. Joseph. The city was right close by. Didn't take more than three, four hours by wagon. She dropped us in front of the orphanage, and that man, he came out and showed us into the house. Mrs. Gulch, she was waiting for us. We stayed there until we was sold off."

Rory and Cap were studying each other as the story came out. Rory asked, "Have you heard this part before, Cap?"

"Only that they were with a wagon man across Nebraska and into Wyoming."

Rory turned to the kids. "Is that true? You crossed Nebraska and Wyoming with the wagon?"

"We walked most of the way. Cold. It turned almighty cold before we got into Wyoming. Stayed cold. Cooper, he finally found a shack we could overwinter in. We stayed there for I don't know how many weeks. Stock came near to starving with the grass under a foot of snow. Grub about near run out, and finally, Cooper shot a skinny yearling steer that was desperate for graze.

Must have got free of some herd, but we never saw no herd. Just that one animal. It weren't much for taste, but it kept us from starving. When the weather started to break, we moved out again.

"We walked, mostly, holding the loose stock close to the wagon. Except Emmalou. Mr. Cooper kept inviting her to come sit beside him on the wagon seat. Mr. Cooper's woman didn't like that very much."

"I didn't like it either," said Emmalou.

Rory didn't have much else to do on a rainy afternoon, so he said, "Finish the story, please. How did you come to be on that stage?"

"The two older fellas, they kept talking about running off when they got anywhere close to a big town. Running in the middle of Nebraska or Wyoming would make no sense. But Cooper, he seemed to be avoiding any kind of settlement. Went a long way around a time or two. But when we came to Laramie, Cooper said they needed supplies, so he turned the wagon toward town. The very first night in Laramie, after Cooper had loaded the wagon with enough to take us all through to wherever he was heading, the other two figured they had their chance. At first, we weren't sure if we should run too.

"Mr. Cooper had been warned that it was too early to be heading into the mountains, but he was sure they could make it. We had fought snow all across Wyoming, and it wasn't hardly even spring in Laramie yet. Cold of a night. Fearsome cold trying to sleep on the ground, under the wagon.

"Emmalou and me, we didn't like the sound of mountains in the winter, which it still was up high, but Cooper, he was in an almighty rush for some reason. We had a few dollars in our pockets that Mrs. Gulch hadn't found. That little bit wouldn't go far, but it was a start. So, when the others lit out, we did too. Only we didn't stay together. They were talking about maybe robbing a store for food and such. We'd rather have been on the wagon than in jail, so we hid in Laramie until Cooper pulled out. Just him and his woman. We saw them searching the town, but we managed to stay out of their way. Hid in lofts and behind barns and such.

"When the wagon was gone, we bought some crackers and cheese and waited for someone heading south, where we figured it would be warmer. A farmer and his wife picked us up and gave us work on their homestead for a few weeks till spring. Weren't much of a place neither. I don't see how they hope to survive in that country.

"I knew they wanted to ask questions, but they didn't. Figured we was runaways, I'm guessing. Their place was nothing fancy, but it was warm, and the woman was a good cook. Taught Emmalou a fair bit. We worked just for the bed and the food, but we still had most of those few dollars. When spring seemed to have really come, we bought us a stage ticket heading south. South just as far as our bit of money would take us. Wasn't far neither. But when our ticket ran out, we just stayed on the rig. We sure didn't want to find ourselves walking up there. There's no real ranches nor no settlements. Not much of anything a man might need to stay alive. Just a couple of small stage stops.

"We stayed on the rigs, and no one asked or seemed to bother. Not many folks riding it in the cold weather. We had no food left and only one blanket each, but we made do. We were cold, tired and hungry. We wrapped up in our blankets just to keep warm. I guess we both went to sleep. Next thing we know we're here, in this town and with Cap caring for us."

The afternoon was about timed out. Cap took the kids out to the house and, with an approving word from Rory, Scout went with them.

Rory leaned back in his chair, picked up the papers, and reread the notes he had taken.

30

KNOWING THE STORY OF THE TWO KIDS COULD NOT END
there, Rory determined to continue the conversation at
their earliest opportunity. But first, he had to complete
the investigation of the Rad Harbinger and Bat Kelly
matter.

As he had decided earlier, he took a room in the
hotel. The poorly built structure allowed him to listen to
the roar of the wind and the thundering of the downpour as it rattled off the shingles. Sometime after
midnight, he awoke to silence. He sat up, as if to listen
better. Then he stepped out of bed and pushed aside the
curtain on the one window in the small room. There was
no sign of light anywhere in the town. Nor was there any
sign of wind or rain. The storm had blown itself out. He
raised the window, loving the smell of the rain-washed
air, and closed the curtain. He lay there planning his
movements for the morning, but somewhere along the
way, he fell asleep.

About the only thing he remembered from his night-
time planning was his determination to find alone time

with Julia Gridley. The storm had kept them apart the evening before. He was going to have to get creative. But first, he had to ride out to the Kelly ranch.

Marshal Wiley rode into town around the time Rory was finishing breakfast in the dining room. Wiley came in for coffee. The two-hour ride from the Double J, after his surprise but welcome visit to Hannah, had pushed a chill into his very bones. Rory waved him over.

"How are things at the ranch?"

"Wet. Everything was wet. But perhaps the wettest was me. I believe I was still in the saddle when the worst of that storm hit. One of your cousins lent me a pair of pants and a shirt while I hung my own duds up by the cabin stove."

Chuckling, Rory said, "That probably drew a lot of sympathy from the girls, and that can't hurt your relationship with Hannah."

"Might have got some sympathy from Hannah and your aunt. But Nancy, she's another matter altogether."

The two men laughed and then turned to the business of the day. When they had looked at all the possible alternatives, they agreed the rewards were to be split where both were involved. For cases they solved by themselves, the rewards would go to the one bringing the problems to an end.

RORY SADDLED up and rode to the B/K Ranch. Not knowing what to expect, he was pleasantly surprised to have Micah Wardle waiting for him beside the corral. The two men shook hands while Rory said, "I need to speak with Mrs. Kelly. Is she up to the house?"

"Ida. Yes. She'll be caring for the kids and getting them ready for their schooling. I'll walk up with you."

Micah rapped on the door with two light taps of his knuckles and then turned the knob. Two kids looked up from their books. Mrs. Kelly turned from where she was washing breakfast dishes in a pan of stove-heated water. Micah said, "Ida. This is Sheriff Rory Jamison. He wants a few minutes with you."

As if she had been expecting his visit, she wiped her hands on her apron and said, "You kids go outside. Maybe Micah can find something productive for you to do. I'll call you when we're finished up here. Won't you please have a seat, Sheriff?"

The interview went about as Rory had expected from what he had learned from Cap. Bat Kelly was not a nice or good man, and his hired man, Reef Malkin, was worse, a gunman and troublemaker, and proud of it. Mrs. Kelly confirmed that she was saddened to lose her husband, and the kids, their father, as anyone would expect, but she hadn't been particularly surprised.

"Bat wasn't made for a civilized country. He told stories of the fights and troubles his father and uncles had been in, seeming to move from one situation to another, and all the time believing they were in the right. I seemed to have heard endless stories about the family. I loved my husband, Sheriff, as strange as folks figured that to be. I kept hoping he would change. We came here to get away from a difficulty in Texas. We have a good ranch here. We lived a good life with everything we could ask for. Life is different here than it was in Texas. Better. Much better. But Bat was never satisfied. He kept talking about what the Kellys were going to do, making a mark for themselves, as if we were some Hill Country feuding families.

"With that hired man, who never did more than a minimum of work, egging him on, Bat was growing worse. I could see it. Still, how he convinced himself that he could simply ride onto some other family's spread and demand they get off, like the ranchers were doing to homesteaders in the open range areas, settlers they named as nesters, I'll never understand.

"When your deputy and Mr. Harbinger rode into the yard with the bodies—that was a sad time for me and the children, but not unexpected. Mr. Harbinger was truly apologetic, but as he said, he was only protecting his family. And his holdings.

"Now, Sheriff, if you're going to ask me if I'm angry or if I wish Mr. Harbinger punished, I can say that I do not. It's done and over with, and the kids and I will somehow carry on. I'm very thankful for Mr. Wardle. We could not have stayed without his help. I'm hoping he will stay on, but that doesn't seem likely. I understand the family is looking for ranchland. Mr. Wardle's younger brother, a man they call Junior, was out here last week reporting on what he had found. When I'm alone again, I will have to figure something else out."

Rory had remained quiet throughout the talk. Mrs. Kelly answered his questions without him having to ask them. Now, looking at this pretty and well-put-together young woman, the thought entered Rory's mind that Micah might be better off to stay right where he was. He would look a long way for a better ranch or for a better woman. But since that was none of his business, he would offer no advice.

The sheriff talked a few more minutes with Micah and then mounted and headed home.

～

213

BACK AT THE FORT, Rory settled in at the hotel lobby, where there was a fully supplied writing desk, common in frontier hotels. He began a new document headed Harbinger / Kelly killings. Over the next hour, he wrote out in detail everything told to him by both remaining parties. He emphasized that there were no third-party witnesses to the shootings.

When he was done, and the document reread twice, he cleaned the nib on the pen, tightened the lid on the ink bottle, and placed the paper into a large envelope supplied by the hotel. He carried that to the marshal's office, sat across from Wiley, and said, "Put on your lawyer's hat, my friend, and read this."

Leaving Wiley alone in the quietness of the office, Rory walked to Mr. Sales's saddle and gun shop. Julia greeted him with a smile. Not wishing to upset Mr. Sales by taking his employee away from her work, he simply said, "How about the dining room at seven this evening?"

Her response was "Yes, how about that?"

He turned to the door with a tilt of his hat and left.

31

Rory returned to the hotel lobby and retook the seat at the writing desk. He intended to sort out the worrisome tale the two kids had told him about the afternoon before. He spread his notes on the table before him and started in. The more he wrote, the more he was convinced that a serious wrong had taken place and, perhaps with other children, was still taking place.

When he was done, he returned to the marshal's office and greeted Wiley with, "If you're finished with the Harbinger / Kelly write-up, I'd like you to take a look at this. Wiley slid the document he had already read across the desk and picked up the new one.

"My opinion, my 'unlawyerly' young friend, is that a trained lawyer would have used three or four times as many words and not said it as well. Personally, I wouldn't add or change anything. Are you simply filing this for your own defense in case something arises in the future to question your actions?"

"That's partially what it's about. But mostly, I have a need to get it right. And you are, of course, correct. I am not a lawyer. Except for you, and the judge, I'm not sure I've ever met a lawyer. The real reason for the report, though, is for my superiors in the state office. Since starting out in this job, I've written up every incident in the same manner. Then I copy the notes out and keep one copy for myself. The difference now is that we have a judge in town. I'll be taking this over to his office for his opinion."

Rory left the office, knowing Wiley's mind would be fully focused on the new case write-up. He walked down to the judge's office. Judge Anders P. Yokam welcomed the sheriff with a handshake and invited him to sit. After a brief chat about nothing important, the judge said, "How did your trip to Texas go?"

Rory felt the man deserved the story, but not in detail. He outlined the issues and the results in just a few minutes, while the judge nodded his head as if he was, by that action, locking the details into his own mind. Then, to prevent the conversation from flashing off into another time-wasting direction, he laid the Harbinger / Kelly write-up on the desk.

"Judge, I'd like if you would read this. It's my write-up of the shooting out at the Harbinger farm while I was away. Cap handled it and, in my opinion, did a fine and proper job of it. But I have also interviewed everyone involved, and this is my report. You will see that I've decided it was a clear matter of self-defense. But if you see it differently, I would like to know that, and perhaps receive guidance from you on the case. I'll be sending this to the people at the state office, so I need it to be accurate and defensible before I mail it off."

With no words spoken, the judge picked up the document and appeared to be immediately absorbed in it. Rory quietly stood and left.

TWO DAYS LATER, Rory had received Judge Yokam's response. Two small changes were suggested. Although Rory considered them to be minor, still, he rewrote the document and then copied it. He had, by that time, figured out what he was going to do on the matter of the kids' missing parents.

"People don't just disappear," he had said to Cap and Wiley as the three lawmen were discussing it in the office, while avoiding another rainy afternoon.

"What do you plan?" asked Wiley.

"I'm going to make some noise. We forget sometimes that we can cross the nation in seconds with the telegraph and in days with the railway. Last year when Block and I were trailing the Lance Newley Gang, Block used the telegraph to alert every law enforcement man in the area. Within hours, men were riding to our aid from four or five directions. Enough lawmen to bring down every crook in the nation if we could have gathered the crooks together as effectively as that telegraph gathered the sheriffs and marshals and their posses. Newley didn't have a chance.

"I'm thinking there's a good possibility the kids' parents are still alive. I can't explain why they didn't return to the wagon and their kids, but I'm gambling on there being an explanation. And how are we going to get the kids back to their parents if we just sit here at the fort? I'm going to ride up to Cheyenne and send some wires. Then I'm taking the train to Denver. We need the Federals involved. Lost parents. Stolen wagon and stock. An orphanage that sells kids. Kids bought and dragged halfway across the nation. No sheriff can handle all that. We need the Federals, and I know just who to talk to. And face-to-face is always better than a letter that takes three days to get there. I'll leave in the morning, and I'll be away a few days."

Grinning, Wiley said, "What about Julia?"

Not wanting to discuss personal matters with anyone, Rory responded with a smile, "Yes. What about her? Fine girl, I'm thinking."

~

HE STAYED one night in a Cheyenne hotel after sending his message to an open wire. Every lawman from Missouri to California would have access to the wire. He had simply given the names of the kids and said,

SEPARATED FROM PARENTS. STOP. WATCH FOR MAN AND WOMAN NAMED STAKES. STOP. REFER TO SHERIFF AT THE FORT, COLORADO.

He then sent a second wire on the open line that said,

WATCH FOR MAN NAMED COOPER. STOP. HEADING WEST FROM LARAMIE BY WAGON. STOP. APPREHEND AND HOLD. STOP.

He followed that short note with his name and location.

~

THE NEXT AFTERNOON he was sitting in Oscar Cator's office in Denver. He turned over the report on the Harbinger / Kelly shooting and then, with little other talk, walked to the federal marshal's office. He was welcomed as if he was one of them, and invited to take a seat, along with his friend Block, in Donavan Gaines's office. After a bit of small talk, mostly about Block's recovery from the shooting, Donavan began to mention the impounded cattle driven up from Texas. The money received for the herd was apparently still on his mind. Rory waved his hand, interrupting.

"That's all behind us now. What I came all this way to talk about is much more important."

With that, he laid the document on the desk and said, "Lost parents, stolen wagon and stock, kids being sold from an orphanage, far more important. And nothing can be done without your federal marshals. Let's talk about that."

They did talk about it, and the more the marshals' chief heard, the angrier he got. He had been scribbling unnecessary notes, but Rory finally stopped him.

"It's all in the report, Donavan. Every name, every location, every date. Or at least as much as we could get from the kids. You just have to get one of your secretaries to make some copies of that report and mail them off to your head office or whoever controls the movements of the marshals. I'd be cautious of using the wires. There's nothing secret on the wire. You don't want to scare the pigeons off their roost before you get men onsite."

Knowing it was as yet premature to hope for any conclusion on the Texas cattle matter, except for the guarantee from Donavan that the criminals were still in jail, and Washington had not yet been advised on the matter, there was little discussion or rehashing of the story. Donavan did, though, confide that the local lawyers were digging into the law, along with Donavan himself, in an attempt to figure out how to handle the matter.

A dinner with Block and his family in their home that evening, and one night in the hotel, and Rory was back on the cushions watching the land go past the window at a speed no horse could hope to match. He would be in Cheyenne that afternoon and back at the fort the next afternoon. With any good fortune at all, there may be answering wires waiting for him.

32

AS HE HAD HOPED, THERE WAS ONE WIRE WAITING FOR Rory in Cheyenne. It was from Laramie, a small settlement not too far west of Cheyenne. It simply stated,

COOPERS IN CUSTODY LARAMIE. ADVISE.

He immediately wired back,

HOLD.

Remembering the kids saying they had watched the wagon heading north and west and assumed they had resumed their journey, Rory was facing a mystery. But the only way to solve the mystery was to ride to Laramie and confront the Coopers. He borrowed a deputy from the Cheyenne sheriff and rode out. The country was dry along the way. The growth sparse, and trees almost nonexistent. The altitude threatened the breath and lungs of both horses and riders.

A good horse could have made the miles on level

ground in a single long day. But the constant hills and valleys, plus the altitude, forced the lawmen to go to camp for a night. They had seen no water and little firewood anywhere along the way. And then they did. A small trickle, enough to satisfy horses and men both, if they were patient with the modest flow, invited them to dismount and throw their bedrolls on the ground. Rory scoured the area for anything that would burn while Caleb, the borrowed Cheyenne deputy, led the horses to the small stream.

The high elevation cold and the rocky ground made for a poor night, but shortly after noon the next day, they were riding down the street in Laramie, keeping their eyes peeled for the sheriff's or marshal's office. They found it at the farthest north end of the street.

The two men pushed the office door open and walked in. A big, bushy-haired man, bulky in shoulders and chest and needing a shave, was wearing a star and smoking a cigar. He greeted them with a sparseness of words. A simple "howdy," was the sheriff's welcome to Laramie, while his eyes were searching the two men at the door for any possible trouble.

Not bothering to ask for a name, Rory said, "Sheriff, I'm Rory Jamison. Sheriff from down at the fort. I received your wire in Cheyenne. This man with me is Caleb, sheriff's deputy from Cheyenne. Came along to give me an extra hand. Your wire said you had someone here named Cooper."

"Welcome, men. Yes, Cooper. Two Coopers, actually. First time we've ever held a woman in the jail. Come, I'll introduce you."

Rory and Caleb followed as the sheriff opened a door and led the way to the three cells at the rear of the building. Not attempting any form of introduction, the sheriff said, "These the two you're looking for?"

Rory had no clear answer, knowing nothing more about the man who had bought the kids, other than his name. He looked long and hard at the man and then stepped to the last cell. The couple had been locked up with an empty cell between them. After another long pause while he studied the woman, Rory asked, "I understand you've recently come from St. Joseph. Is that true?"

The man in the first cell hollered, "Don't you be telling him anything, Gert. They got nothing on us."

Rory, tired from a lack of sleep and weary with riding, slowly paced off the few steps to the first cell.

"Alright, Mr. Hero. Why don't you tell me where you've been and where you're going."

"I ain't telling you nothing."

Rory returned to the woman but spoke to the sheriff.

"I believe we should release this lady. Just for a few minutes, you understand, while we take her somewhere more comfortable for a longer talk."

The sheriff turned the key in the big lock and opened the door. Gert Cooper backed up and sat on the bunk, huddling into a corner. Rory slid the sides of his coat back to reveal the two .44s racked there. And the badge hooked onto one of his belt loops. He studied the woman for longer than she was comfortable with before he said, "Come on, Mrs. Cooper. It's a bit chilly back here, and the fire sure feels good in the front office. It would be a fine place for you and me to have a talk. Kind of get acquainted, you know what I mean?"

She huddled even farther into the bunk and almost squealed out, "I ain't no Mrs. Cooper. I'm no kin to that," she said, as she pointed a thumb toward the other cell. "I just needed a way out. Cooper promised me a free ride to California if I'd come with him. I was to do the gathering of wood and the cooking of grub. I guess it was free alright, as far as money goes, which I have none of. But it weren't no way free altogether."

She seemed to stop talking to allow the men to figure out what she meant by that. Afraid he did understand, Rory was immediately incensed.

"Tell me, Gert. Was it something in St. Joseph you were trying to get free of?"

Her answer was a simple nod. There were tears running down her face now. Then she clarified, "A little village in the hills a short way from St. Joseph."

"And did Cooper make arrangements with an orphanage back there to get the services of four kids?"

Before she could answer, Cooper was again on his feet and shouting threats to the terrified woman. Although she was clearly confused as to who to trust, the three lawmen all saw her repeated nod. She then said, "I knew it weren't no way right, but I was so desperate to get away I said nothing at all. I just sat on the wagon hoping we could get on our way and not have no troubles. And Cooper, he had made me the kind of promises a girl likes to hear. I'm ashamed of it now, but at first, I kind of got sweet on him. But he's just an awful hard man. Thinks of no one but himself."

"She's lying. That's all it is. She's lying."

The Laramie sheriff looked at Cooper and said, "You shut up, or I'll tie you outside and let the town dogs loose at you."

Cooper returned to his bunk and sat, but Rory knew he hadn't heard the last from the man.

He turned again to Gert. "Gert, I have two questions for you, and then we'll get you both out of here. First, where is the wagon and livestock? The second is, why did you return to Laramie after you headed farther west a while ago?"

"Wagon is at the livery. Animals too."

"Good. Now, why did you return to town?"

"After we got farther west, that is, after quite a few days, Cooper, he didn't like the looks of the snow in the passes we saw in the distance, nor the snow we was driving through. And he was having trouble finding graze for the animals. Finally, he said, 'Ain't spring up here yet. Not by a long shot. We'll go back and wait.' With the four kids gone off, I had to walk and herd the animals."

Rory smiled to himself, having heard what he needed.

"So, you did have three boys and one girl with you?"

"Cooper, he bought them from this place he heard about at a tavern along the way somewhere. That was back in Missouri."

Rory turned back to the front office. The sheriff relocked Gert's door and joined him.

Rory and the Cheyenne deputy were chafing their hands over the wood heater, trying to work some warmth back into them. Rory looked over at the sheriff and said, "I'm hoping you won't have a problem with me taking those two off your hands."

"None at all. I have nothing to hold them on. They're here because of your wire."

RORY AND CALEB took advantage of the town to get their horses grained and rested while they themselves enjoyed a night in the hotel and a couple of decent meals. In the morning, they hitched Cooper's team and readied the wagon for the trip south. They left the few cows Cooper had been driving for the livery man to sell, with instructions to send the money to Rory.

Cooper had been traveling with one saddle horse which Gert had said he occasionally rode. Rory tied it to the back of the wagon and drove the rig over to the general store. He called Caleb over and said, "I have no idea what all's in those boxes and the two small barrels. Must be Cooper's traveling provisions. But we won't bother with it. We'll take our own fixings. Take this money and get grub for three days for all of us. Check the water barrel on the wagon and make sure it's filled. I'll get Cooper and the woman."

Cooper was pushed onto the wagon seat with his hands free but his ankles in cuffs. Caleb had climbed into the wagon and moved everything away from the back of the seat so Cooper couldn't reach a weapon of any sort. Gert was allowed to walk freely with a warning from Rory that if she tried to run off, he would catch her, and it would go hard on her. When she was about to climb onto the wagon, Rory asked, "Do you think you could ride that bay gelding?"

"I can ride about anything that wears hair, Mr. Sheriff."

"Alright, wait until I throw Cooper's saddle on him. That will be better than being on the wagon with him."

Two nights on the trail, along with three long, hard days at the speed of the plodding team, all the while listening to Cooper whine about the injustice and shout his innocence, had the entourage riding down the main street of the fort. The first stop, of course, was the livery. Only when the animals were placed in Keg's capable hands was Cooper allowed to climb off the wagon seat. The chains clanked against each other and dragged dust behind them as he was led toward the jail.

That evening, while taking dinner together, Rory, Cap, Wiley, and Caleb discussed how to proceed with the Cooper matter. Earlier that afternoon, after school let out, Cap had led the kids to the door of the marshal's office and let them have a good look at Cooper. At first glance, Peter looked as if he'd like to find a weapon to attack the prisoner with. Emmalou cringed back against Cap's legs. There was no doubt at all about the man's identity.

Now, knowing Caleb would be back in Cheyenne the following evening, they needed to discuss what to do and say. Rory had informed the federal marshals, hoping they were active around St. Joseph. What could they say on the wire without causing a problem for the marshals? They finally decided on a few simple words:

WAGON MAN IN CUSTODY STOP. ADVISE.

The message would be sent to the Denver marshal's office. Donavan Gaines could decide where to take it from there. Perhaps he had thought of a way to inform the Missouri marshal's office without being public on the wire. Rory gave Caleb a few dollars for the telegraph and some for his own troubles and his able assistance. Caleb started to object and then, with a grin, simply said, "Thanks."

33

THE SMALL MARSHAL'S OFFICE AT THE FORT, WITH ITS single cell, was an inappropriate temporary home for Cooper and the woman. With a stern warning, which Gert appeared to take to heart, Rory led her across the street to the hotel. He signed the register on behalf of the county and told the clerk that the woman was a prisoner on trust. She would be using the room.

At the clerk's question about Gert's possibility of violence, Rory looked at Gert and said, "Answer the lady, Gert. And dump out your reticule to show her you're not armed."

Gert did as he asked, trembling with fear at all that had come upon her. Studying her anew, the sheriff thought, *I was wrong by a couple of years. She's younger than I first thought. Not much more than a kid herself.* After going to the dining room with Gert to arrange for meals, he sternly warned the woman again. "This is too big a territory for you to run in. If you try to escape, I'll be sure to find you."

"I won't run."

"Alright, you stay in your room. I'm going to send a lady over later in the day to take you shopping for some new clothing. Her name is Julia. You can trust her. You might want to ask at the desk if they can arrange hot water for a bath."

Rory then walked over to the gun and saddle shop. When he opened the door, causing a tinkle from the small bell hanging above the door, Julia looked up and smiled. Her employer, Mr. Sales, looked up from the saddle he was working on and mumbled something past the heavy thread he had hanging from his mouth. The words didn't sound altogether friendly, as if the sheriff was taking too much of Julia's time and interrupting her work.

Rory decided to make light of his visit.

"Mr. Sales. I've come to believe this young lady is the best thing that ever happened to your shop. Everything looks all cleaned and wiped down. The glass in the showcase is all polished and sparkling. That new window I got for you is clean as the day it was made. Everything is dusted and shining, ready for the next customer. Yes, sir. I'm thinking she might deserve a raise in pay."

Mr. Sales pulled the thread from his mouth, and replied, "Sheriff, you may have got me that window, but before you had that out-of-control rancher shooting up the town, I already had a window. I ain't no way better off with the new one. And as for this lady, when you marry her, you can take her away and have all the time in the world with her. But until then, I need her to be busy with my work."

"That will be a sorry day for the Sales Gun and Saddle Shop. You're just not going to find a better worker. Or a prettier one."

The two men finally dropped the pretending and grinned at each other.

Rory told Julia what he wanted her to do for Gert and laid a ten-dollar gold piece on the countertop.

Julia picked it up and dropped it into her pocket. She had not said a single word during the visit, but her smile was radiant and gripping. Rory tipped his hat and left the shop.

Thinking about the kids and the Cooper incident, Rory smiled to himself. *The way that dog has taken to the kids, I fear I may have lost him.*

LEAVING the work at the fort in Cap's hands, Rory headed south. He had been fussing about how long it had been since he was up in gold country.

34

WITH HIS HALF OF THE DOUBLE J RANCH NOW SOLD TO the family, Rory's private cabin was turned over to his cousins. Although there was no doubt about his welcome or the enjoyment of the dinner his aunt Eliza and Nancy put together, still he felt it best to ride on to the Stevensville hotel for the night.

He planned on spending the day in town, catching up on the local happenings with Ivan, his county deputy, and Key Wardle, town marshal. After that, he had planned to tackle the steep slope up to MacNair's Hill, up in gold country. Buck, his appointed deputy, had been on his own for the winter. Rory wasn't sure if the snow would be off the steep trail yet, but he was going to give it a try. The miners would soon be flooding into the area, and Buck would need help, perhaps another deputy. He'd rather keep ahead of potential troubles than try to catch up after things went wrong.

The plan ended, though, when Marshal Key said, "Sorry, Sheriff. There was no way to tell you except sending a note on the stage, and Ivan didn't figure to wait that long.

"Buck sent a note down with a fella who was coming this way. He figured he needed help. The story was, according to the note, that a couple of hard cases had ridden through the snow, coming up from Idaho Falls. Buck figured it looked like trouble. That, and a few miners had returned. He managed to keep the lid on with a couple of fights, but he feared fists might give way to guns.

"Ivan had been up to Kiril's old cabin a few days before. Tempest had wanted to see it, so he took her up. You can read into that whatever you wish. Anyway, he said most of the snow was gone so far as he could see up the trail. He rode off four days ago. I expect he's got things under control by now. Him and Buck."

Rory thought through his choices. To ride after Ivan didn't seem to make much sense with all that was going on up at the fort. Ivan was a good man and a wise one. He wouldn't start anything he couldn't finish. Rory trusted him. So, he changed the subject, asking Key about his marshal's job and what was happening around the town.

They were just delving into the subject when Cousin Nancy rode down the street, catching the eyes of both lawmen. When she turned to the marshal's office, and Key jumped up to take her reins, tying them to the rail, Rory said nothing. He was so surprised he wouldn't have known what to say anyway. And when Key and Nancy smiled at each other and kind of touched hands, his surprise was complete.

Key went inside and dragged another chair out. Nancy settled into the half-barrel chair vacated by Key, smiled over at Rory, and said, "Morn'n, Cousin."

With thoughts bouncing around in his head, he stood and said, "Well, I'm not needed here. I do believe I'll just ride on up north. There're things to do up there."

He untied his gelding and spoke to Key.

"When Ivan gets back, have him send me a note."

"Will do."

Saying no more and receiving no explanation or comment from either Nancy or Key, the sheriff stepped into the saddle and turned for home. He waved at Mr. Browning, sweeping the boardwalk in front of his mercantile. He saw no one else. Had he been gone from Stevensville so long that he was feeling a bit like a stranger? It didn't seem possible.

35

Life at the fort appeared to rest easy for about one week before Rory was pacing the small office. Five paces in one direction, three the other, leaving the cell block from the calculation. Cap and Wiley watched, first with questions on their minds, and finally, with grins on their faces.

Wiley, fearing the man would wear out the floor, or his boots, either one, said, "If I was sheriff and I was hoping for a wire or a letter advising on a couple of major cases, I'd probably ride up to where there was a telegraph station." He left it at that, pretending to be studying the newspaper on his desk.

Rory paced out the floor and finally said, "I think I'll ride up to Cheyenne."

Cap answered, "Good thinking, boss. That's why you're sheriff, and I'm just deputy. Good thinking."

Rory knew full well what was going on, but he just grinned and let the two men enjoy their moment.

~

IT WAS a bit late when he left the fort, but he was registered in the hotel in Cheyenne just after the sun had escaped the high-country sky. He dropped his saddle-bags on the hotel bed and left, locking the door behind himself. He headed over to the station, hoping for news. Cheyenne was a busy rail center. The telegraph office never closed. The night man was just settling in for his shift when Rory greeted him from the door. The two men had met briefly on Rory's last trip north.

"Howdy, Sheriff. I was about to fold a couple of wires into an envelope and put it on the morning stage for you."

"Thanks. I'll save you the cost. What have you got?"

"Two wires, both marked confidential. Now, you understand, when we talk about confidential on the tele-graph, that depends on the integrity of a lot of other telegraphers. But we do the best we can. I've got them right here for you."

Rory thanked the man and found a chair in the big station waiting area. He stuffed one wire into his pocket and opened the other. The sun was long gone from the sky, and the lamp light was dim. Unable to read, he made his way to a writing desk, similar to the one he had used at the hotel. Here the railway had thoughtfully provided a lamp just for that small area.

The first wire was from the St. Joseph federal marshals. It was short.

HOLD WAGON MAN TILL FURTHER WORD.

The second wire was a little longer. It was from Donavan Gaines at the Denver Federal Marshal's Office.

Texas matter deepens. Stop. Come to Denver soonest.

～

Suddenly Rory felt the need to talk with his father. It had been many months since he last felt that need. His father probably hadn't been quite as wise as young Rory had remembered him to be, but still, he longed to hear the older man's voice. It had been the murder of that good man that eventually led Rory into carrying the badge, although he only carried it in his pocket, most days. Of course, Rory knew he would have to make his own decision, but the longing for the advice of his parent persisted.

He couldn't do anymore that evening, so he went back to the hotel for dinner, thinking it all through as he ate. His decision was eased by the comfort of having Cap on duty at the

fort. That was a comfort because the trips to Denver often took longer than he liked. On previous trips, he had left the northern portion of the county with no sheriff on duty. That had troubled him greatly. But Cap was a competent lawman. Rory could leave with some confidence that the town and surrounding countryside were in good hands.

Knowing what his duty to both the county and the Federals demanded, he made a decision.

The hotel had a lamp-lit writing desk almost identical to the one at the station. There was no one using it. Rory eased into the delicate-looking chair and lifted the hinged desktop. Hidden beneath the top was a supply of paper and a variety of envelopes. He chose what he needed and started to write.

Cap. The enclosed wires will answer most of your questions.
Keep a close eye on both Cooper and Gert. Hire a night man
if you feel it is necessary.

I have gone to Denver on the other matter. The less said
about this, the better. I will be some days but hopefully not too
many. Please tell Julia where I am.

Thank you,
Rory

By the next evening, Cap sat reading the note, handed
down to him by Tate from high on the whip's box on the
stage.

Rory, making good time on the rails, was having
dinner in the hotel with Block.

"WHAT'S GOING ON, BLOCK?"

"Nothing good, I'm afraid, although I could yet be
proven wrong on that. Two federal marshals from Washington arrived a few days ago. They didn't seem to have
much interest in what I, or Donavan Gaines, had to say.
It was almost as if they were prepared to push our work
aside and start an investigation again themselves. I found
myself having a hard time trusting them. But after
finding that list of names in Webster Cunningham's file,
I find myself suspecting everyone.

"The Washington men were downright unhappy to
hear that you, a man from outside the marshal's organi-
zation had been involved. I'm not even sure they were
happy about the arrest of Webster Cunningham. And
they were downright cross over the arrest of Glover
Harrison.

"They spent barely any time at all in Denver, before

heading down to the state lockup. The only connection I can think of there is Mike Wasson, and I doubt if Mike knows anything at all beyond what he and that phony judge were doing.

"They arrived back in town two days ago, but from then to this afternoon, they've spent all their time at the city lockup talking to Glover Harrison and Webster Cunningham. They stormed into the office this afternoon, shouting about overstepping our bounds and demanding that the two men be released into their trust. They were to be returned to Washington.

"For once, Donavan found a backbone. He shouted just as loud as those eastern oafs had. He said the criminals belonged in jail, and that's where they would stay. He then detailed off two more of our marshals to stand guard at the jail. The city police aren't very happy about all the goings on in their building, but Donavan pulled rank on them too. So right now, we're at a stalemate. And for some reason, the eastern agents are determined to talk to you. You can expect some face time with them in the morning."

Rory had completed his meal while Block talked. As he pushed the empty plate aside and reached for the slice of peach pie the waitress had laid there, he said, "I don't really have any information you and Donavan don't have."

"I know that, and so does Donavan.

"The Washington boys are Marshals Carlton and Byway. They don't use first names apparently—yours, mine or their own, even among their peers. They're determined that one of us is keeping secrets, and that you are the most likely suspect. 'Small-town hillbilly would-be sheriff,' Carlton called you. I tell you that just to make you smile."

Not knowing quite where to go with the conversation, Rory changed the subject, asking about Block's recent wound and then his family. After another short time, the two men parted.

In the morning, Rory, a little later than he had at first planned—walked into a packed room at the marshal's office. It appeared as if everyone was waiting for him. There had been no conversations to interrupt and no one who had to turn toward the door. Every eye was glued to the half-glass oak door, and when he opened it and stepped in, it was almost as if a sigh of relief, or perhaps anticipation, escaped some lips.

Donavan was the first to speak.

"Good morning, Sheriff. Good of you to come down."

Rory had unfastened his fringed buckskin coat, not simply to make access to his .44's but because the day had turned out warmer than he had planned on. Still, the guns were immediately noticed by the gathered men.

A broad-shouldered man wearing a big badge on his shirt, with his hat tipped almost to where it covered his eyes, said with a sneer, as if speaking to someone well beneath his own station, "Place those weapons on the table, Sheriff, and step away from them."

Rory laughed at the man, an action that would rile most people. He said no words.

Donavan said, "Hold up there, Carlton..."

Carlton brushed Donavan's words aside. Angrily, loudly, and grimly, the words were shouted, "I'll not interrogate an armed man! Nor will I have a potential enemy armed in our midst! Now, do as I say, or my men will take them from you!"

Rory glanced around the room before he spoke. Then, in a penetrating voice so quiet, each man leaned a little bit forward as if they couldn't hear the words. "Pick your men carefully before you give that order, mister. Make sure they're expendable. There'll be blood on the floor before you have my guns. And the first of it will be yours."

The room fell to such a depth of silence that it almost hurt the ears. Here was a small-town sheriff threatening a room full of federal marshals, and not a man among them doubted his words.

This time when Donavan spoke, his voice rang with authority, and perhaps of fear. "They're not actually your men, Carlton. They're under my authority, and no such order will be given in this office or anywhere else in my jurisdiction. Now, stand down."

From his first trip south, Rory had ignored the city ordinance against carrying weapons. But he didn't often carry his carbine in the streets. Why he had done so that morning, he could not have explained. During the short confrontation, he had tipped the barrel of his .44-40 carbine in the direction of the loud-mouthed marshal from Washington. He had made a decision, and he meant to act on it. That he was strong and adept enough to handle the heavy weapon with one hand caught the attention of some of the men. Having the carbine at the ready held a sobering effect on the room's tenants.

"I'll be going home now. This trip was a fool's errand and a waste of my time. Thanks for speaking for Donavan. Perhaps we'll meet again soon."

Watching every move the marshals made, he backed out the door, before he turned and left the building. The walk to his hotel took less than a half hour. He was soon packed and checked out of the room. He hailed a carriage and directed the driver to the rail station. The Cheyenne train had left an hour earlier. The only thing going north was a cattle train. Taking advantage of his position as sheriff, he managed to bribe his way onto the caboose.

The train moved slowly, but a small breeze still blew generous portions of coal smoke and cattle stink into the open window of the caboose. The conductor sat high on his raised chair, looking out the small window that gave him a view over the length of the train.

When Rory mentioned possibly closing the window, the conductor refused, leaning on what he called his love of clean, fresh air. Rory took a long look, wondering if the much older man had already breathed in too many years of coal smoke and needed it, like a pipe smoker needs his tobacco. Thinking the man, who was doing his best to ignore the sheriff, may have held the job too long already, he resigned himself to the facts.

After a long, slow day with no food or coffee, and little conversation with the conductor—who obviously resented Rory's intrusion into his personal kingdom— the train pulled into Cheyenne. Rory was soon back at the hotel from which he had started. The next day he would gather his horse from the stable and ride home, in a land where the air was truly fresh, if a bit nippy from time to time.

36

ANOTHER WEEK WENT SLOWLY BY. RORY AND JULIA SPENT a lot of time together, often out at the steadily rising house. The pertinent question still had not been asked. The time together and the planning for the house, was all done on the presumption that they had an unspoken agreement. Only once did Rory consider formalizing that agreement. That was when he realized they were going to need furniture. He finally said, "Might be good for you to borrow a couple of catalogs from the general store and sort out some furniture."

"Silly man. It's already done. I just need your approval to order it. Perhaps you and I could study on it together later this evening."

"No need. Just order it."

Rory had clearly missed the intent of Julia's suggestion, but she let it go. She had the feeling that there were more moments like that in their future, but she would make up for it. Somehow.

~

RORY RODE to Stevensville in the hopes that Ivan had returned. He had.

"Afternoon, Ivan," Rory said to the deputy, speaking through a broad smile. "I take it by the fact that you're sitting in the sun while collecting those big county wages, that everything is right with your world."

"The word, 'everything,' takes in a whack of territory, my northern friend. But, if by its use you mean has Browning's Mercantile been robbed this morning or the bank raided, I would have the privilege of telling you that neither of those things has happened. If you're looking beyond those facts, we might have to go across the road and discuss it over coffee, and one of Hip Dawson's donuts, which Ma has taken to offering in her dining room."

"Coffee and donuts it is, then. Can you get out of that chair on your own, or should I toss you a rope?"

Not waiting for an answer, Rory stepped down, flipped the reins over the tie rail, and shook hands with Ivan. Together they crossed to Ma's dining room. Sonia, Ivan's sister who had worked in the dining room for several years, brought coffee and a plate with two donuts on it. Without being asked, she said, "Don't ask for more. The baker is working half the night now just to keep these rolling out. It's one per customer."

Sonia had worked up a soft spot for Rory when he first returned from the goldfields. They had taken a couple of buggy rides together. But now, after some time had passed, they had both moved on to other interests. She satisfied herself with a light touch on the back of Rory's hand and a quiet, "Good to have you back, Sheriff."

~

THE TWO MEN ate their donuts in silence, enhancing the delicate taste with sips of coffee. When Rory swallowed the last small bite and brushed the flakes of dried sugar glaze from the front of his shirt, he said, "So, how was it up the hill?"

"The hill itself was passable until the last quarter mile. I had to walk in the brush beside the trail to get a footing, and practically drag my horse along. But the snow is melting fast, and soon it will be all rock and exposed tree roots that lie there in wait, ready to trip up an unnoticing horse, or man.

"The town itself, by that I mean MacNair's Hill, is just waking up from their winter nap. There were, perhaps a dozen or so miners back at their claims. Still pretty cold work, but gold fever seems to be without feelings for hot or cold.

"Buck Canby is still content with his part-time deputy job. He's moved into MacNair's store full-time. Lives there too. He's taking both positions seriously. Since MacNair won't be returning, Buck waits in anticipation of some relative or friend of MacNair's claiming the business. So far, no such thing has happened, so Buck cares for it as if it was his own."

"Taking a certain young lady seriously too."

Rory grinned, and asked, "By that do you mean that waitress Buck used to harass? I believe her name was Gloria."

"The very same. They appear to have let bygones be bygones. It looks good on both of them."

As was his habit, Rory's mind didn't hover long over small talk. He moved immediately back to thinking about business.

"Did he have any trouble to deal with over the winter?"

244

"Apparently there were a few fistfights. No gun problems. He stopped the fistfights by closing the saloon whenever he saw something heating up. He says that after the saloon was closed for a couple of days, the boys were anxious to take it as it was and leave other fellas alone with their thoughts."

"So, he's good for now, is he?"

"That's what he says. I passed on to him that he could deputize another man or two if that was needful. Told him, too, that either you or I would be up soon with a pocket full of money."

Rory thought for a minute while he sipped coffee. The idea seemed to sprout out of thin air. "How would you like to take a raise in pay and be responsible for the care and feeding of Buck and whoever he hires? I would tell Jesse Ambrewster, over at the bank, that you can draw wages from the county account. I have to go there this afternoon, so that I could arrange a deal for you at the same time."

Not at all sure about what Rory was saying or expecting, he asked, "Are things that busy up north?"

"They wouldn't be if I could shed the federal marshal people off my back."

The two men walked back over to the marshal's office. In answer to Ivan's questions, Rory explained about the Texas matter and the difficulty of dealing with the federal people.

When Rory rode back to the fort the next morning, he found himself to be the center of a gathering storm. Not a storm of lightning and thunder, but a storm of federal marshals.

DEPUTY MARSHALS CARLTON AND BYWAY WERE THERE, along with Block and two other Denver marshals.

Rory walked into the small office with a wire in his hand and his mind on the matter of Cooper and the kids he had bought. The wire was from a St. Joseph marshal, sent to Cheyenne and forwarded by stage to Stevensville. Rory had read it as he rode home, but he was reading it again, concentrating on the message to the exclusion of other matters. He liked to have things fresh in his mind when he intended to take action. It wasn't until he looked up from the wire that he became aware of the crowd in the office.

Carlton was waiting with a Colt in his hand. The smirk on his face reflected what was in his mind. He said, "Come in, Sheriff. And this time, you will do as I say or pay the consequences."

Rory was seldom without his Big Fifty on the left side of his saddle and the .44-40 carbine on the off side. As a matter of habit, his right hand had folded around the action of the .44-40, lifting it from the scabbard. He had entered the office with the wire in his left hand and the carbine in his right, hanging down along his leg, obviously not noticed by the federal men. When Carlton surprised him, he automatically tipped the carbine, as he had done in the Denver office.

The two men stared at each other for a long three seconds, before Rory said, "Marshal, you're just bound and determined to go home in a box. But I don't think that's in any way fair to these other men. You need to know that when I start shooting, I won't stop until you're all down.

"Block, I'd like it if you'd step outside. You too, Cap. Take Wiley with you."

Cap stood his ground.

"I believe I'll just stay right here, boss."

Wiley chimed in with, "And this is my office. I plan to defend it."

Block, clearly defying a man who was his superior, stepped to the center of the room between Rory and Carlton, facing the federal marshal.

"Carlton. You're a fool. And if you get me fired for saying so, that's fine. You have no idea what you're threatening to unloose. We need to end this nonsense. Rory is the best deputy I ever rode with, and I've ridden with a few. Let's answer a question or two, Carlton. Just to help you understand why Sheriff Jamison was along, leading in fact, on that ride to Texas.

"Have you ever crawled on your belly through grass, cactus, and broken gravel? Grass so short that no one would believe it could be done without being spotted? Crawled until your clothes were filthy and torn, and your hands raw from gripping the gravel while you pulled yourself along? Crawled until you had the drop on a murderer, and then took that murderer without a shot being fired? This man has done that more than once. But you haven't.

"Have you ever ridden into a heavily armed camp of murderers and bank robbers unarmed and with your hands held out in the air to negotiate a surrender; and then get that surrender and the leader's Sharps Big as a gift to boot? This man did that. I watched it all take place, and I made the arrests, after the men had dropped their weapons. Have you done anything like that?

"Have you ever faced three murdering thieves and rode away, leaving three bodies on the ground, and you just eighteen years old? This man did.

"Have you seen the stories in those foolish penny dreadful magazines? The stories are flowered up and awful, but every tale told about this man is true.

"I could tell you more stories, Carlton. Things I've seen with my own eyes. And I don't know the half of it.

"You're a fool, Carlton. I'm proud to have ridden with this young man. You couldn't have a better man siding with you, or one you could trust more, and yet you insult him and make an enemy of him.

"Go home to your big comfortable office, Carlton. Leave the law work to the likes of Sheriff Jamison and these good marshals who have followed you out of loyalty to the marshal's service and the nation. Go home. You're out of your depth out here."

The silence in the room was like a tomb. Marshal Byway, who had remained silent in the Denver office, now in the fort office, stepped around Block and held his hand out for Carlton's gun.

"This man is correct, Marshal Carlton. Not only is he right, but I believe you have taken the situation beyond repair. You and I are going home."

Even though Marshal Byway was of a lesser rank

than Carlton, Marshal Carlton backed off. As a compromise, Carlton slid the gun back into its holster and pulled his jacket over it, signifying an end to the confrontation.

Again, there was a slow count of three or four, while silence held the space. Then, with no words, Carlton shouldered his way past Byway and Block, making no eye contact with anyone. Rory stepped aside to prevent more confrontation.

The two eastern marshals mounted their horses in silence, turned, and rode back toward Cheyenne and the railway.

38

T<small>HE</small> <small>ROOM</small> <small>HELD</small> <small>ITS</small> <small>SILENCE</small> <small>WHILE</small> <small>THE</small> <small>REMAINING</small>
marshals looked at one another, as if wondering what
came next.

When Carlton and Byway were out of sight, Rory
stepped from the office and untied his horse. He walked
the animal over to the livery and left him in Keg's care.
When he originally had tied his gelding, he had plans for
lunch. Now those plans were forgotten. In their place
was the information in the wire he had received.

H<small>E</small> <small>WAS</small> <small>MET</small> outside the office by Block and the other
marshals. Block said, "Rory. There's another problem,
but we think we've figured out what to do." Without
waiting, he continued.

"Carlton insisted on bringing the prisoners from
Denver. He planned to take them to Washington. Now
they're in the Cheyenne lockup, under guard by
another of our boys. We can't allow them to get away. If

they get to Washington, I fear our entire case, and all our hard riding, will be for nothing. But Deputy Pegs Drury here, is a rider. I mean he's a distance rider. He figures if you can find two fast horses for him, he'll outride those two that just left. If he can get to Cheyenne well before Carlton and Byway, he can get the prisoners loaded on a stage and bring them down here. From here, we'll find a place to stash them away for a while."

Rory looked at the man named Pegs Drury and said, "You figure you can do that?"

"With two good animals, I can. I'll pass those other two in the dark of night, and they'll never see me."

Rory looked from man to man, knowing his decision was important.

"Well, you're light enough. Won't be much strain on the animals. Come with me."

Together they walked into the livery and called Kegs from his little sleeping space. Rory gave the brief request.

"Kegs, we need two of your best horses. From our county stock—if possible—but anyway, the best. Runners and stayers."

Without unnecessary questions, Kegs said, "Come with me."

Rory held Block back and said, "Go to the general store. The county has an account there. Buy whatever you think your man will need. Food that will keep him in the saddle without the need for cooking. Get two canteens. Maybe three."

Within minutes Deputy Drury was in the lightest saddle Kegs had, comfortably sitting atop the fastest horse and leading what Kegs said was the close second. The only extra load on the animals was a light pair of saddlebags carrying food that could be eaten right from the package.

The final word from Kegs was, "If one of those geldings starts to drag you down, turn him loose. He knows where home is."

THE DOOR to the room where the single cell held Cooper had been closed while the confrontation with the marshals had taken place. Now Rory went directly to it and turned the knob. He spoke to Cooper from the doorway.

"Got a wire here, Cooper. Seems like you stole that wagon and team. The cattle too. Since you also stole the gelding and saddle, I'm assuming you had nothing at all of your own. Stole them all, way back in Missouri. There're folks back there who would like to see you. Perhaps see you on the end of a rope. Or in prison for a good long stretch.

"What do you think, Cooper? Would you rather be hung here or back in Missouri? I'll leave you to think on that while I talk with the judge."

He closed the door again and sat down.

Wiley grinned at him. "I will say, Sheriff, you have a way of making things happen. Bringing them to a head, you might say."

Cap said, "A bit hard on a couple of marshals too."

Ignoring the awkward teasing, Rory stood and said, "I'm going over to see the judge."

Judge Anders P. Yokam listened to the sheriff's story and reread the wire. Rory's question that he wanted advice on, was what to do with Cooper. It was a far distance from the fort to St Joseph. Of course, with the rails offering travel between the two locations, although admittedly there were many stops and a couple of transfers between rail lines involved, the distance shrank to just a few days. Crossing the continent, or in this case a portion of the continent, didn't appear anywhere near as formidable as it once had.

Rory was familiar with the way the judge was in the habit of studying the evidence. In this case, he studied the wire and the fact that Cooper was locked down in the fort's small holding facility. The options, in Rory's mind, were simple. In fact, they were reduced to just two —hold trial for Cooper where he was already securely behind bars or move him east and let the folks there deal with him. If they moved the suspect back to St. Joseph, the marshals could dig up live witnesses. At the fort, the evidence would all be hearsay.

Rory was becoming impatient with the slowness of the judge's considering, but finally, the wire was laid on the table, and the judge leaned back in his chair, his fingers intertwined on his somewhat corpulent belly. Rory may have leaned forward just a bit in anticipation of the unofficial ruling.

"As I see it, Sheriff, you have little to go on here. In fact, you have only the word of the children and Miss Gert, whose family name she has yet to divulge.

"That would be little enough to take to court when the man has only to deny and present an alternate story. He could somewhat convincingly claim that he offered to provide a home for the youngsters and that they were entrusted to him on that basis. Who could argue against that with facts? The same could hold for the young lady. I remind you, my friend, that in court, it is provable facts that count. Opinion and circumstantial evidence seldom win court cases.

"The crime, if crime there was, took place in another city in another state, far from any jurisdiction either you or I can claim."

Again, there was a long pause.

"I think, Sheriff, that if I were in your position, I would arrange for the transfer of the prisoner to the jurisdiction where the crimes took place. As to witnesses, the two older boys who escaped Mr. Cooper are gone, and we'll likely never find them. But I would be prepared to take a deposition, under oath, from the children now in your care, as well as Miss Gert, who would then have to admit to her full name. That deposition, taken before me and this court, should suffice for witness statements in the other jurisdiction, where the court could hear supporting testimony. You could leave your own deposition with the court in St. Joseph if you were in a hurry to get home.

"That is my advice to you, sir."

THAT EVENING, as Rory and Julia took dinner in the small cantina, where they had gone for Mexican food, and to escape from listening ears, Rory, in a totally uncustomary move, reached across the table, wrapped Julia's hand in his, and said, "I'm going to have to make a trip to Missouri. Cooper is needed there for trial. Of course, I'll ride the rails, so there won't be too much time involved. Wiley is going with me to help secure the prisoner.

"The house is nearing completion. We have a decision

to make, so I had best get to doing my part. Julia, I would very much love to have you share that house with me and make it into a home. Now, after some weeks in town, you have seen my life. You know the risks. You know the travel and the nights when I'm away. You know the kind of people I have to deal with. You know that I would not be home every night. Knowing all of that, would you still consent to be my wife? To marry me?"

"Silly man. Of course, I'll marry you. And you're correct. I've seen and considered all those things you mentioned. But, Rory Jamison, I love you with all my heart. I know the risks. But they wouldn't stop me from wanting you."

"I love and want you, too, Julia. Can we plan on standing before the pastor soon after I return from down east?"

"Of course, we can. I'll talk to him. Make some arrangements. Do you think you'll be home in two weeks?"

"Sooner, I hope, but allowing for the unforeseen, that should still work."

"I'll plan on three weeks from Saturday. If we have to change it, we'll change it. It's not as if the pastor is overly busy in this little bit of a town."

They laughed together on that fact before Rory said, "I have to leave right away. I'm not going to have time to ride out to the ranch to talk with your father. But as soon as I'm home, I'll make it out there."

"Silly man. You don't need to worry about my parents. I'll ride out this weekend when I'm off work. They'll be delighted to hear the news. And if it will make you rest easier, I'll make your excuses for you."

The young couple smiled across the table at each

other. Julia noticed the Mexican couple at the next table smiling, too, after taking several surreptitious glances during their conversation. When she thought Rory might not notice, she grinned back at the couple.

By the time Rory and Julia visited most of the night away and the cantina was about to close, a light rain had started. They stepped out the door to where their horses were tied. Rory held his hand out, as if to confirm that the weather really had changed. "I should have rented Kegs's buggy."

"We'll be alright, but we must hurry along."

WITH JULIA safely escorted to her boardinghouse, Rory took her horse by the reins and turned his gelding toward the livery. The rain had increased, but there was still enough light to pick shadows out of full night. He slowed the horses' walk to stare at what looked like riders coming in from the north. The muddy clop of hooves was the only sound disturbing the night. Always suspicious and conscious of his duties, Rory stopped and waited. As the two riders came close, he called out, "Evening, folks. Late for riding."

Neither of the riders spoke until they came closer. Rory could see that it was a man and a woman. Strangers. When the man spoke, Rory didn't recognize the voice, confirming his first judgment that they were new to the town.

"We're much later than we planned, but we're hoping to find Sheriff Jamison. Can you help us on that?"

"I believe I can. I'm Rory Jamison. What can I do for you?"

"We're Gunter and Birdie Stakes. We were told by the

sheriff in St. Joseph that you were looking for us. When we found out that your town doesn't have the telegraph we jumped on the train. Loaded our horses and got off in Cheyenne. We've ridden for hours, but it will be worth it if you have news of our children."

They sat in silence, getting wetter by the minute, as Rory thought it through. It was late. The kids would be in bed and asleep. Cap, too, likely. Still, it was no small matter for parents to be separated from their children. Also entering into his decision was the work he had to do in the morning to prepare to accompany Cooper to the train. He had arranged for an early, private stage. He would have no time for the Stakes in the morning.

"Follow me."

He dropped Julia's horse at the livery before turning toward the house.

As they rode through the wet night, Rory could almost feel the tension in the couple. He decided to allow the silence to continue. It wouldn't take more than a half second to know if these were the parents to Peter and Emmalou. One look would be all it took.

As was his habit, Cap had left a lit lantern out, over the door of the small barn. Rory led the couple right inside, against his own rules of mounting and dismounting outside. But it was a wet night, and the folks were tired. They stalled the horses, leaving the saddles in place, and turned back into the night. A very short walk took them to the cabin door. Cap would not normally lock a door, but with the kids living there, he had taken on the habit. Rory wrapped his knuckles on the wood and waited. The dog growled immediately. It didn't take long for Cap's sleepy voice to come through.

"Who is it? What do you want?"

"Rory here, Cap."

The scratching of the bar sliding out of the grooves sounded into the night. The door opened enough for Cap to confirm Rory's presence. He stepped and said, "Wait till I light a lamp."

Rory moved in far enough for the three of them to get out of the rain and waited. The dog lunged at Rory, knowing him even in the dark.

Rory loved him up a bit in return.

The flame of the newly lit lamp grew and turned into a glow as Cap replaced the globe. The small kitchen came into view. The dog immediately noticed the strangers. He had probably smelled them as they stepped through the door, although the wetness may have disguised the odor of a strange human. At the first growl, Rory ran his hand through the animal's ruff. "Quiet now, Scout. Quiet."

As if in explanation, Rory said, "Scout has really taken to the kids. I don't believe anyone could get near them without coming through their four-legged protector. But he's a good fella. Give him a little scratch behind the ear and let him get a smell of you. He'll be fine."

Cap's study of the visitors was full of questions. Rory didn't give him time to ask them. He simply said, "Go wake Peter up. Bring him out here."

With another questioning look, Cap turned to the bedroom door. Rory could hear him say, "Peter. Wake up. I need you to come with me."

The boy emerged from the bedroom, rubbing his eyes. He saw nothing, but as soon as Gunter Stakes said, "Peter," the boy's head snapped up. He had clearly recognized his father's voice. His look was a picture of disbelief. After all the months, all the hardships, and all the tears, his parents were standing in the kitchen. Without a word, he leaped across the kitchen, throwing himself into the waiting arms. All he said was, "Pa. Pa."

"It's me alright, Son. And here's your mother."

Peter let go of his father and rushed into his mother's wet but welcoming arms.

Cap, seeing the story unfold, turned back to the other room. In a moment, he returned with his hand on Emmalou's shoulder, leading the half-asleep girl toward her parents. Rory and Cap stood looking at each other with nothing to say. A bit choked up, Rory finally suggested, "Let's light another lamp and build up the fire. These folks are wet and cold. So am I, for that matter."

Rory lifted the stove lid, assessing the remnants of the supper fire, and then shook the grate just a bit before adding several sticks. He closed the lid and reached for the coffeepot. With the room heating up and the hopes of fresh coffee in a few minutes, he turned to the happily reunited family.

At the beginning, when Cap thought Rory would be moving into the cabin along with the kids and himself, Cap had found a cot somewhere and set it up in the farthest corner of the kitchen. The Stakes family, all four of them, had sat down on it. He knew his young protégés would be answering questions for days to come, but right now the questions were secondary. It was all hugs and kisses and groans of happiness.

With the initial flush of joy passed, Gunter looked at the two men.

"I'll never be able to thank you men as you deserve to be thanked. There's no telling what at all has gone through our minds these long months. And to find them here in a warm cabin being cared for by the sheriff is more than we ever dared hoped for. Thank you. Thank you."

259

Emmalou burst in with, "I've got my own room, and Mr. Caps bought us each a horse so we can ride to school. And I'm doing some of the cooking."

The lawmen heard the first laugh when that was said.

Mrs. Stakes looked from Cap to Rory and back again before she said, "I, too, thank you men. It's wonderful to see what care the Lord laid on our children. Thank you for being His willing servants."

Cap, embarrassed at the praise but at the same time thinking back to his own family, came close to tears. To cover his embarrassment, he turned to the coffee, burning his fingers as he lifted the lid to drop in some grounds.

Mrs. Stakes asked the kids, "Is it true that you're going to school?"

Peter answered, "Yes. And when we have trouble with our work, Cap helps us."

"If you have to get up in the morning for school, perhaps you should get back to bed."

"Aw, Mom. We can miss one day."

Cap grinned and said, "Peter's right, Mrs. Stakes. One rainy day ain't going to set them back none."

After more visiting and even more hugs, reluctantly the kids returned to their beds. Although they were really past the age, the parents went and tucked them into bed. When all was quiet again, the four adults took seats at the table. Rory poured coffee while Cap dug a chocolate cake out of the cold pantry and set it on the table with a knife.

"Would you like to cut some for each of us, Mrs. Stakes?"

"My goodness, Cap. Are you a baker too?"

"No, ma'am, but we have a pretty good baker down on the main street. I leave making of the sweet stuff to him. Not that we have sweets very often, if you know what I mean."

Rory had already figured out that he was going to have to delay his trip for at least one day. Reverting to business, as was his habit, he said, "Mr. and Mrs. Stakes, I was supposed to leave in the morning. I'm due in St. Joseph in a few days. I'm escorting a prisoner and staying for a trial. The prisoner is the man who apparently bought the kids from an orphanage and brought them west.

"It's a very long story, and we're not going into it tonight. I'm thinking, Mrs. Stakes, that if you can share the bed with Emmalou and Mr. Stakes, you take that cot over there; you can make do here in the cabin. But I'll be needing your testimony to take to the St. Joseph court. I'll make arrangements for you to give a deposition before our local judge right after lunch tomorrow. That will give you and Cap and the kids the morning to wind through the story. And perhaps you would care for your horses tonight. Take the dog out with you. He needs a bit of a run before you all settle back down."

"Where do you live, Sheriff?"

"I'm in the hotel for a while. I'm having a new house built right here on this property, but it's not ready yet. You can find me tomorrow in the marshal's office. Cap and the kids all know where that is."

39

LATE IN THE AFTERNOON THE NEXT DAY, RORY HAD THE depositions of Gunter and Birdie Stakes and again was set for the stage ride to Cheyenne and then onward by rail to St. Joseph.

Listening to the Stakeses give their evidence, provided Rory with one critical piece of the story that had been giving him pause.

Gunter Stakes was speaking: "I went looking for work for a winter stopover. We had no intention of risking the prairies in the winter. Unfortunately, my horse lost his footing on a bit of snow on a steep grade. He fell, and I couldn't kick free quickly enough. Thankfully, he didn't roll over me, but he did catch one of my legs. I heard it break. Felt it too; you can be sure of that. The horse wasn't hurt, but he scrambled some getting back to his feet. That did more damage to the leg. The fool thing then wandered off looking for graze, I suppose. He stayed within sight, but he refused my call. I lay there two full days praying for help. Finally, Birdie showed up."

Birdie jumped in with, "My horse picked up the scent of his stablemate and led me right to Gunter."

Gunter took over again. "I thought I'd never be able to get back on the horse, but with Birdie's help, we got it done. We found a small village with an old, half-retired doctor. He put the bones right. Or as right as they'll ever be. But it was several days before I could be moved. Then, with the borrow of a wagon, the old sawbones drove me to where we had left our wagon and kids. Of course, they were gone. To say we were frantic would be too light a statement.

"We never found the team or our goods, but we did find the wagon. It was under a hay shelter at a livery outside St. Joseph. The livery man claimed innocence. Said he had bought the rig in good faith. We didn't argue, although he was clearly lying.

"When he went back inside, Birdie climbed underneath. We had built a small enclosure under there that held our cash money and some of our valuables. She dug it out and we left, knowing there was no use hanging around or asking more questions. We went to the law but found no interest. 'Kids run away all the time,' the lazy sheriff said. We've been searching and asking questions ever since."

RORY CAREFULLY FOLDED the several depositions and placed them in an envelope. The next morning, he and Cooper, along with Wiley, were on a stage to Cheyenne, hoping to avoid any contact with the Washington marshals.

With Cooper handcuffed to the bench seat in the

passenger car, they made their long, tedious way to St. Joseph.

After considering the sweltering heat on his first cattle-buying trip, Rory had Wiley arranged for a bath and new clothes for Cooper before they left Cheyenne, all at county expense. He couldn't face sitting beside the man any other way.

The other consideration was to arrange for a one sleeper unit on the train. He and Wiley would take turns resting and guarding. Cooper could stretch out on the floor if he wished to escape the hours of sitting.

40

THE VOICE WAS LOUD, GRUFF, AND PROFANE, BREAKING into the dinner conversations in the hotel dining room.

"There she is. That's my wife. Run away, she did. Left me. Ain't no woman going to show up, Crash Tobin. Not on yer life. Promised myself I'd find her. Take her home. Drag her if the need should be. Git yerself out here, woman, lest I should come and git ye."

Wiley and the sheriff weren't even all the way to St. Joseph yet when Cap found himself facing a situation. He heard the loud voice coming from the dining room, all the way out to the boardwalk. Not knowing what was happening but sure it wasn't good, he rushed inside. A tall, lanky, filthy straggly-haired man was standing at the door of the dining room. It appeared he was shouting at Gert. The poor girl was cowering in fear. Other diners were startled from their dinners, cringing at the crudeness of the shouting man.

Cap strode to the man's side and said, "Calm down, Mister. Calm down and come with me. Outside. Now."

The man brushed Cap's hand off his arm, shouting, "I

ain't neither leav'n till I have my woman back. Git away from me."

Cap could clearly see there would be no reasoning with the man. He flicked the man's timeworn hat off his head and wound his fingers into the greasy hair. Stepping away, he pulled the man after himself. Someone held the door open, and Cap dragged the man backward until they were on the boardwalk. The fella's arms were windmilling. His vile mouth was still uttering curses, now directed at Cap.

Cap needed to bring an end to the confrontation, but the struggling, repulsive man was in no frame of mind to give in to the lawman.

Junior Wardle was in the process of tying his horse at the nearby rail. Without being asked, he took one of the windmilling arms and pulled it behind the man's back. The man screeched in pain as Junior pressed his advantage. He then reached for the other arm. With Crash Tobin now screaming in pain mixed with anger, Cap pulled one hand free and reached for the handcuffs hanging from his belt. Crash Tobin was soon helpless and on his way across the road to the jail.

Once inside the locked cell, Tobin's anger played out on the steel door. He rattled it fiercely until Cap finally warned him.

"You do that once more, and I'll open the door and lay into you with a club. Now settle down and tell me your story. But no more shouting and no more cursing. I'll not have it."

Cap then turned to Junior after picking up the bar of homemade soap from the small washstand.

"Bring that bucket of water and the dipper and come out here."

With Junior sloshing water over Cap's hands, the

deputy came near to scrubbing the skin off his fingers. He rinsed and sniffed his own hands. When he could still smell the greasy hair, he started again. Only after the third washing did he begin feeling clean again. Back inside, he took a seat behind the desk and studied the prisoner. When the man seemed to have settled down a bit, he said, "Now, speak to me. Decently and quietly."

"That woman, Gert, her name is, she's my wife, or near enough. Promised to me by her old daddy just afor his dy'n. Made me promise to care fer her, and I mean to keep that promise. My wife she was promised, and my wife she'll be."

"Did Gert have any say in the matter?"

"It ain't for womenfolk to have no say. Her daddy spoke for her."

Cap and Junior looked at each other and left the office. As they crossed the road, Junior said, "That story sounds like something right out of the hills from a century ago."

"We'll talk to Gert and then somehow deal with the man."

THEY FOUND Gert upstairs in her hotel room. At Cap's knock, she quietly asked, "Who is it?"

Cap introduced himself. She still hesitated, but at Cap's second assurance, she asked, "Is he with you?"

"No, ma'am. He behind bars. Now open the door."

She opened the door just a crack. She had clearly been crying. She looked so young and defenseless, that it was difficult for Cap to believe this was the same woman who had run from a foolish promise made by her father, wagoned across two northern states, most of it in winter, and walked across most of another, herding cattle. And all the time fighting off Cooper, who had the same intent as the man he had just arrested, although he expressed it in a more genteel manner.

"You had best let us in, Gert."

"Who's this with you, and why is he here?"

"This here is Junior Wardle, ma'am. He helped me with the prisoner. He's concerned about your welfare too. So far as I know, he's trustworthy."

Junior doffed his hat before he said, "I just want to help, Miss. You wouldn't know me. In fact, I just arrived back in town. I was tying off when the deputy dragged that fellow out. I was glad to be able to assist him. But I'll leave if you'd rather."

"No. It's alright if Cap knows you."

Gert sat on the bed. Cap took the single chair. Junior squatted on his heels with his back to the door.

"Now, Gert, what's this all about? The man claims you're his wife by promise."

"There's nothing further from the truth. The man that made the promise was not my father. He was my mother's husband. Her third. My father and another one died. Then when my mother died last year, her husband took up drinking with Crash Tobin. Filthy drunkards, the two of them. I accepted that wagon ride offer from Cooper in a desperate attempt to get away from those two. This so-called promise of marriage was hatched up between the two of them during a drunken wallow in the mud of their own minds. I'd die before I'd marry a man like that. Cooper was no prize, but he was a far sight better than Crash Tobin."

Cap looked at Junior as if to say, "What do I do now?"

He then turned to Gert and said, "I don't imagine being filthy or shouting in a restaurant is going to give me grounds to hold the man. I can hold him till morning, but then I'll have to let him go. I'll warn him, but I doubt that he'll listen. From there, Gert, I don't know. I just don't know."

A few silent seconds went past before Junior said, "I have an idea. My brother Micah is holding down a job for a widow woman out east a few miles. She's a recent widow. Young. Two small children. I'm willing to believe she'd make room for you and enjoy the company to boot. If you don't mind finishing the ride in the dark, we'll go now."

Cap and Junior waited for an answer that was slow in coming, but when it did come, the words were, "I'll clear my room out, and if Cap will let me ride that big black Cooper had, we'll do as you say."

They were gone within a half hour.

THE NEXT MORNING Cap released Crash Tobin with a warning. But it was clear the man had heard nothing beyond what he wanted to hear. After an hour of making a nuisance of himself around town—looking in every store, every barn, every possible hiding place, and shouting about his wife and telling of the horrible things that would be happening to anyone hiding the woman—he spotted Cap walking to the livery.

Crash Tobin, never the smartest man in the hills, made his final mistake. He rushed across the road, dodging horse and wagon traffic, waving his pistol, and shouting threats. When he cleared the last wagon, he stopped and leveled his gun at Cap, shouting the whole time. The deputy did the only thing left to do. The crash of two .45s being fired at almost the exact same time was a thundering noise on the street, gathering lookers from every direction. Cap was a bit late to lift his Colt because Tobin already had his in his hand. But in his excitement and his unreasoning fury, his shot drove lead into a top piece of siding on the livery stable. Cap shot true, taking the last breath and the life of Crash Tobin.

41

By what at times seemed like an eternal trip, one with many changes, stops, and plain confusion, the train pulled into the station at St. Joseph. The three men were tired, sore from sitting, out of sorts by the repetitious meals, the never-ending coal smoke, and lost. None of them had ever been in the city before. They emerged from the station, along with the crowd, only to arrive among another crowd on the sidewalk. There seemed to be horse, wagon, and cart traffic jamming the road in every direction. Teamsters were shouting warnings, and cabs for hire were pleading, first for a paying fare, and after that, for others to move aside.

Rory flagged a cab, directing the cabby to somehow get them to the city jail. The frightened man looked at Cooper with his hands in cuffs and chains and whipped his horse into extra motion as soon as the traffic allowed.

At the jailhouse, Rory paid the cab costs plus a bit extra for the driver and entered the building. Several pairs of eyes fell on him. One uniformed policeman laid his hand on his holstered pistol.

Stepping to the counter while Wiley held the resigned and docile Cooper by the elbow, Rory said, "Sheriff Rory Jamison, the fort, Colorado. I have a prisoner to hold for the federal deputy marshals. We've been days on the train. I'm hoping you can take this man off our hands while we make connections with the marshals. And that could be speeded up if you could provide some guidance to their office."

Another uniformed officer who had been listening from the doorway of a small office stepped forward. "We can do that for you, Sheriff. Is this man dangerous? Does he need any special guarding?"

"His name is Cooper. He's not dangerous in the normal sense if you're talking about guns, murder, and such, but he desperately wants to get away from the charges facing him. Those charges would include theft, cattle and horse rustling, and kidnapping of children. Some bars and a secure lock should hold him."

"Sounds like a nice fella. I'm glad you brought him to us. There's much we can learn from a fella like that. Yes, we'll take care of him for you. And if the thefts and whatnot took place in our area, we may find his talk interesting. A fella just never knows about a thing like that.

"If you want to connect with the marshals, you're going to have to go out that door, wave a cab down, and have him take you to the address I'm going to write on this paper. Say hello to the boys over there for me."

"Thanks, I will."

A half-hour later, the fort law officers were standing among six gathered federal deputy marshals. The trip had ended successfully. Cooper was out of their hair and in the custody of competent guards. They were free of responsibility, at least for this one evening. Suddenly all the energy seemed to be drained from Rory's body. A quick glance at Wiley said the city marshal felt about the same. Rory was wishing they had taken a hotel and left the marshal's visit until morning.

After Rory had outlined the reason for their presence in St. Joseph, the marshal in charge looked at the big ticking clock on the wall and said, "That can all wait for one more day. Why don't I guide you to a good hotel and we'll get at this in the morning. You fellas look about done in."

Rory could have kissed him. But he settled for a nod and a quiet "thank you."

❧

THE BRIEFING of the federal men took a good bit of the morning. An officer named Deputy Marshal Kent took notes and seemed to be in charge. When Rory finished his story, Kent drew a line under his notes and leaned back in his chair.

"I must say, Sheriff, you have laid out the case clearly. It will be a great help to us. We wouldn't normally put as much manpower as we have into a case of theft. Even horse and cattle theft. Of course, if that was all there was to the case, we would leave it to the city and state folks. But the selling of children from an orphanage and transporting them across the country raises the bar considerably. Your testimony is going to fill in many blanks for us.

"We won't be ready for trial for a while yet. But I'm thinking you must be anxious to get back home, rather than waiting around here for a trial that could be weeks away. Or months, the way lawyers work."

"We are, although I wish we could somehow fly instead of remounting that smoke-belching, rattling train. But, then again, it's better than riding a wagon for weeks on end. I'm assuming you'll put Cooper in a safe place."

"Indeed, we will. The lawyers will want to question him, so we'll keep him here. We have cells in the basement. But the other matter is getting the lawyers to take a deposition from you, similar to these you've brought from the fort. How would it be if I arrange that for tomorrow morning? Then you can get on your way home?"

The meeting with the lawyers took longer than Rory expected, but finally, it was done. He reread the document the secretary had produced and signed it. Wiley had gone to the station to purchase tickets and arrange for a sleeping room for each of them. They would be on their way home in the morning. The thought and hope in Rory's mind was that the affidavits would be adequate. He cringed inwardly at the thought of returning to attend the trial of Cooper and whoever else the marshals managed to find, to complete their search for the orphanage and all that had gone on there.

42

WITH ADEQUATE REST IN THE SLEEPING CAR AND NO prisoner to deal with, the trip home was more pleasant for the fort law officers, although Rory hoped to never smell the acrid stink of coal smoke again.

Once home and up-to-date with local happenings, Cap told him about the incident with Crash Tobin and Gert, finishing the story by advising him to check with Junior Wardle at his first opportunity.

Over the months of spring, Rory had found that dealings with the Wardle family had mellowed when Boon, the father, was taken out of the picture. It was as if the three sons and Tempest, the daughter, were discovering their own direction in life once they were away from the big thumb under which they had been raised.

Rory made a point of finding Junior.

"How did your search for land go, Junior?"

"There's lots of land, but new complications have risen. When Pa had us gather the herd to take our leave of the Roaring creek area, there was no thought of our mother or what her wants might be. Pa's motive was to

275

keep the family together as much as possible. Meaning his sons and Tempest. Ma would make her own decision. He'd have to try to deal with Mother separate from the move of the Mirrored W.

"He's not the deepest thinker you'll ever meet, but he knows cattle, and he does love the family. All that shouting, way back, about Key and Tempest being removed from their inheritance was all nonsense. We all knew it at the time, but no one ever got very far challenging Pa, so we all let it go, as we had let so many of his other poorly thought-out declarations go.

"Key and Tempest had already found town life to be to their liking. Mother pulled out a couple of years ago. Her leaving had nothing to do with her feelings toward Pa or her kids. She was simply tired of the hills. Tired of the isolation. She had lived years with hardly ever seeing another woman. And then, Ma never said much, but some days she was feeling poorly. When she said she wanted to see a doctor, Pa didn't take her seriously. We had all lived through illnesses, broken bones, and what-have-you, without a doctor.

"It took her leaving to get Pa's attention. Even then, he didn't do anything more than grump around the ranch and stubbornly hold to the hills.

"A man can live, and even enjoy the hills and isolation for all of his life. But not a woman. In any case, it's not fair. Eventually, she'll want to get to town and visit with another woman or two. Enjoy a bit of a social life. Get to church. Buy a new dress. Maybe eat a meal someone else cooked.

"Even after Mother pulled out for Laramie, Pa could see none of that. He insisted her leaving was all about seeing a doctor, and that she'd soon be back.

"It took Key's leaving to start us all thinking in

another direction. A direction that would take us out of the hills.

"Neither Micah nor I said anything at the time, either, but that first trip we all took to visit Key was an eye-opener. Of course, that's when we lost Tempest to the town too. And then, we saw quality cattle that had replaced the longhorn crosses we were familiar with. When we got home and opened our eyes to the truth, our cattle looked like scrubs, and we all knew it. But, again, we didn't really talk about it. But there was some discontent that we could all feel."

Rory had listened intently. He had a question.

"What caused the final break?"

"Two things happening almost at the same time. The three of us left on the ranch, that's Pa, Micah, and me; we finally had an open talk. Pa could sense that he would be alone on the Mirrored W if no changes were made, and he reluctantly started to think. Finally, as if it had been his decision all along, he announced that we were to get the crew working on a roundup. We were moving the ranch south. He said it almost blindly, or perhaps I could daresay 'in ignorance of the facts,' as if there was land everywhere with adequate water and yearlong graze, just waiting for the arrival of the Mirrored W.

"It helped that a neighbor, and by neighbor I mean a man from twenty miles west, came and offered to buy the ranch, land, buildings, and all. Put together with everything, it was too much for even Pa to resist. So here we are."

Rory stood, saying, "Lunchtime. Let's go see what surprises Amber has for us today."

With their food in front of them, they ate in silence. Obviously still thinking of his search for ranchland,

Junior laid down his knife and fork and said, "It's different from the hills, but it's lonely, just the same."

"You lost me a bit there, Junior."

"I suppose. My mind was on the grasslands I've looked at buying. Miles and miles of grasslands. Some here on the eastern flatland and some up higher. South some miles west of Pueblo and tucked behind the hills, there's some great grass. Like the hills of home, it's a bit lonely, but lovely country. This country up here, around the fort, it's a bit tight on water in places, but there's no shortage of grass. I guess what I was thinking is that a woman could feel just as alone on the prairie as she does in the hills, given distances. Takes some consideration to work that all through."

"Did you find anything you liked?"

"I did. But I'm thinking the old Mirrored W is broken up and gone forever. I watched Pa sitting on a tipped-back chair exchanging lies and wild stories to the liveryman down in Stevensville. He looked as happy as I've ever seen him. And he and Ma are sharing a small house they found vacant. They'll not want for money, and by himself, Pa is no longer able to do the work of ranching. He'd need Micah and me, or a bigger crew. And I'm not sure that's going to happen.

"Micah seemed pretty content holding down the B/K for Ida Kelly. I saw that clear enough when I delivered that Gert lady out there. Mrs. Kelly, she's a pleasant and fine-looking woman. I asked no questions on that line of thinking. I'll leave big brother to keep his own secrets and do his own thinking."

"So, I'm hearing that leaves just you, Junior."

"That leaves me. I still feel the need to ranch, but I'll never have such as the Mirrored W, nor do I want that. I'd like to have something I can handle myself. Of maybe me and one man. Fenced like your Double J. Make a decent life for a woman, whoever that might turn out to be. A woman and kids.

"I'm thinking I never told you that I visited the Double J. Your uncle George showed me the animals. I'd never seen their like. Made me long for the same. And the fencing that eliminates a crew that needs paying every month."

Hoping to encourage Junior, Rory said, "It was not so many years ago my father started the Double J. Started with near enough to nothing. He was maybe about your age but married with a family. There's nothing saying you can't do the same with a bit of seed money from the Mirrored W. Go your own way. Let your brothers go their way, and your father to share stories with Tippet. Might be good for all of you."

The conversation lagged until Rory finally said, "I've got work to do, Junior. Keep in touch. I'll be waiting to hear what your final decision is."

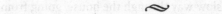

RORY WATCHED Junior walk away and then pushed all other thoughts aside while he did the one thing he had been putting off in the days since his return to the fort. He saddled his gelding and rode out to the new house. Sticks Willoughby waved from the rooftop and shouted a greeting.

As Rory was tying the horse, Sticks was descending a ladder. His form of greeting was, "Just putting the last of the shingles on 'er, Sheriff. The inside's about finished. Ready to move into, mostly. That girl of yours, she's a pusher. Difficult to say 'no' to. When she said to get the inside done, that you'd put up with the boys hammering and sawing to get the porch and siding completed later, I couldn't find a way to deny her wishes. Careful with your boots, going inside, there's carpets on the floor and furniture about everywhere you look. She's a pusher, as I said, and a stickler for detail, that girl."

As Rory was trying to sort all that out in his head, Sticks said, "I gotta get back to the shingling, my friend. Don't want your lady catching me not working." He accompanied those few words with an uproarious laugh.

Rory stood at the front door in amazement. It, indeed, was as Sticks had said. There were even a few books lying on a set of shelves in the oversized kitchen. He knew he had given Julia the freedom to order the furniture, but he couldn't help wondering at the cost of everything he saw. It had arrived so quickly he was tempted to wonder if she had already ordered it when she first brought the subject up.

The kitchen counter and cabinets, extending from both sides of the big nickel-trimmed stove, caused him to pause in wonder.

He made his slow way through the house, going from room to room. Contrary to most house designs, the sitting room was at the back of the single-story house, with one bedroom to the left side and two smaller bedrooms to the right. The back door of the sitting room opened to a garden of flowers and fruit trees planted by the previous owner of the land.

The beds were all made with store-bought sheets and blankets. The top quilts were obviously handmade. Rory had no idea where they came from, and he didn't much care. Between two of the bedrooms was the bath space. The only thing in that space was a large, galvanized metal tub. Rory hunched his shoulders and moved on, with many questions forming in his mind.

He untied his gelding to return to town. Mounting, he glanced back just once. *Sure a far cry from a tent on a sidehill, beside a gold stream in the mountains of Idaho, Father.*

He was always conscious of the fact that it had been his father's idea to ride north in search of gold. And that everything Rory had or ever owned was credited to their success on a gold-bearing stream.

HIS HORSE HADN'T TAKEN a dozen steps when a call from the cabin halted him.

"Sheriff. If you have a minute."

He looked over his shoulder to see Gunter and Birdie Stakes calling from the front porch of the cabin. He turned the gelding and walked him over to the tie rail. He remained in the saddle for what he hoped would be a short visit.

"Hello, folks; how goes it with you?"

With the sound of Rory's voice, the dog came bounding from the side of the cabin, whining happily and wagging its tail. Rory bent from the saddle to give the dog a moment of love, listening as Gunter said, in answer to Rory's question, "It goes better with us than we could have ever hoped for. Largely thanks to you, Sheriff. And Cap, of course. Peter and Emmalou are doing well in school. Or at least that's what the teacher claims. And we've found a place right in town. We'll be moving in the next few days."

"Have you given up on your hopes for a ranch of your own?"

"For now, we have, anyway. I got talking to Kegs, down at the livery. When he found out I was a millwright and a wheelwright and could do some smithing, he offered me a deal. Space to work at the livery, and all the shoeing and smithing business he's been turning away. We'll give it a try, anyway. All my tools were stolen when the wagon was driven off, but I'll replace or remake them as they're needed.

"Maybe the ranch idea was a pipe dream. Or maybe I'm just being honest about my abilities. The leg hasn't healed quite straight, and it will never improve. Hours of riding and working cattle with a damaged leg might not be the wisest course in life. We've always been towns-folk, so settling in at the fort will be no hardship. We're finding we like it here.

"But what can you tell us about Cooper and the orphanage back east, and the theft of our team and wagon?"

"It's doubtful you'll ever see the wagon again. And searching for one team in this vast country is a monumental task too. You might put an ad in a few newspapers describing the team and the brand. We've found homes for a few stolen horses that have come into our hands that way.

"As to the orphanage and Cooper. Cooper is in the federal jail, under guard by the marshals. They found the orphanage and have arrested the woman who ran it. Her and the man the kids told us about. I've given the marshals all our affidavits. If they need more when they go to trial, they'll contact either me or you. That's all we can say for now."

Knowing the feeling of wanting justice, or at least something closer to justice than what they had now, and thinking of the unsatisfactory conclusions to most of the crimes he had been involved with, Rory said, "It's a hard thing. And every lawman I know would love to be able to do better. But sometimes, we have to accept that this is an imperfect world. You and the kids are back together, and you can rebuild whatever else you lost. That might be the best you can hope for. Take Kegs up on his offer, enjoy your family, and be happy. If something comes of the happenings down east, that will be a bonus."

Birdie spoke for the first time. "You are undoubtedly correct, Sheriff. And we've talked the same way. I'm pretty well over losing the wagon and team. A few things I was given by my mother and grandmother I will always miss. And of course, Gunter's tools were a big part of his life. Still, we can rise above all that.

"But what happened to our children should not be allowed to go unpunished. I've lost many nights of sleep wondering what happened to them, and more nights since we are back together, as I find myself praying in thankfulness. I've been very thankful, too, for your presence in all of this, Sheriff. You and Wiley and Cap and, I'm sure, some others whose names I will never know. Thank you."

Rory wasn't comfortable with praise. Never had been. He smiled at the couple, tipped his hat just a bit, told the dog to stay, and turned back toward town.

43

JULIA HAD BEEN A BUSY LADY WHILE HER FUTURE GROOM was riding the rails across the country and escorting fugitives. Besides hiring a freighter to bring the furniture down from the depot in Cheyenne and installing it in the house, she had also arranged a wedding, sending a rider to the Double J Ranch and then to Stevensville, with the news. She intended to ride herself to talk to her parents. But thinking of how Mr. Sales had come to depend on her assistance, and all the other things she had to attend to before the wedding, she settled for writing a long letter. Again, for a few dollars taken from her meager wages, she found a boy who was prepared to ride out to the ranch with the news.

In her letter, she had explained that Rory was away, but he had asked the question. She had answered on behalf of herself and her parents. She then provided the date for the wedding and advised that she had reserved a hotel room for them for three nights.

Rory knew none of this, but she was anxious to tell him all about it at dinner that evening. When that time came, they sat at the corner table in the cantina. They both enjoyed the food at the cantina. Normally a place where men gathered, she was pleased with her gracious welcome. And the one other lady diner, plus the girl waiting tables, seemed to appreciate her company, although it would have been against everything any of them would have deemed appropriate to involve themselves in another's business or interrupt their talk.

They placed their order and leaned back in their chairs, looking at each other. After just a few seconds, Julia leaned back toward the table, folded her arms in front of her, and cupped her chin with her hands.

"You have been very busy, Mr. Jamison. Are you going to be able to clear your mind as I tell you how much I love you and how anxious I am to become Mrs. Jamison?"

Rory grinned a reply. "I'll do my best to accommodate you, future Mrs. Jamison."

"Well, alright then. First, have you been out to the house?"

"I was. Sticks was tearing his hair out, saying what a tyrant you are and how he'll be happy to finish the work so he can get on to something else."

"He said no such a thing. In fact, he's been an absolute dear to work with."

"I maybe didn't hear it quite right."

They grinned at each other for another moment before Rory said, "You had better tell me what all you have planned."

For the next hour, while they ate and drank coffee, sometimes whispering and sometimes laughing out loud, Julia outlined all the plans. When she was done, she asked, "Does that all suit you? There's still time to make changes."

"My dear, I wouldn't change a thing unless it was to go right now and get married. That way, we could just make the gathering in town a family celebration without all the fuss and fidgeting."

"My dear, Mr. Jamison. Don't you even joke about taking away the only wedding celebration I will ever have."

Rory could have said he wasn't really joking, but he thought better of it.

That brought on another short silence before Julia had another question.

"I have been wondering about that Texas gold problem you worked on for so long. Is that completely behind you now, or do you think there will be more? I know how much you didn't want to go to St. Joseph. I can't imagine you in Washington, facing all those politicians and lawyers."

"All the evidence I have, or ever had, is written down in witnessed and signed affidavits. I can't see what else the marshals or the lawyers could want from me. I'm hoping it's finished. But I can't promise that."

There was really nothing more that could be said on an open-ended investigation such as that one. It seemed to be reaching into the higher levels of government, far above any knowledge Rory might have. The conversation returned to the wedding and then back to the house. It was a better subject to end the evening on than talking about crooked politicians.

44

TWO WEEKS LATER, ON THE SATURDAY OF A SUNSHINE-filled weekend, the little town of the fort was looking as if everyone with a horse or a wagon had made the trip to town. Surrounding ranchers, the parents and siblings from both the Double J and the Gridley ranches, Ivan and Key from Stevensville, along with Tempest and Sonia, were all in town looking forward to seeing the two young people entwined in marriage. Even Tippet had made the trip. And much to Rory's surprise, Block and his wife managed to take the train to Cheyenne, and then the stage down to the fort.

Every hotel room was taken. Townsfolks opened their homes to visitors. Ivan and the Wardle boys took up Kegs's offer of space in the loft. Cap had a house full at the cabin.

Rory and Julia had their new house, and they intended to use it, keeping it to themselves.

At the appointed time, Rory and Ivan, both decked out in their fine new suits, stood at the front of the little church. The young pastor stood beside them, taking one last look at his notes that were folded neatly into the crease on his open Bible.

Rory and Ivan looked to be unarmed, but a closer study would have shown a neat holster tucked into the tops of their pants, each carrying a small .32 pocket model. Outside, stationed front and back of the small church, the Wardle boys had taken it upon themselves to stand guard. Across the street, Gunter and Cap stood under the awning of one of the local stores. At the entrance to the church, dressed to where few would recognize him, stood Tippet. His double-twelve gauge was held so closely to his pant legs that few noticed it.

The sheriff was getting married. Who was to know what enemies he had made in his time as a lawman. It was possible that one of those enemies would think the sheriff's mind would be on other matters, and that the wedding would be an ideal time and place to right their perceived wrongs. His friends were there to see that nothing was to spoil the occasion.

Julia, lovely as always, and especially so in the flowing white dress she had chosen from the catalog at the mercantile, was smiling as she had never smiled before, standing at the back of the church, waiting for the signal which would come from the pianist, as she struck the opening chords of the chosen song. Beside Julia stood her brother's wife—her sister-in-law—and her father, who would happily escort her to the alter.

Considering all the work that had gone into the planning and the preparations, it should have taken longer. The high point in a young bride's life shouldn't be over so quickly. But the fact was that in a short fifteen minutes, Julia Gridley had become Mrs. Julia Jamison, and she couldn't be happier.

The celebration, the food, and the dozens of hugs and

well-wishes went on into late afternoon, and then early evening. Finally, as darkness fell, Rory gathered up his new wife and whispered, "I've had about enough of this."

She grinned, nodded, and took his hand. She waved as they headed for the door. Rory had turned his back already and didn't notice the wave. He heard the cheers and shouting but ignored them.

Rancher Williamson, who had first loaned a buggy to Rory when he was attempting the rescue of Julia and her parents, had driven to town. He had the buggy parked in front of the church, all cleaned of the road dust and looking grand. The rancher himself was on the seat, holding the reins. With another wave and the responding cheers, Williamson turned the rig toward the new home on the hill, just outside of town.

They would be alone at last, although Rory, knowing the ways of cowboys, wasn't at all sure they had heard the last of the crowd for that night.

No one, not even Rory, knew that Tippet, now dressed in his livery clothing, stood guard in the darkness beside the little brick house. On the other side, Ivan had found a comfortable spot to rest in, while he cradled his carbine across his knees. There was to be no risk, and no disturbing the sheriff and his new bride that night.

CRIME WITHOUT CONSCIENCE

A SNEAK PEEK AT BOOK FIVE

AVAILABLE AUGUST 2023

For the past several months there had been constant rumors about the telegraph coming to Stevensville and the fort. Other parts of the West, centers much smaller than the two towns Sheriff Rory Jamison patrolled, had already been blessed with the modern, fast communications. But the towns in question still relied on stagecoach-handled mail or a fast rider making the trek to Cheyenne or, even further away, to Denver to reach a wire.

The sheriff was riding toward his newly built home. He was expecting to join his wife of only a couple of weeks for lunch. As had become her habit in the short few days since the marriage, she stood at the edge of the covered porch, waiting. She held her hand over her eyes to shade out the sun's glare. Grinning in happiness, Rory knew that under the shaded face, her lips were holding a welcoming smile.

A rider, pushing a sweating and heaving gray gelding almost to exhaustion, was heard hollering, "Sheriff! Sheriff!"

Rory pulled his Double J Ranch-bred, blood-red bay horse to a stop. He half turned in the saddle to see who it was that was flagging him down. Waving his hat in the air while kicking the last of the gelding's strength out of the animal, Wat Preveau, the young man Kegs often hired to help in his livery, hollered for the sheriff to wait up.

Wat was so out of breath, a listener could be forgiven for thinking the kid had been the one doing the running. He started to speak, stopped to catch his breath, started again, and, while the gelding heaved and trembled in exhaustion, managed to say, "Fire. Livery. Marshal's office. Bank an' a couple others. Bank robbed. Horses burned up. Banker shot."

Rory said, "Alright, Wat. I get the idea. Now you step off that animal before he drops from under you. Walk him back to the livery. Slowly! Get Kegs to help you. He knows more about horses than anyone around. He might be able to save the animal. You stay and care for the horse. There's nothing you can do down to Stevensville that others can't do. I'll ride down."

Rory turned back to his house and the woman waiting on the porch. A few seconds of riding brought him to the tie rail. As he walked up to the house, he was about to speak when Julia said, "I heard. I've got lunch ready. You sit and eat. I'll grab a change of clothes for you to take along."

Before the wedding, the young lovers had discussed the demands of the sheriff's job in a large county. That they both had hoped the call to action would take a break while they settled into married life, hadn't held off whatever was happening twenty miles to the south. Nor was there any guarantee on how long the sheriff would be gone. This would be the first test of their new marriage.

One-half hour later, Rory turned the red horse back to town and the road south. Julia kissed him goodbye.

"I'll pray for your safe return."

ABOUT THE AUTHOR

Reg Quist's pioneer heritage includes sod shacks, prairie fires, home births, and children's graves under the prairie sod, all working together in the lives of people creating their own space in a new land.

Out of that early generation came farmers, ranchers, business men and women, builders, military graves in faraway lands, Sunday Schools that grew to become churches, plus story tellers, musicians, and much more.

Hard work and self-reliance were the hallmark of those previous great generations, attributes that were absorbed by the following generation.

Quist's career choice took him into the construction world. From heavy industrial work, to construction camps in the remote northern bush, the author emulated his grandfathers, who were both builders, as well as pioneer farmers and ranchers.

It is with deep thankfulness that Quist says, "I am a part of the first generation to truly enjoy the benefits of the labors of the pioneers. My parents and their parents worked incredibly hard, and it is well for us to remember".